THE SWORD MASTER

Also by Kate Heartfield

Alice Payne Arrives
Alice Payne Rides

The Chatelaine
The Embroidered Book
The Valkyrie
The Tapestry of Time
Mercutio

THE SWORD MASTER

KATE HEARTFIELD

REBELLION

First published 2026 by Rebellion Publishing Ltd,
Riverside House, Osney Mead,
Oxford, OX2 0ES, UK

www.rebellionpublishing.com

ISBN: 978-1-83786-418-8

10 9 8 7 6 5 4 3 2 1

A CIP catalogue record for this book is available from the British Library.

Designed & typeset by Rebellion Publishing

Printed in Denmark

MIX
Paper | Supporting responsible forestry
FSC® C021394

For libraries and librarians everywhere.

CAST OF CHARACTERS

Françoise de Montesquiou d'Artagnan: a young daughter of a country lord in the south of France

Queen Catherine de' Medici: widowed mother to King Charles IX

King Charles IX: eldest son of Queen Catherine and King of France

Henri, the Duke of Anjou: the second-eldest living son of Queen Catherine

François, the Duke of Alençon: the youngest living son of Queen Catherine

Queen Marguerite: daughter of Queen Catherine and husband to Henri, King of Navarre

King Henri of Navarre: a Huguenot, invited to Paris to marry the Catholic Marguerite. Fourth in line to the throne.

Charlotte de Sauve: One of Queen Catherine's ladies of honour, and lover to the King of Navarre

Joseph Boniface de La Môle: A Huguenot count from Provence, lover of Queen Marguerite and friend to Coconnas

Annibal de Coconnas: A Catholic count from Piedmont, lover to the Duchess of Nevers and friend to La Môle

Henriette, Duchess of Nevers: Best friend to Queen Marguerite and lover of Coconnas

Henri de Sainct Didier: A fencing master from Provence

Chicot: The nickname of Count Jean-Antoine d'Anglerais, a Gascon gentleman of modest means

Madame Charbonneau: Innkeeper of Le Chat Noir in Orléans

Maître La Hurière: Innkeeper of La Belle Étoile in Paris

Maître René: Rene Bianchi, perfumer (and poisoner) to Queen Catherine

Cosimo Ruggieri: Sorcerer, astrologer and adviser to Queen Catherine

Sister Anne: A nun at the abbey of Montmartre

Sister Marie: A nun at the abbey of Montmartre

CHAPTER ONE

The Hills of Gascony

For two full days, nobody could wake Françoise de Montesquiou d'Artagnan. The eighteen-year-old lay in her bed, oblivious to her nurse banging pots and pans, to the prayers of the priest, to the complaints of her fiancé, to the lancet of the physician, and to the exhortations of her parents. The latter would have preferred to keep the fiancé in the dark, but the second day of their daughter's long nap happened to be her wedding day.

Françoise's mother was convinced that this was no coincidence, that the girl had somehow contrived to get out of it. Had she ingested some sort of potion? Dabbled in black magic? The physician could only shake his head sadly, touch the girl's lips with theriac—a greasy panacea that was, he explained, made with sixty-seven exotic ingredients and cost more than gold—and fill another pan with the girl's blood. Drip, drip, drip.

By sunset on the day of the cancelled nuptials, the news had spread through the village and even to other parts of Armagnac, running along as quickly as the clouds scudding over the foothills of the Pyrenees. The manservant was pleased every time another anxious visitor came by, giving him a reason to open the door to fresh air. What a relief to let out a little of the smoke from burning rue and partridge feathers. The smoke was meant to calm the patient's womb—the source of all mystifying feminine behaviour—and the stink of it, the doorman privately thought, could have woken the dead.

Through it all, Françoise slept on. Her body was perfectly still. No fever, no apparent pain. She was just *asleep*, so deeply that the doctor had to put a mirror to her snub nose to be sure she was breathing.

As far as Françoise was concerned, she was not lying in the bed at all. She was loping over the hills in the form of a brown hare.

She'd always had vivid dreams, but this was something new: she felt entirely awake, but in borrowed form. This small, furry body was hers, just as much as the body lying in the bed was hers. She smelled, not burning feathers, but wild cowslips and sun-baked grass.

Her back legs beat a rhythm as they followed her front legs, and her heart beat a strange new rhythm, too. Underneath her gallop, there was a pulse like the beating of a giant drum that seemed to come from the earth but at a great distance, speaking directly to her. It drew her onwards. If she could find the source of that drumbeat, she would be released. Released from what? She could not have said, in that wordless animal awareness, but she felt it more strongly than she had ever felt anything in her young life.

She ran through a field of yarrow, their pale flowers like umbrellas overhead, forming a canopy.

Then she emerged onto shorter grass, cropped by goats. Up, up a long hill, with the sun now winking behind it. The air was cooling at the end of the day. Thud thud thud. The drum beat, calling her forward. With these eyes, she could see so much of the world. She could see a small fox loping over to her right, in the same direction. She could see an eagle gliding overhead. Strangely, she did not fear either of them.

And she could see a jumbled black shape up on the top of the hill, lit from the sun setting behind it. A collection of stone ruins. Later, with her human mind, she wondered whether it might at one time have been a church, or perhaps something even older. A temple.

As the animals approached the ruins, their pace slowed. They approached as if they were expected: the fox, the eagle, the hare, and many others. Next to Françoise, a small lizard slithered between two blades of grass and then transformed, silently stretching upward into a tall, thin shape, something like a woman, but not a woman. This giant wore a cloak and bowed her head to the others as they transformed from their animal shapes into something like people. As tall as church doors, thin and stretched as shadows, they nodded to each other.

But not everyone transformed. Françoise did not know how to be anything but a hare, in that moment. The deer stared back at her companionably, also unchanging. A brown sparrow hopped on the stone table around which they had all gathered.

The drum stopped.

There was a voice, and it came from a greyhound, although its muzzle did not move. A voice from its mind to the minds of all those assembled. A man's voice.

It has been long since we were summoned. It is not safe.

In her hare skin, Françoise could feel the anxiety of the others, a current on the air. Feathers rose on the necks of the birds, and canine ears stood at attention. Behind them, the crumbling skeletons of three stone arches stood against the bloody glow of the horizon. Here and there, other stones were scattered, weathered blocks that looked as though they had once had faces or vines carved into them, but now the shapes were meaningless, unreadable, only slightly unnatural.

She sidled closer to one of the blocks, the heavy texture of the sandstone in her peripheral vision, giving her some small sense of shelter.

The giant who spoke next was very old. He held a long stalk of yarrow plucked from the field below, still straight as if it had not yet had time to realize its life was over. His posture stooped just enough that he did not block the moon, his grey beard swaying, but his voice was strong. *It was necessary. The queen is moving.*

Dry laughter from the giant woman who had been a lizard. *She is always moving. Wheels within wheels. We cannot oppose her in numbers, only in stealth. We must work as she works, in the darkness.*

Some of those here, said the eagle in the voice of an old man, *are new to this life.*

He looked directly at Françoise. The wind picked up a little, down at the base of the hill, and moaned.

Another reason why this meeting was necessary, said the old man. *Why do you think there are so many of us? It is a sign that we will be needed. We must ready ourselves.* He paused, seemed to sigh without breath. Françoise sat back on her hind legs, trying to gather her courage to ask a question, to find the words. Every question she considered seemed to have another, more fundamental, question beneath it. She was afraid to try to speak as the others spoke. Afraid it would come out as a squeak, or nothing at all.

While she was considering, the old man spoke again.

We may not have time for the traditional ways. I may not be here to help.

The giant woman glared at him. *You're leaving us?*

I am going to the court.

The woman laughed again. *To the lion's den?*

At the same moment, the greyhound asked, *To Paris? Is that wise?*

It may already be too late, the old man said.

The black cloud that flew up from behind the hill moved faster than the wind, faster than thought, and Françoise was down in her haunches, below the grass, before it had finished darkening the moon. A cloud made of scraps that moved together and apart.

Vampires!

The word came at once from many voices: a hissed warning, an echo of the panic that was already running through every vein in Françoise's small brown body. She was as low and small as she could get, but she moved quickly, behind the stone block, into a thorny bush that bit through her fur and into her skin. The bats filled the windows of the ruins, adding to the darkness until it filled her hare's vision. More and more darkness. The bats were everywhere. On this side and that, behind her, cutting off escape. Where the bats were, suddenly there were people, dark shapes against the evening sky.

In front of her terrified gaze, a cloaked figure wrenched the neck of the deer just as it was leaping, and sank its teeth into its neck. The smell of blood poisoned the air. A bat alighted on the shoulder of the giant woman and was, in an instant, a woman too, crouched on her shoulder. The woman clawed at her attacker and the old man tried to pull it off her, but a fountain of blood issued from her neck and she seemed to shrink, to collapse in on herself, a woman of ordinary size now, younger, dying.

Françoise retreated deeper into the bush. She could run, down the hill. Would they notice her in the tumult? Surely she was not important, but she knew in every fibre of her animal body that she was prey, nonetheless. It did not matter that she kept herself still, that she was the colour of the earth and the grasses. These creatures could smell her, just as she could smell them. They would find her.

A strange thing then happened to Françoise. All her terror seemed to build up to a swell and then transform into something else. Anger, perhaps, although she didn't name it in the moment. She knew only that she was not safe in hiding, that she would not be safe in running, that safety was no longer a useful goal. She felt revulsion at the blood polluting the earth, wetting the plants that should know only sweet rainwater, seeping into ground that had no desire to gorge itself on so many bodies.

The anger built up in her until she knew, when the moment came, that she would buck, and buck she did. A vicious hand, with sharp nails, sank into her neck. She bucked, her front and back legs stretching to impossible length, her body twisting, harder and faster than she had ever moved or even thought in her life as a woman or as a hare. She was free, for one eternal moment, twisting in the darkness, a ballet of limbs and muscles, thinking not of up or down or left or right but only of away.

When she landed, wriggling herself into a running position, the vampire was bent over her, both hands now outstretched, one set of fingernails red with her blood.

The tall old man came up behind, holding his yarrow stalk. It whipped through the air, curling around from the side, and then something happened that made Françoise freeze, not from terror or self-preservation but from sheer confusion. She had seen dozens of impossible things already that evening, but this was beyond impossible. Where the thin stalk struck the neck, in the front where the cloak did not protect it, the flesh sizzled and burned red. The old man took hold of the other end and pulled it back like a garrote that burned clean through the neck of the vampire, and left the grinning, grey-skinned head, a scrap of cloak falling off it, on the ground.

Run, said the old man.

CHAPTER TWO

Departure

Françoise saw nothing when she opened her eyes. Pitch-black as deep and unwholesome as the cloaks of vampires. A thud, and another, as if she were inside a beating heart. When she put her hands up to her face to check that her eyes really were open, she felt the lid.

Wood, an inch from her face.

Her scream was a human scream, from human lungs, that sucked in too little air when they had finished. Her world was small and smelled of mildew, of death, of small unspeakable creatures. Her hands felt the wood at her sides. Her legs bucked and kicked. She was lying flat. This was not merely a box; this was a coffin.

Thud, thud.

There was someone, or something, outside. It might be a monster, but a monster would be more welcome than this prison. Let her take one breath of clean air, just one breath, and then come what may, but let her breathe.

She was still beating against the lid and screaming, her eyes screwed shut, when the thuds stopped.

There was a long silence, then. She screamed again, but it ended in a kind of strangled choking as her lungs were squeezed within aching ribs. Her head swam.

Then a distant tumult, like voices in a dream, like the voices of her murdered colleagues as they whispered their last words on the hilltop, as their blood drained into the dirt. Many voices. A symphony. Perhaps, she thought, as her stomach rebelled and she choked on bile, perhaps these were the angels, greeting her.

Then a scraping, a terrible light, and dirt falling into her nostrils and into the eyelids she couldn't help but open, and then squeeze shut again, the dirt making her cry. She couldn't see anything, but she could hear her mother's voice.

"God preserve us!" her mother said. "The girl is alive!"

She sat straight up in her now lidless coffin, pushed the arms of strangers away, wiped the muck out of her eyes, and glared up at her mother. God, the day was bright.

"Of course I'm alive," she croaked.

Her mother crossed herself. It did not look like joy.

THE MARRIAGE WOULD certainly be off. Her parents made sure she understood that in the carriage on the way home, as if everything else paled next to that. As if their daughter returning from the dead were not cause for thanksgiving. They acted as though Françoise had done it on purpose, as if she had pretended to be dead just to give them all a scare, and get out of the wedding.

Truth be told, getting out of the wedding was a happy consequence, but she had no desire to be treated like some sort of vampire herself, after her narrow escape.

That it had been an escape, and no mere dream, she did not doubt. Under her second-best dress, in which her parents had buried her (no use sending her to heaven in her best), her back bore fresh red scratches from long fingernails. She stood backward in front of her looking glass and twisted to see as well as she could, wishing she still had the vision and liquid muscles of a hare. Even though she had to strain to see them, there was no mistaking them. And anyway, they hurt like the very Devil.

A long bath had made her feel a little better about whatever those fingernails had left behind, but only sharpened the sting.

Her old nurse Sancia had been with her since she was a baby, and was now her maid and companion. She helped her dress, gingerly, taking care not to touch her and saying nothing about the scratches.

"Won't you fetch me some of the salve?" Françoise asked.

"Will it help?" Sancia asked.

What an odd question! How many hours had they spent gathering, drying and grinding the eight yellow flowers, mixing it with honey fed on bees that only fed on yellow flowers, too. They kept a hive in a meadow specifically for that purpose. And now the nurse asked whether it would *help?* "You taught me yourself that the Golden Salve can heal anything."

"I have never tried it on marks from the grave!"

"The marks are not from the grave. What, do you think I was buried on top of someone else? Go, fetch the salve, and I'll put it on myself if you won't touch me."

Sancia was not a monster, and did help with the salve, although she applied it with a cloth. She had just finished tying up Françoise's sleeves when there was a knock, and the door opened.

Her parents stood there, looking at Françoise as if she were a leaky drain or a tumbled barn. A problem to be solved.

"We had the cook make you some gruel," her father said, holding out the bowl as if offering meat to a rabid dog. "And we'll have the doctor here as soon as we can."

"I don't want either." Françoise was, as it happened, very hungry. Even more hungry than she was stubborn. "On second thought, give me the gruel."

"The doctor," said her mother firmly, "and then the priest."

Françoise sat on her bed and shovelled gruel into her mouth as if it was the finest thing she had ever tasted. "I should have thought the priest had prayed over me enough for one day."

"Blasphemy," whispered her mother.

"The priest is coming not only to pray, but to help us find a good place for you," her father explained coldly, as if discussing a business arrangement. "The sisters of Saint Amable may be willing to take you in, for the price of an endowment. They have well-born girls there, and you won't have to do much rough work. If you are a good girl when the priest comes, he will put in a good word for you."

"A good girl!" Françoise was astonished. "A good word!"

"Have you lost your wits?" her mother hissed at her. "You ought to be dead and you are not. If the sisters of Saint Amable do not want the Devil's bride among them, you will have to be packed off to the Poor Clares, whose charity is boundless, or so they say."

A convent! Françoise looked from one face to the next, searching for some sign that this was all a joke or a bad dream. Her parents were rarely affectionate, but they had never been downright cruel to her before.

"Life in a convent won't be so bad," Sancia cooed, seeing her face. "You may be able to work in a garden, and read. And you won't have to put up with a husband. And there, you'll be safe. In the bosom of the church."

Françoise remembered the clouds of bats, darkening the ruined arches. She shivered; she did not think she'd be safe anywhere, and truth be told, she did not have any desire for safety. She wanted to find those creatures and take her revenge. She wanted to find her comrades, the creatures and giants whose names and waking faces she did not know, but who felt like her family now. They had faced death together, in a secret that felt bigger than anything she had known until now. But what was it? What was this momentous thing that had happened to her? She had gone into the grave and come out again; she had found a secret confraternity of night; she had escaped vampires. She wanted, more than anything, to understand it. And what understanding could there be behind a convent's walls? Constrained, moving only where and when as the bells told her she might, speaking when she was allowed to speak, making only those potions and salves that were believed in by fearful old women?

"I thank you all for your concern," she said coldly. "But the illness has passed. I am recovered. There is no need to fear for my safety." Then she looked at their faces again, and a sick understanding took hold of her guts. "Unless it is not *my* safety that concerns you."

Sancia crossed herself. "I hoped it would be all right," she said, as if in confession. "I hoped and prayed it would be all right."

Her mother glared at the nurse. "Quiet, foolish woman!"

"I've been quiet long enough!" Sancia wailed. "I knew well enough when the child was born in the caul, as if born in her own shroud, I knew then that she was destined for no other bridegroom but the Devil. Babes born in the caul are not for this world. And yet, how could I not have loved her? That angelic face! They say the Evil One does hide his handiwork."

"The Evil One's handiwork?" Françoise was so shocked that all she could say was, "What a very rude thing to say!"

Sancia let her head fall, shaking it sadly. Her mother had covered her mouth in horror, and her father's eyes were hard.

"Leave me," Françoise said, and let the half-empty bowl of gruel clatter down to the floor. "I'm very tired."

"You slept for three days," her father said. Jean de Montesquiou, seigneur d'Artagnan, was not the most intelligent man in the world, but he had found that putting matters plainly had gained him a measure of respect in and around the village; people tended to agree with what he said, because it was so obvious, and thus they had the vague impression that he must have a head on his shoulders. "You slept so long and so hard that we thought you were dead. And now you wish to sleep more?"

"I wish to be alone," Françoise hissed, not caring about playing the dutiful daughter. She did not want to play a part ever again; she had never been very good at it.

Her parents obliged. Sancia, looking slightly guilty, hesitated at the door.

Françoise grimaced at her, and she left.

After that, Françoise felt guilty herself. Sancia was not a bad woman, and she had been through a shock. Then again, she had called her charge the Devil's handiwork. And Françoise was, despite her long sleep, very tired. All her muscles ached. She lay on her bed, and stared at the ceiling whose pattern of imaginary flowers she knew better than her own hands. She made a plan for what to do next.

SHE WAITED UNTIL the very darkest part of night, which held no terrors for her. She had seen terrors at sunset; she knew that there was a darkness deeper than night. She dressed herself in the plain linen and red wool dress she wore to work in the garden, with her red travelling cloak, hood and boots, and she put her second-best set of clothing into a sack: Spanish shoes; linen stockings and garter ribbons; extra smock; underskirt; petticoat with bodice attached; yellow kirtle; blue gown; white lace partlet and ruff; blue cap and white veil.

Perhaps it was the memory of being a small, hunted creature, a creature of fur and shadows, but Françoise found it very easy to creep down the corridor outside her bedroom and towards the servants' stairwell. The household had once been a bustling one but these were harder times, and there were only six servants to worry about: Sancia, who was sleeping in with the housemaid and the lady's maid tonight since Françoise had banished her from her own room; her father's manservant; the groom, who was also the coachman when required; and the cook, who slept in a narrow room near the kitchen. But the kitchen itself was as quiet as the grave.

Into the sack went oranges, nuts, the salty, hard white cheese the neighbours made, and a loaf of crusty bread flavoured with lavender from her garden. And, upon reflection, a sharp knife. A flask of fresh water, wrapped in a cloth so it would make no sound.

Finally, Françoise went to a cupboard and took the cook's petty strongbox out, filled with coins to be used on market days. When she put it into the sack, it made what seemed to her to be a horrible racket, but nobody in the house stirred.

Even the moon had gone to bed, so when she crept outside, she was but one shadow among others, and caught no one's attention.

This would be her last walk through the garden where she and her nurse had worked so many hours together. She said farewell to the bishop's wort and comfrey, to the lime tree and the plantain.

The horses dozed in their stalls, all except her favourite, a deep grey mare named Mistral, who was looking at her now with her dark eyes.

"You can keep a secret, can't you?" Françoise asked her, easing the door of her stall open, and putting her hand on the mare's neck. She breathed in the familiar smell of the stable, the last part of her childhood home she would see in her lifetime. "Not a whinny, and step softly. We're leaving, you and I."

CHAPTER THREE

The Road to Paris

IT TOOK LONGER to get to the top of the hill on horseback than it had on hare's feet. She led Mistral on a winding upward path, approaching the ruins from the other side—the side from which the bats had come. Not merely bats. Vampires.

Françoise had heard stories, most of them from Sancia, about humans who had traded their souls for the chance to live for centuries, feeding on the blood of mortals. They could change their shapes, even take the forms of animals.

And what other creatures had that ability? Werewolves, certainly; her nurse had been fond of stories of the loup-garou when Françoise was misbehaving. But there had been no wolves at the hilltop the night before. What had happened to Françoise did not feel like a curse or a spell, and the others around the stone table had worn their forms as if proud of them, as if born to them.

Born to them. Born in the caul, Sancia had said. Françoise wasn't sure what that meant; she had witnessed only one birth, human or animal, in her short life, and Mistral's befuddled, damp foal had not had any wrappings or shrouds on it. Her father had sold that foal years before, so at least Françoise's adventure wouldn't separate the mare from her child. Only a daughter from her parents, and despite her parents' evident fear and contempt, that did make Françoise feel very cold and alone as she rode up that hill.

Alone and at the mercy of whatever creatures might hunt her here. But she had to know. She had to understand.

Everything was in reverse of how it had been the night before. As she approached from the other side, the sky lightened in the east, rather than darkening in the west. She rode high above a beast whose feet beat the ground, rather than running low and noiselessly on her own lean muscles.

Her arms twitched. She remembered that form as if it were her true life, and this one a dream. But if she was neither vampire nor loup-garou, what was she? What other beings could take the forms of animals in the night?

One word reverberated in her mind: *Witch*.

But surely witches were witches by choice. Surely she was not the Devil's servant from birth, as her nurse believed. Surely the old man, the deer, the eagle—they were not about the Devil's business. They had gathered because—she cast her mind back, trying to remember the conversation—because they were worried about the queen. Queen Catherine de' Medici, the mother of the king. The old man said he was going to the court, to Paris.

She reached the top of the hill just as the sun was peeking over the far horizon. In the soft light of morning, it was not fear that seized her heart, but grief, as she looked over the bloody patches on the weeds and bushes, even on the stone table itself.

Slowly, Françoise walked the horse toward the fallen stone where she had hidden. From this height, it looked so small, and yet it had been her shelter. There was the thorny bush behind it, and on the bush, streaks of dried blood and a scrap of torn brown fur.

Her own.

There was no one left behind. Those who were killed had vanished, their bodies taken by their killers, or by scavenger beasts, or by some magic. Perhaps Françoise was the only survivor, saved by the old man who had told her to run. And run she had, making a straight line for her village, for her family home, until the rhythm of her own exhausted legs seemed to lull her into a kind of sleep.

Until she had woken up back in human form, in a coffin.

And yet, there was fur left behind on the bush. It may have been her mind alone that left her woman's body behind, but when it took a hare's form, it took on the fur, and sinew, and blood of a hare, too. If the vampires had killed her in that form, she had no doubt her mind would never have returned to the body in the box.

One way or another, she had been in danger, and was probably in danger still. In danger from an enemy about whom she knew little but their name.

And what of the man—if it was a man—who had saved her life? She wanted to find him, if he was still alive. To find all those from the battle who were still alive, and if she could, avenge all those who were dead.

Françoise leaned down from the saddle and plucked a yarrow stalk, much like the one the old man had wielded like a sword. Holding it like a knight holding a lance at rest, she turned her face to the left, to the north, to Paris.

FRANÇOISE KNEW LITTLE of the geography of France, only that Paris was about three weeks' journey to the north. She kept the sun on her right in the morning and on her left in the afternoon. For the first day, she kept to the quietest roads she could find and did not stop anywhere for fear of being recognized. But it didn't take her long to run low on food and run out of water, and she found she did not much like riding at night, in the dark, knowing what she knew about the creatures it held.

So, on her second night, when she reached the village of Mont-de-Marsan, she paused, and doubled back, apologizing to the exhausted Mistral. At a quiet spot by a farm wall, she slipped down, let Mistral graze, and pulled the strongbox out of the sack.

A few whacks with the butt of her knife broke the lock. There was a jumble of small coins that the cook would have used to buy bread, wine, butter, meat. All together, it came to a little more than a dozen francs.

Françoise put a few coins into her pocket and dropped the rest back into the box, returning it to the sack with the clothes and food, all of which she buried under the farm wall.

It was a very tired, bedraggled and dirty Françoise who presented herself at the inn in Mont-de-Marsan and asked for a room for herself and board for her horse.

The red-eyed, stocky man serving behind the counter looked her up and down, and then spoke quietly to the groom, and looked at Françoise again. "Where did you get that horse?"

A very rude question, but Françoise knew to be on her guard. It was important not to let anyone see that she was a rich man's daughter, who might have something on her to steal—who might even be worth something to someone. She did not think she could pass for a peasant. So she copied the one woman she knew who might have found herself in an inn: Sancia.

"My master sent me with it," she said, haughtily and defensively.

"Your master?"

"Indeed. I am on an errand. A family matter, for a very important family."

A small smile. "And did this very important family give you money to pay for your room?"

She reached into her pocket, trying not to let her face show that she had no idea how much an inn charged for a night's lodging. "What do you charge here in Mont-de-Marsan?"

The landlord looked her up and down. "Two francs."

"I'll pay you one franc, for which I'll want supper, and board for my horse, and a bed to myself."

He was quiet for a moment, scheming, subtly putting himself at such an angle that the groom and the two other guests eating their dinners would not see what he held. He spoke softly. "I don't ask questions of my guests, and I'll take your payment, but I warn you, I want no trouble. If anyone comes looking for you, I'll tell them what I know."

Her heart stopped briefly. He knew—he knew! What had given her away? And then she realized, looking at the dull gleam in his eye, that when he spoke of someone looking for her, he didn't mean her father. He meant the master he presumed she had stolen from. The money, and probably the horse, too. He thought her a thief.

She was about to object when it dawned on her that this misunderstanding was likely to keep her safe and housed for the night, so she swallowed her pride, nodded curtly.

But the innkeeper was not done with her yet. He leaned over the counter and spoke even more softly. "And if your master is a Catholic, and you a Huguenot, I'll turn you in with pride."

The threat chilled her. For much of her life, France had alternated between civil war and uneasy peace.

The widowed queen Catherine de' Medici had been left as the mother of a boy king and then, when he died, another even younger. Factions of powerful nobles had fought tooth and claw to see who could control the boys and, through them, rule France.

Some of those noble factions espoused the protestant forms of religion, and those who followed the teachings of John Calvin gained the nickname Huguenot, for reasons mysterious to Françoise. When the Huguenot nobles wanted to make war on their Catholic enemies, they called them corrupt and immoral. When the Catholic nobles wanted to make war on their Huguenot enemies, they called them heretical traitors funded by foreign powers. Thus every skirmish became a holy war, and the people of both faiths suffered, even women and children massacred at their prayers.

The queen mother tried to keep a fragile peace, by never allowing either side to get too powerful. She kept both Catholics and Huguenots at court among her counsellors and friends, although she and her son, King Charles, were both Catholics. But every time there was a peace treaty, some rumour or insult would create suspicion and the violence would begin again. Of late, Catholics had been attacking Huguenots. As a gesture of conciliation to show her support for the beleaguered Huguenots, the queen had offered her daughter Marguerite as a bride to the Huguenot King of Navarre, and the wedding was soon to take place in Paris.

At the night battle, someone had spoken about the queen, about opposing the queen, working in the darkness as she did. Could that have had anything to do with these wars of religion? Françoise could not see how. But then, she knew little about the fighting between factions. War and peace were distant events that people spoke about every time a traveller came through the village. There were some in her village who professed the reformed religion; they had always got along well enough with their neighbours. She had never seen contempt in someone's face as there was in this man's when he said the word Huguenot.

"I was baptised a Catholic, and I have never practised any other religion," she said truthfully.

He leaned back. "Then I warrant you'll find no trouble here, nor anywhere else on your journey. Where did you say you were travelling to?"

"I'll take my supper now. With a cup of your best wine, please," she said, and sat down at the nearest table, facing away from the innkeeper, keeping her hands under the table so no one would see them tremble.

It got easier after that, even though it made for slow going, burying her treasure every time she stopped at a town, and digging it up again in the morning. She used loose bricks and rabbit-holes when she found them. She felt at home in the world of roots and dirt. And yet, she never again took the form of a hare at night, or if she did, she didn't remember it.

There were other dangers than robbery facing a woman travelling alone, she knew, but though she found herself nervous once or twice, she avoided those, too. On the rare occasions when another woman was at an inn, she saved money and anxiety by sharing a room, sometimes a bed. Perhaps it would have been safer to ask for lodging at religious houses, but she didn't know where the convents were, while the inns seemed to be wherever the roads took her. Besides, the very idea of finding herself inside the walls of a convent now made her skin itch, made her feel as if they might close the gates on her and never let her out.

It was a long three weeks, in the heat of August, washing with a basin where she could, wearing the same smock as she kept all her clean things in the sack and buried it every night. A moment might arise, she thought, when she would want to be in fine clothing again, and she protected it against that eventuality.

Sometimes, when she did not find an inn before nightfall, she was forced to rest in the open, lying next to Mistral in a field. Françoise slept very little, those nights.

It was coming towards evening on the day she left Tours when she turned a corner around a hedge and saw a vast procession walking toward her.

Dozens of people, all on foot, carrying nothing. Dressed in ragged and torn clothing. Their faces grey, their expressions blank.

These wayfarers did not respond to her nods or tentative smiles, or indeed acknowledge her presence at all. Why were so many travelling south on the road from Paris, and on foot? Were they pilgrims?

Mistral stepped to the side, right into the field by the side of the road, and Françoise let her stop and wait for the procession to pass. It took several minutes, as there were so many of them, walking slowly. What inn could provide beds for so many? She was reminded of the stories her father used to tell her of an ancestor who went on Crusade, walking the whole way, although whether out of humility or necessity was never clear. A shudder went through her as she watched the strange people pass. It was several minutes more before Mistral could return to the road and turn her tail to the silent walkers.

BY THE TIME she reached the outskirts of Orléans, August had nearly ended, and she had grown quite comfortable in her own skin, even if that skin was grimier than custom would dictate for the daughter of the seigneur d'Artagnan.

The innkeeper in Orléans was a thin, brisk woman with piercing eyes who told her they were full, and she would have to share a bed with a German woman. Françoise told herself to be grateful on behalf of her depleting stock of coins.

Here, at the edge of a large town not far from Paris, no one looked at her curiously. Everyone seemed wary, in general, and too occupied with their own worries to wonder about an ill-dressed young woman travelling alone.

She ate heartily of roast pork, turnips and salad, and was just tucking into her second cup of thin red wine when the door of the inn opened and a man carrying an arquebus strode in.

Behind him, two other men walked, flanking him and glaring at the occupants of every table.

"We are here for Nicolas Allard," declared the man with the arquebus, loudly.

Nobody said anything.

The innkeeper with the piercing eyes walked toward the invaders, showing no fear. "We have no guest by that name here tonight."

"No, I am sure you do not. If I were a treacherous Huguenot spy, I would not give my real name either. What is *your* name, then?"

The innkeeper answered evenly, "My name is Odile Charbonneau, and I want no trouble."

"Trouble will find you, Madame Charbonneau, if you insist on protecting heretics. The people of Paris have put an end to a plot by the Huguenots against the Royal Family, against the monarchy itself, against the kingdom. Ordinary folks have taken up arms to rid the city of these invaders. It now falls on Orléans to do its part."

"You will find no spies here, I am sure," said the innkeeper sourly. "What information would they hope to glean? My recipe for lemon cake?"

General nervous laughter. One of the thugs behind the leader stepped forward and put a knife to the woman's throat, and the laughter collapsed.

A man stood up in the corner, pushing his chair so that it scraped loudly on the floor. About fifty, thin, with greying stubble, dirty spectacles and a philosopher's manner. "I am here. You seek Nicolas Allard? You have found him."

The thug with the knife strode toward him and without a word, knocked him down on the table and slashed his throat.

Someone screamed.

Françoise stood up, not willing to be a bystander again, but not sure how to be anything else. Her whole body felt out of joint, as if the wrongness of the man's actions had taken her apart without putting her back together again. Her hands were fists and her breath came quickly.

"Get off him," she growled.

The thug, surprised, backed away from his victim, mockingly holding up both hands as if obeying her command, but it did not and would not matter. Blood flowed from the Huguenot's neck as he fought to right himself, moving his arms and legs to no avail. Françoise watched the red pool forming on the floor and thought of the small patches of dried brown on the hilltop, of the vampires sinking their long teeth into the necks of her nameless comrades.

The other guests had all left their tables and were now retreating by the stairs going up to the rooms, jostling each other, getting as far from the three killers as possible. Only Françoise and the innkeeper remained standing like stone where they were.

Then the innkeeper roared.

A blast of terrible wind blew the three killers against the walls with such force that they fell, broken and bloodied like rag dolls.

Françoise felt as if she were turned to stone; she could not move. Not her little finger, not her eyebrow, not her bottom lip, nothing at all. But her heart beat like a tide as she watched the innkeeper leap upon the dying Huguenot. The man was beyond saving, but the innkeeper's objective was not the man himself but the thin river of blood that still ran down from his body to the floor below. The innkeeper's long pale tongue licked the red pool, as she crouched on all fours beside it. The innkeeper called Odile Charbonneau lapped the blood, her face in a state of ecstasy.

Françoise heard the word as her companions had spoken it on the hill, a whispered warning: *Vampire*.

She was still frozen when the bloody-mouthed woman stood up and walked to her, put both hands on her shoulders, and sniffed her neck.

"Who are you?"

The question seemed to loosen her invisible bonds. She shook Madame Charbonneau's hands off her shoulders, and took a step back, bumping a table.

"Just a servant. From the south."

"A servant of whom? Or should I say, of what?"

The vampire smelled of roses, and Françoise was suddenly aware that she was very beautiful, this thin, middle-aged innkeeper who seemed so inconsequential a moment before. The hollow of her cheek was haunting, so Françoise looked away from it, up into her violet eyes, which were worse.

She found herself telling the truth. "I am travelling to Paris, because my parents disowned me. Are you going to kill me?"

"Kill you? No." Madame Charbonneau stepped back from Françoise, as if coming to her senses. She chuckled softly. "No, I had enough of killing, which is why I left Paris, and yet it seems Paris has not done with me. Even here, she sends her gifts my way. But I am not so easily bought. You are on your way there. Why?"

"I am going there to find an old friend. Someone who once protected me. Someone who might need my protection now."

Madame Charbonneau smiled sadly and shook her head. "There is no protection except for the queen's. Paris is a charnel house. And Orléans will be by morning. These three were just the vanguard." She gestured at the bodies on the floor, the ones she had killed with a single roar.

"The queen's..." Françoise began, gathering all her courage to ask the vampire a question.

But Madame Charbonneau put one finger to Françoise's lips. She held it there for a moment, and Françoise had an unaccountable urge to take that finger into her mouth, to taste whatever remnants of blood might be upon it.

Then Madame Charbonneau leaned in close and whispered in her ear, "Get the hell out of my inn while you still can."

CHAPTER FOUR

The Inn of La Belle Étoile

PARIS WAS INDEED a charnel ground. Françoise rode all through that night, the next day, and another night, stopping only to drink water and rest the horse. At one point during the bright heat of afternoon, she found a quiet spot under a windmill wall, curled up and went to sleep. But she was woken an hour or two later by screams, somewhat distant, yet still too close.

From then on, she saw the signs of violence everywhere as she approached Paris. A tree with two men dangling from it. An abandoned carriage with blood on the glass window. Crows circling.

She arrived at Paris in the grey dawn. Françoise had never been to a city so large, with such an enormous gate, like that of a castle, with men walking on top.

The gate seemed a bad joke, with its implication of keeping violence *out*, as Françoise rode north on the Rue Saint-Jacques. Corpses lay scattered in the street, bloodied and bashed. One of them was lying in a shape her mind could not recognize at first, until she realized that what she had taken for another limb was a crooked line of entrails, and then she was sorry she had looked and puzzled it out. Children looked out of windows and watched her pass with idle curiosity. In the streets, a few women with mournful faces were collecting the dead, laying them out on carts. A man wheeled a cart full of fresh bread, an incongruous sight, but the living had to eat.

Even decorated in blood, Paris was beautiful. For a girl from the country, it seemed a wonder. Tall houses, three and four storeys, crowded next to each other, so that the churches came as a surprise. Mistral plodded her way across long shadows.

Françoise knew very little about Paris, but she knew there was a cathedral called Notre Dame on an island at its heart, and she knew that the court was usually in residence at the castle called the Louvre. As she crossed the Seine and gazed at the cathedral, a priest walked past her horse, striding as if to an appointment, keeping his head down. She called to him and asked where she might find the Louvre.

"Carry on over that bridge," he said, pointing to one ahead of her. "Then it will be on your left."

On that second bridge, at last, life seemed ordinary. Butchers of the quotidian sort were preparing their tables and sweeping their thresholds.

Then the Seine again, past small barges tied up. Heeding what the priest had told her, Françoise turned left, riding along the quay until her path was stopped by a drawbridge at the base of a complex of high walls and round towers.

A sentry watched her as she steered Mistral onto the drawbridge. Without dismounting, she said, "I would like to enter the Louvre, please."

The sentry looked her up and down. She and her mare no doubt bore the signs of a long journey, and truth be told, they had not been that impressive to start with. But that long journey must have been for a reason, and this was it. The old man said he was going to court; the court was usually to be found at the Louvre; therefore, she had to get inside.

"Give the password," he said.

"I don't have any password."

"Then you can't get in. Are you mad? At a time like this, you expect me to open the door to anyone who asks?"

"Where can I learn the password?"

"Someone would have to teach it to you."

"But how can I ask them to teach it to me if I can't get in to ask? Isn't there a way to ask for an appointment?"

"An appointment with whom?" The sentry was clearly amused, by this point.

Mistral stamped and huffed, which expressed her rider's feelings perfectly, but it also reminded Françoise that her horse needed a stall, food and water.

"Then will you at least tell me if there is an inn nearby?"

The sentinel had lost interest and his half-smile dropped. "La Belle Étoile. Go back the way you came, then turn left after Saint-Germain L'Auxerrois—that's the big church. You cannot fail to find it."

Françoise did not share his faith, but he was proven right. A large metal sign swayed from one of the buildings, showing a roast chicken hanging in the sky like a star.

In the narrow postern, a boy leaned against the wall. He looked her up and down.

"You are staying at the inn?" he asked.

He was younger than Françoise, skinny, with dirty fingernails. She immediately trusted him.

"If there is a room available."

"Oh, there are rooms available, believe me. We've very few guests because of all the killing, you see. We lost our maid and our cook, too. The master says that Huguenots must have slaughtered them. So we are short-handed, but your horse will be well looked after. That's my job."

"Oh, you're the ostler?"

"Everyone calls me Charlot."

The young ostler held out his hand and helped her dismount.

"What's your name, madame?" His voice was a soft murmur, which saved Françoise some embarrassment as she realized in time that he was talking to the horse.

"Her name is Mistral."

"And a fine strong mare she is. Come on, I've got a beautiful stall waiting and the coldest water, fresh out of the Holy Innocents fountain."

And with that, the young ostler was gone, leaving Françoise to her own business.

Inside, La Belle Étoile was quiet except for a middle-aged man wiping a glass, and a younger man writing on a piece of paper in a dark corner.

"You're too early for food," said the glass-wiper, barely glancing at her.

"That's all right, but in the meantime, I want a room, please."

He straightened and looked at her. "As it happens, business is a little slow since the events of the last few days, so you can have your pick, mademoiselle. Don't tell me you've travelled alone to Paris, now of all times."

She nodded, trying to look confident and sure of herself. "I have business here. I did not know when I set out that there was such an upheaval in Paris."

She was keenly aware that the last time she had been alone with an innkeeper, she had been alone with a vampire. At least here, there was another person in the room. The man in the corner had stopped writing and was now staring at her fixedly, without disguising his interest. She stayed close to the door.

"An upheaval long overdue, if you ask me," said the innkeeper, stoutly. "All the same, not good for business."

"Will you tell me what happened?"

"Do you know nothing, then?"

She bristled. "I come from the south."

"Ah, yes, many visitors from the south lately." He looked at the man in the corner, then back to her, warily. "I would ask your religion, but you would certainly lie to save your own skin, so what is the point in asking?"

"To save my own skin!" Her fear turned to indignation. "Do you mean to say you would murder a woman, a guest in your own inn, over her religion?"

He shrugged.

The man in the corner spoke. "A great number of women have lost their lives, and men too, and even children, since Saint Bartholomew's Night."

The stranger's accent, Françoise noticed, was Gascon, like her own. She had left home on the sixth of August, and it had taken her three weeks, making it the twenty-seventh now. "That would have been, what, three days ago?"

The innkeeper nodded. "Coming from the south, you have heard, no doubt, of the kingdom of Navarre."

"Certainly. And I know that the King of Navarre was to marry the sister of the King of France." One of the neighbour girls was fond of sighing about how beautiful the wedding would be. The lord and lady of Artagnan had taken great pride in the fact that their daughter would be married in the same month as Marguerite, the beautiful princess.

"That's right," said the innkeeper. "They were married. And you may also know that the King of Navarre is a Huguenot."

"Was," interjected the man in the corner. "He converted, I've heard."

The innkeeper shrugged. "Who can tell truth from rumour, these days? But it would not surprise me to learn he changed his colours to save his life. After all, he still lives, when so many of his co-believers do not."

"But he is now the king's brother-in-law!"

"Indeed," said the innkeeper. "Some say the wedding was a trap all along, laid by the queen mother."

Françoise shivered, remembering the words of the old man on the hill. Everyone had said that the queen's plan to marry her daughter Marguerite to a Huguenot was a gesture of peace between the religious factions.

"Do you mean that Queen Catherine arranged the wedding to bring Huguenots to Paris, to make them feel that all was well and we were now at peace, and then... arranged their slaughter? Surely not."

"Oh, I do not say this. I am reporting what others say. But she is a wily one. And why shouldn't she be? She knows what is in the best interests of France, after all these years. She and her son, the king, made everyone believe that they wanted tolerance, harmony, a France where any man could believe whatever nonsense he chose. Pah! I'm glad that's over."

"But what changed? How did the massacre begin?"

"After the wedding, someone took a shot at old Admiral de Coligny, adviser to the King of France and an unrepentant Huguenot. A snake in the very breast of the nation. The Huguenots took offence, and then everyone knew they were surely going to take revenge on the people of Paris, perhaps even on the Royal Family. So we defended ourselves."

With a chill, Françoise remembered the men hanging from the tree, the entrails in the street, the silent procession of grey-faced people walking south from Paris.

"Did the Huguenots have any warning?"

"Warning? What do you mean?"

"Never mind," she said. "I never imagined that so much death could come just because some people believe... what do the Huguenots believe, anyway?"

The man in the corner cleared his throat. "They believe that the Church is corrupt and has too much money and power, and that it's God who chooses which sinners are to be saved, not the priests."

"They are fanatical rebels who rail against the divine right of kings and deny the presence of Christ in the Eucharist, among other heresies," snapped the landlord.

"That too," acknowledged the stranger amiably.

"So, you see," summed up the landlord, "you have chosen a strange time to travel to Paris, a young woman from the south, all alone. What business do you have here?"

No business of yours, Françoise wanted to retort, but she needed help and advice wherever she could get it. She was here to find the others of her kind, the comrades who had fought the vampires beside her. And she could only find them here; the only clue she had was the old man's talk about Paris, about the queen, working in the shadows. Could he have known that the queen was setting a trap?

She replied, "I am seeking an old friend. I don't know where he is staying in Paris, but I know he has business with the court, so I must seek him there. But I don't know how to gain access to the Louvre."

"Nothing could be simpler," said the man in the corner.

"Careful, Chicot," said the landlord, in a low, serious tone. "This seems a virtuous girl."

"I suggest nothing untoward, Maître La Hurière. Mademoiselle, the one thing that unites every person whose blood or business brings them to the Louvre is a desire to leave that gloomy castle. Most afternoons, you can find certain members of the court walking in the gardens of the Tuileries, which you can find by going back toward the Louvre, and then carrying on in the same direction until you leave the city gates. I have a feeling you will find the man you seek there."

IT TOOK FRANÇOISE a little time to dress herself in the robin's egg blue gown she had brought with her, which was now quite rumpled and had a faint musty smell, after having been buried in a sack several nights running.

The afternoon was warm, and by the time she passed the Louvre and reached the city wall, she was already sweaty in all places she had carefully washed with the cloth and basin back in her room at the inn.

At least the sentry at the gate paid no mind to her now. A well-dressed young woman going out in the daytime, even one with no escorts or companions, was doubtless less concerning than a dirty traveller at dawn.

There was a long palace under construction, only a short walk from the Louvre. It was only half-built, without roof or windows, but was very imposing all the same. On the far side of it were the gardens, latticed with pathways, creating squares of green grass, flowers, shrubs, fruit trees or patterns of rocks. There was even a small labyrinth in the middle. Françoise was delighted, walking from one square to the next, her skirt swishing, discovering new worlds. She might have forgotten to pay attention to the couples and small groups of people walking on the other paths, if it weren't for the fact that her entire purpose was to find her rescuer.

One of the squares had four benches arranged on each side, staring outward. Within was a cluster of five lime trees, arranged like the points on a die. She stopped, suddenly homesick for the first time. Françoise used to drink a tisane of lime leaves in hot water when she had a sore throat, and it always made her feel comforted. She had no tree of her own, now, no place of her own either, and might not for some time.

She reached out to the nearest tree, touched a leaf between finger and thumb, leaned forward to sniff it, and put her left foot onto the grass.

From there, it was nothing to take another step, into the square designated for viewing, not for touching. She settled herself down at the base of the centre tree, leaned against the bark and breathed in the scent of home, of childhood, of safety. No one could see her, thanks to the benches set around the square. It was a chance to take the first deep breaths she'd taken in weeks, and to think about her predicament.

When she opened her eyes she saw, to her horror, a pair of fine gentlemen's heels in grey velvet peeking out from the bottom of the bench in front of her.

Françoise dropped low, and turned around to crawl out the other side.

Another set of heels confronted her: black ones, belonging to a lady. She could see the woman's jaunty cap above the back of the bench.

There was no wriggling out without being perceived.

She'd have to wait, then, until both visitors stood up again and walked away.

The gentleman spoke, softly. "Noctu pro more?"

Françoise knew very little Latin, only enough to recognize it. There was something familiar about the voice, though. She had heard that voice inside her own head, telling her to run.

It was the voice from the old man on the hill. She was certain.

She got to her feet ungracefully and strode out into the pathway, looking with excitement to the occupant of the bench.

But this was no old man dressed in rags holding a yarrow stalk. He was perhaps forty, dressed in a cerulean velvet cloak, with silk ribbons on his knees, and a handsome face that Françoise did not recognize. He looked up at her with astonishment, and sat up straight, like a schoolboy caught passing a note.

"Pardon me, sir," she said breathlessly. "I thought you were someone else."

He smiled, politely but not warmly. "No need for pardon. In these gardens, it is easy to make such a mistake."

Françoise's heart beat faster. There was no mistaking that voice.

"I think I know you, sir."

His smile vanished. "I am quite sure we have not met."

"But we have. On a hill in Gascony."

Faster than thought, he was on his feet, his hand on her arm, his breath in her ear. "Not here. Be at the church of Saint-Germain L'Auxerrois in one hour. In the Chapel of the Virgin. And watch yourself in the meantime."

Then he laughed loudly, kissed her on the cheek, let go of her arm and strode off in an ambling fashion down the paths.

When Françoise had recovered from her astonishment, she looked at the other bench, where the lady had been sitting, but there was no one there.

CHAPTER FIVE

Two Encounters with Gentlemen

FRANÇOISE WAS ALREADY acquainted with the church where he had suggested they meet—in fact, it was the only church in Paris whose name she *did* know, as it was between the Louvre and La Belle Étoile.

She wanted to skip with elation as she went back through the city wall. The old man had proven easy to find, after all! Yes, he looked nothing like the tall spirit who had saved her in Gascony, but he spoke with the same voice. Surely she was on the right track.

Deep in these thoughts, she ran straight into another pedestrian as he turned a corner into the street she was on.

He bowed low, sweeping away a black cape. "My pardon, mademoiselle."

"Not at all," she responded, flustered. "I was not paying attention."

"A risky practice, on these streets. Did you find who you were looking for, then?"

It was then she realized he spoke in a Gascon accent, although this voice, unlike that of the old man, had not yet seared itself into her mind.

"Ah, you are the man from the inn!"

"At your service. My name is Count Jean-Antoine d'Anglerais, but my friends and enemies call me Chicot, and I would be delighted if you would do the same."

She remembered her manners and held her hand out for him to take. "I am Françoise de Montesquiou d'Artagnan. Am I to be your friend or your enemy?"

"We shall have to find out! But you did not answer my question. Was my advice good? Did you find the one you sought in the gardens?"

After a moment to consider, she prudently said, "No, I did not."

"Ah. Well, I can't say I'm sorry."

"Why not?"

"Because I would have been jealous."

She blushed. "I am not in Paris to conduct love affairs, sir."

"Why are you here, then? Why now, when the city is stinking with blood?"

"To settle a matter of honour."

She expected to be laughed at, but instead he nodded seriously. "That sounds like a story. Will you tell it to me?"

"No, I cannot."

He shrugged. "A pity. Then may I accompany you to La Belle Étoile? These streets are not safe for a woman alone, not even in daylight."

"But how do I know you are safe?"

"You don't. Although I submit that, if my plan had been to rob you or carry you off, I would have done so by now."

Françoise looked up and down the street and saw only a few distant figures scurrying in various directions on their own business.

"Then I accept your offer," she said, and took his arm. "But I am only going as far as the church. Saint German L'Auxerrois. I wish to give thanks to God for my safe journey to Paris."

"I will content myself with a short walk, then, and perhaps we will have a longer at another time. I don't meet many people from our part of the world here."

She realized they had slipped comfortably into her own Gascon dialect. It did make her feel safe, although some more cynical part of her mind warned her that she could not make her decisions based on instinct, given that she was a young stranger from the countryside in a city full of terrors.

"Monsieur Chicot—"

"Not monsieur. Just Chicot, if you please."

"It is a very odd sobriquet. How did you come by it?"

"Don't you think it suits me?"

"Not really, because where I come from, chicot means tree stump, and you are quite tall."

"Perhaps it is ironic."

"Perhaps?"

"You were going to ask me a question, Mademoiselle d'Artagnan."

She almost said that if he was just Chicot, he should call her Françoise, but couldn't bring herself to be that forward. "All right. I was going to ask whether you understand Latin."

"Are you going to preach me a sermon?"

"I want to know the meaning of the phrase *noctu pro more*."

His face showed first confusion, then amusement. "I take it you overheard this in the gardens? It means, my new friend, that two lovers are arranging a tryst. The translation would be 'tonight as usual.'"

"Oh," said Françoise, blushing. She had interrupted the gentleman and lady; that explained why the lady had vanished. How ordinary!

"It seems your visit to the garden was entertaining, if unsatisfactory."

They had come to the church; they both looked up at the belfry, which seemed impossibly tall.

Chicot pointed. "The bell in that tower is named Marie, and she sang on Saint Bartholomew's night, to tell the people of Paris to take up arms, and take up arms they did."

She wanted to ask him whether he had killed any Huguenots, but it was impossible to ask the question, somehow. It was too big and terrible a subject to speak of, and too big and terrible a subject to ignore. The streets of Paris seemed quiet enough tonight, at least. Perhaps the killing was over and done with.

"I thank you, monsieur, for your kindness," she said, and curtsied.

He bowed in response. "It was not out of kindness I escorted you, but curiosity. It is a flaw in my character. Quod me nutrit me destruit. That is Latin, too. I will tell you what it means at supper, if you return to La Belle Étoile."

With that, he walked across the street, leaving Françoise looking up at the great carved entrance that loomed above her. There was a wooden door to one side, ajar, and she made for it.

With her hand upon the door, some feeling made her pause and turn to look where he had gone. But Chicot was walking away from her, whistling.

She went inside.

THE CHURCH OF Saint Germain L'Auxerrois stretched up to heaven, filled with holy silence and dust that swirled in the light from its narrow windows. On those few occasions when Françoise had been inside a church as big as this one, there had been crowds and sonorous piety. This church was empty save for the shuffling of clergy in the shadows, making no more noise than rats' feet, and save for a single figure kneeling at the front near the altar.

She recognized him by the cerulean cloak, and by the posture, so straight, even in supplication. Was she meant to approach him here, while he was at prayer? She hesitated, then took a few steps forward—they seemed to ring in that hollow place—and knelt beside him.

"What fur did you wear when I saw you last?" he whispered.

She recovered from her brief confusion and answered, "That of a hare."

"I thought as much. And my own appearance was different then, was it not?"

"You took the form of a very old man, and very tall. Impossibly tall."

He breathed out, although in relief or grief, she could not say.

"Do I pass the test?" It came out a little more loudly than she intended, and he winced.

"Be on your guard," he whispered. "This place has no protections. I chose it for that reason, because they do not suspect it, and thus will not watch it. Here we are in plain sight, which is often the safest place, until it isn't."

She did not ask whom he meant by *they*. Suddenly the statues, who had gazed sternly at her as she walked into the church, seemed more sinister and she resisted the urge to look behind her. "Are not all churches protection against evil?"

"If only that were so. Symbols can ward off some of the older ones, if they are wielded by someone of pure faith, but a person of pure faith is no more frequently found inside a church than anywhere else, alas. Yes, you pass the test. You are who you claim to be, more's the pity. And you recognized me—how? By my voice?"

She nodded.

"But I spoke only a few words."

"There was no mistaking it, monsieur. I was taken aback by your appearance, and yet I was sure you were the man I sought."

"My spirit is much older than my body. This is a skill you may learn yourself, in time. You say you sought me? You have travelled many leagues, then. For what purpose?"

"To offer you my thanks and my service. You saved my life in Gascony, in more ways than one. Whatever assistance I can provide, it is yours."

"Assistance!" He was startled out of his whispers, briefly. Then, softly: "I do not ask for your assistance, and you should go home immediately. It is not safe here."

"Clearly, it is not safe there either."

"But Paris is the centre of the spider's web. The best way you can repay any service I did you is to survive. Go home at first light tomorrow."

"I cannot," she said simply. "My parents have disowned me, as they consider me... unnatural. I have nowhere to go. Perhaps I could join your household."

"I have no household. I am a guest at the Louvre, and I only arrived a few days ago myself. Though I travelled as quickly as I could from Gascony, I was not in time to prevent the massacre..." His voice trailed off. Then he continued gruffly: "I do not even keep a servant. There is no haven I can provide for you. Indeed, I fear it may already be impossible to get you safely out of Paris. Who knows you are here?"

She thought. "The sentries at the city walls and at the Louvre know my face and my name. So does the landlord at La Belle Étoile. Oh, and another guest there, who calls himself Chicot. It was he who told me where to find you."

"Then you told this stranger you were looking for me? By all that's holy, you have no wits at all!"

"I did not tell him anything about you. I merely said I was looking for someone at court, to... to settle a matter of honour." It sounded ridiculous and childish now, and she blushed, but better to sound ridiculous than foolhardy. "He said many people walk in those gardens in the afternoon."

"And did you see many people, in those gardens?"

She was taken aback. The fact was that she had not: only a few small groups and couples. "I don't understand."

"Clearly." He sighed. "Is there anyone else on the list?"

After a mere moment's pause, she ventured, "I had an encounter with one of *them*. A vampire. This was in Orléans, though, not Paris. I do not think I told her my name. I do not think she knew I was… anything but ordinary. Her name was Madame Charbonneau."

He did not move, but his hands were fists, where they lay atop his knees. "You had an encounter with her? And you escaped?"

"She seemed to be… satisfied with the victims who came before me. She let me leave. Encouraged me to leave, in fact."

He was silent for a long time. "I believe you have been lucky."

She could not help but snort. "Lucky! It was a moment that will trouble my sleep forever."

"I do not doubt it. Tell me: she did not seek you out? It was a coincidence, you meeting her?"

"I was simply looking for a place to sleep. Why? Do you mean that it was not a coincidence, that I encountered her because… because of what happened in Gascony?"

"No. If she had known what you were, she would not have let you live. If it seemed to be coincidence, it likely was. I am sorry to say that many people in France are encountering vampires these days, as their ranks grow among us. Most who get close enough to witness their crimes do not escape, or if they do, their minds lose the memory. People are very good at forgetting horrors, and some vampires have a kind of influence on the minds of those around them, which can hasten the forgetting. But I am speaking of ordinary people. You are not ordinary, mademoiselle. You are one of us. You do not have the privilege of forgetting. But there are compensations. I said you were lucky, and I meant it. Luck is one of our gifts, or it can be. But we must never take it for granted. You have much to learn about the dangers we face."

"Indeed, I do have much to learn," said Françoise, her anger and desperation winning out over her desire to show her protector deference and respect. "And I wish to learn it. If I cannot do you a service, at least let me learn from you what these creatures are, and what I am. I deserve to know what I am!"

He was silent for a moment. "I agree with that. Which was one reason I convened the gathering in the first place. But I was wrong to do so. It was rash, a miscalculation. I did not know whether it was safer for you and others like you to know what you are, or to remain ignorant."

She shivered. "You were not wrong. You opened my eyes. And now that they are open, I cannot close them again. I cannot. If this knowledge ends in my death, well, it will be no different than what awaits me out in the world with no money to my name and no idea what creatures hunt me."

"In a matter of five minutes' conversation with me, a man whose name you do not know, you provided me with two valuable pieces of information, without even knowing that you did so," he said, but she could hear the hesitation in his voice, so she did not argue. He continued: "But information flows two ways, and the fact that you are unknown here, and so clearly innocent in the ways of the court, could make you valuable." He sighed, and concluded, "If you join us, you will have to learn how and when to keep your mouth shut, and you will have to learn quickly. You will have to be able to lie and dissemble. Your spirit chose the form of a hare: like the hare, you must be always vigilant, still, and ready to move quickly and forcefully when danger threatens you."

She nodded, and said nothing, waiting for him to realize he'd talked himself into it.

He rubbed his face. "I suppose the time has come to introduce myself. I am Henri de Sainct Didier. What is your name?"

She told him.

"A daughter of nobility?"

"My father is the lord of Artagnan. We have only a modest estate, but our name is respected."

"Relatives? Anyone who knows you or your family at court?"

"I don't think so."

Sainct Didier thought for a moment. "An ancient countess died recently, a woman of little consequence and no family, but whose antecedents were great. We could give it out that you are this woman's distant relative, that you travelled to Paris to be a companion to her, not knowing she was dead, and that your servants were killed on the road. By Huguenots. People will believe anything of Huguenots at the moment."

Françoise swallowed. "Then I am to live at the Louvre?"

"Not at the Louvre, but at the Hôtel de Guise, where the Duchess of Nevers is staying. She is one of our kind. A Benandante."

Françoise had never heard the word. "Is that Italian, monsieur?"

"It is the only name I have ever known, but I come from Piedmont myself. We are the Good Walkers. Our ancient enemies are a vampire tribe, the Malandanti, the Evil Walkers. They have recently asserted control in Paris, exterminating their ancient rivals and converting new victims to their kind. Anyone in Paris could be a vampire. As for the Benandanti, well, we have the disadvantage that we cannot create new members. We are born, or we are not. And even those of us who are born to it sometimes refuse the call. We are also solitary by nature, and when we do meet, it tends to be in spirit form, out on the land, as you saw that night. I know the names of only two others in the city, beyond you and me. One of them is the duchess."

Françoise's eyes went wide. "Was she—was she the woman who spoke to you, in the garden? Before I interrupted."

"Precisely. The duchess is the closest confidante of Queen Marguerite, the king's sister, who still lives in the Louvre even after her marriage to the King of Navarre, and so you will doubtless have many reasons to go there. Tonight, though, you may sleep at that inn, La Belle Étoile; it is as safe a place as any, I think. Tomorrow, I will write you a letter that purports to be from your father, addressed to the late countess, thanking her for taking you into her service. We will show this to the Duchess of Nevers, who was related to the countess, and present your case to her. We will appeal to her generosity of spirit and she will let you into her service. Everything will be above board and there will be evidence and witnesses to all of it if the queen investigates, and she will investigate. Even a little country mouse coming to live in Paris will not escape her attention."

"The queen?"

"The queen mother, to be precise. Catherine de' Medici. The most powerful vampire in Paris. We know she is the head of the Malandanti tribe now, but the other members of that tribe are as yet unknown to us."

She felt sick. In a city where the queen was a vampire, what justice or mercy could there be for anyone? She had come to Paris looking for answers, and for the companion of her battle in the hills. Now she had found both, and she felt no comfort from either. She said very little as Sainct Didier escorted her out of the church and back to the inn.

CHAPTER SIX

The Duchess of Nevers

THE DUCHESS OF Nevers appeared to be a woman on the threshold of thirty, with tight golden curls, an arched eyebrow and a curious, self-satisfied smile. A thick white ruff of lace framed her chin, and she wore a velvet cap of a very deep blue, matching her gown. She leaned forward in her chair and looked at Françoise closely.

They were deep within the guest apartments at the Hôtel de Guise. In Paris, every private mansion or stately townhome was called the Hôtel of Something. This one belonged to the powerful Guise family, but the lady of the chamber who showed Françoise to the room told her the Duchess of Nevers was a frequent guest, as she had vast estates in the country but as yet, no hôtel of her own in Paris. It was the duchess who had the money and title in her marriage, the lady of the chamber confided. She also spoke the words *frequent guest* in a portentous manner; was she implying that the duchess was having an affair? Clearly, gossip was not discouraged in the Hôtel de Guise.

It might have been easier if there were only the two of them in the room, instead of the three other ladies standing behind the duchess's chair, looking on in amusement. Françoise might have been more frank, with just the duchess, but then again, she was not supposed to be frank, not anymore. Frankness had always been among her most charming qualities. Here, in Paris, she would have to learn to lie.

For the moment, she simply stood stock still and stared back. Sainct Didier had warned her that the duchess might seem to be resistant, but he had assured her she would say yes in the end.

At last, the duchess said, "You were sent to Paris to join the household of a countess, and upon finding the countess deceased, you have decided to trade up for a duchess instead. Is that so? Perhaps we should investigate the death of the countess; murders have happened for less."

The other women smiled, but nervously; the joke seemed to unnerve them.

"I am content with any position madame la duchesse might bestow upon me, and will perform any duties that may be required."

"Hmm. You do not speak properly; you are dressed like a bumpkin. It would reflect badly on me to have such an attendant. And yet… yet it may be an interesting challenge. What do you think, Louise? Marie, what do you think? We could have a little doll to dress up. We could teach her our ways."

Françoise thought she had spoken very prettily. She blushed.

"Let us try it," the duchess said with a wave of her hand. "Let us see what clay we have to mould. What are your skills? Do you have any?"

"I ride, and I am very good in the garden."

The three attendants tittered. The duchess, though, merely tapped her chin, above the ruff. "Yes, I am sure you are," she said, quietly, thoughtfully. Then, more loudly, she declared, "We will make a trial of you. I was going to make a donation of my old clothing to the poor anyway, in thanks for the miraculous deliverance of the Royal Family on Saint Bartholomew's Day. Louise, Marie, go into my dressing room and bring out some treats that might suit this little mouse."

The two attendant ladies inclined their heads, and moved into the next room.

The duchess took the opportunity to step in close to Françoise and speak in a harsh whisper. "Sainct Didier has vouched for you. Do not betray my trust. He says you can go unnoticed where he and I cannot, and perhaps that is so. When I am at the Louvre, I am always in the company of Queen Marguerite. I will give you an errand to the Louvre, but your true assignment is to get lost. Go where you are not supposed to go. See what you are not meant to see."

Françoise only had time to nod before Louise and Marie returned with armloads of gowns, petticoats and kirtles.

"Ah, perfect!" said the duchess, petting the silks and brocades. "When we have dressed you in something suitable, you will go the Louvre and pay a visit to Maître René, the royal perfumer, who holds regular consultations at the palace. When you see Maître René, you will ask him for some orange blossom. It is out of season now, and I need some for my sachets."

A visit to the Louvre already! She inclined her head. "And how shall I pay him, madame?"

There was a long pause. Then, the duchess, in a high, amused voice: "Pay him? Maître René is retained by Her Majesty the queen mother, and I was once lady-in-waiting to the queen mother. He will not refuse you."

At the mention of the great vampire, Françoise stiffened.

The duchess shot her a warning look. "Go now, and get dressed properly. I think pale lavender would suit that wheat-coloured hair of yours. Yes, lavender or perhaps pink, but not yellow."

* * *

Somehow, Françoise ended up in yellow anyway. She felt a little like a buttercup, with a wide ruff at her neck like opening petals.

She did not feel that this would be suitable as a riding costume, although Mistral was now stabled at the Hôtel de Guise. She was not important enough for a litter. So she walked through winding streets, guided by glimpses of the Seine.

Françoise passed a stone cross in the middle of a crossroads, and saw people crowding the public fountain at its base, jostling and trying to move something out of the way. It was a man in rags, lying listless with the water splashing over him. His eyes were rolled back in his head, and he was as pallid as a corpse, but she could see from the frantic movements of one leg that he was not dead. He was in the throes of some illness, she thought.

Then, as the crowd managed to move him out of the way, she saw the marks on his neck.

A poor man, dressed in rags, half-starved with hunger. Surely he had suffered enough in this world without also being subjected to the gluttony of vampires.

This time, when she reached the Louvre, she had a password, but it gave her little satisfaction.

"The lion's tooth," she said to the sentry, feeling a bit ridiculous.

He put up his halberd and let her pass. She was over the moat that separated the castle from the rest of the city, and into the tall square collection of walls and towers. The beating, bloody heart of France.

Inside a marble hall, a doorkeeper passed her off to a lady, who showed her through long, grand rooms into an antechamber reserved for the use of Maître René when he came to the Louvre. So far, she was not seeing many opportunities to get lost.

There were no furnishings in the empty antechamber other

than tapestries hanging on three walls. The fourth wall was almost entirely occupied by a painting of a city. Beside the painting there was a single door.

What was she to do next? There was no one in the antechamber, not even an usher or a footman. After a few moments of anxious reflection, she rapped primly on the door.

It opened, and a middle-aged man in faded black stood at the threshold and looked her up and down. He had a face carved out of rock and a cruel mouth.

"Good afternoon, Maître René," she said and curtseyed.

At that, the mouth moved into a smile no less cruel than the grimace of before. "I am not he. I am his servant. Do you have a message?"

She recovered her dignity. "I wish to speak with him."

"And you have no appointment? Maître René consults by appointment only."

"But I was told... I have come on behalf of the Duchess of Nevers."

An eyebrow twitched.

"All the same, you do not have an appointment."

The door closed again, leaving Françoise alone in the antechamber.

Frustrated, she paced in front of the enormous painting, which covered several panels, and depicted the city from God's own view. A red ribbon painted at the bottom bore the word "FIRENZE" in gold. Maître René must have come from Florence, too, like the queen mother.

There was a spot on the ribbon where the paint looked worn. Acting on some instinct, she reached out her finger and ran it along the bare patch.

There was a click, and a creak. Françoise had to take a quick step backward to avoid the panel swinging open towards her, revealing a dark space inside the wall.

Naturally, she stepped inside. She had a brief glance around a small bare room, the walls simple wood. This windowless, lampless room was not meant as a room at all, she realized, but merely a passage into the antechamber from somewhere else, so that royal visitors could avoid the curious eyes of the thousands of people who had some business at the Louvre. It was such a narrow passage that she could touch either side of it, and when she took three steps, she encountered the outline of a door.

Then she whirled back to the opening in the painting, as she heard footsteps approaching the antechamber the same way she had come. She immediately pulled the painting panel shut behind her to shield her from view; she felt that she was exploring somewhere she was not meant to be.

Now she was in darkness. She could hear her own breath. In the antechamber, the footsteps got closer, and then the other door, to the perfumer's room, opened again.

A young man's voice asked: "Is he ready for me?"

The servant replied. "Yes, Your Highness. Come with me." There was a pause, then, "Maître René, the duke is here."

And the sound of the door closing.

A duke!

There was a sound from the next room, like a chair scraping, and then a man's voice, with an Italian accent, saying *Please, monsieur, take this one.*

The perfumer. It must be him. And she could hear his voice, clear as a bell. It seemed she had found a way to get usefully lost.

More conversation from the next room. This time, a younger man, French, saying, *I want you to confirm Ruggieri's horoscope. I know you use some of his methods.* That must be the duke.

The older Italian man—Maître René—replied, *Yes, I have consulted on all the royal horoscopes, for your brother the king as well as for the Duke of Alençon. I would be pleased to offer you any assistance I can, monsieur.*

She felt her eyes go wide, for all it did her in that dark chamber. The client with Maître René was one of the king's brothers. Catherine de' Medici had three sons living: King Charles IX, the Duke of Anjou, and the Duke of Alençon. The perfumer had just mentioned the first and the third, so this one, the handsome man consulting on his horoscope, must be the Duke of Anjou. The middle brother, heir to the throne. And she could hear every word.

Maître René said, *We will start with the palm. Just like so, if you don't mind, monseigneur. Your palm is very eloquent. You will have a long life.*

The Duke of Anjou: *A long life? Is that what you see?*

Maître René: *It is indisputable. I have never seen such clear signs.*

The Duke of Anjou: *And yet, your friend Ruggieri took a bit of my hair and my blood and all the information about my birth, and he told my mother that I would die very young. Oh, there's no need to deny it; my mother told me herself, as it amuses her to cause us pain. As I am about to turn twenty-one, surely I cannot be considered very young much longer.*

Maître René: *I do not dispute Ruggieri's horoscope, and yet, your palm is clear. Some signs say you will die young, and yet other signs say you will live a long life. Perhaps your fortune hangs in the balance, and one or the other will come true, and all depends on some choice that lies before you.*

The Duke of Anjou: *I don't think that's what it means at all, René.*

A silence.

Maître René: *Oh, you have another theory, monseigneur?*

The Duke of Anjou: *It quite clearly means that my mother will soon induct me into her bloody company.*

A new voice, closer, broke in. A conversation in the antechamber, this time.

"I will wait for my appointment. In the meantime, may I ask your advice?"

Françoise was startled, and a little annoyed at the interruption to her eavesdropping.

The servant's voice, oily and bored. "My advice?"

"On perfume. That is why we are here, is it not? You must know all the master's products. I want to buy a gift. For a certain lady. The trouble is, I can't decide between something very distinctive—something that cannot fail to make her think of me, but something she might hate—and something very popular, that anyone is sure to like. What would you choose?"

She had missed some of the more important conversation, but when the questioner in the antechamber stopped, she heard the Duke of Anjou say, *Why shouldn't she? She has made both my brothers vampires. Why not me? Oh, don't look so surprised. I know you know all about it.*

"I'd ask the lady," the servant murmured in the antechamber.

"Oh, but then it wouldn't be a surprise."

She missed René's response, damn it! But now Anjou said: *If you are suggesting that my mother delays this gift because of her love for me, then you do not know my mother at all.*

Maître René answered: *My pardon, monseigneur. I spoke out of turn. Will there be anything else?*

Françoise barely had time to compose her expression before the far door of her little secret passageway opened onto sunlight and a beautiful, dark-haired young woman stood there, clearly shocked to see her.

So Françoise did the only thing she could: she took her skirt in her hands and brushed past her without a word, as if she had every right in the world to be there too.

Françoise kept walking, room to room to room, and now she was well and truly lost. When a staircase appeared, she went down, then turned to her right.

With every step, she thought about the information she had learned. *Almost anyone in Paris could be a vampire*, Sainct Didier had said. *The other members of that tribe are as yet unknown to us*. Well, not anymore.

Along the way, the guards and ushers seemed to pay her no attention. She felt almost invisible, until she came into a small room where a young, pale man was staring out the window into the courtyard. He was gripping the windowsill in alarm, as if what he was watching was a shock to him.

Perhaps someone outside was hurt—perhaps there was violence.

Françoise crossed to about a foot behind him and tried to see what he was looking at. The glass was not perfect, but she could make out two figures fighting with swords.

"Is it another massacre?" she asked.

The man whirled around. "What? Oh, outside? No, it's just the fencing master giving lessons." He laughed bitterly. "I recognized his style, that's all. I did not know he was here."

"The fencing master? You mean Henri de Sainct Didier?"

"I don't know his name. It might be."

He put a hand to his shoulder, with a small grimace; it seemed turning to greet her had caused him some pain.

"Monsieur, are you hurt?"

"Not really. The wound is a few days old and no reason for concern. It is simply stubborn, as I am."

He smiled.

Françoise smiled back, while she thought: A few days. He must have been injured in the massacre. But which side had he been on? The Catholic one, presumably, since he was here at the Louvre, in the bosom of the Catholic royal family.

"I am Count Joseph Hyacinthe Boniface de Lerac de la Môle, at your service," he said, bowing low, with one arm across his chest. He caught her blinking and frowning on his way back up, and he repeated, "Count La Môle."

She remembered to curtsy. "Françoise de Montesquiou d'Artagnan. I appear to be lost."

He laughed, as best as he could manage with the pain from his wound. "I am new to Paris myself, or I would help you. I'm going down to the courtyard now, though, to see this fencing master before he finishes his lesson with the duke. You could come with me. You might get a better perspective from the middle."

She stared at him. "The duke?"

"Yes, he's fencing with the Duke of Alençon."

The youngest of the three brothers. And, as Françoise had just learned, a vampire.

She rushed to the window, leaned on the sill and looked out. The two men had their swords in a tangle, so close they were nearly wrestling. How would a vampire react to a mistimed parry, a stray drop of blood?

"Yes, monsieur, I will come with you. If you don't mind."

CHAPTER SEVEN

The Fencers

Françoise and La Môle went out into the bright central courtyard of the Louvre. The height of the walls and towers of the square fortress made it feel as if the world outside no longer existed, despite the faint sounds of shouting and horses that made it across the moat from the city outside. They walked diagonally across the open space inside the palace.

La Môle pointed out various parts of the castle to tell her what they were.

"The king's private armoury must be in there, along with the rest of His Majesty's apartments," he said, indicating a tall, rectangular block squeezed between abutting walls. "But the fencing masters and their students among the nobles in the palace must use a general armoury, so that they don't have to go to the university or to the masters' houses to practise."

"Sainct Didier doesn't have a house," she said absently, keeping her eye on the two fencers as they got closer.

"No, I think he is recently arrived, like me," said La Môle. "He's an old soldier of some kind, I think. How is that you know him?"

The question took her off guard. "That is my own business, monsieur."

"Of course, of course. You must forgive my frankness. I am not used to Paris intrigues."

They had reached the area where the fencing lessons were happening. Several young men were watching, with swords in their hands; Chicot was among them, and he nodded briefly to her. It seemed he had found his own way into the Louvre.

Sainct Didier was fencing with a young man in beautiful, voluminous grey hose and a black doublet. Françoise was nearly breathless, watching Sainct Didier move with confidence, prudence and speed, delighting in his own lean muscles: though he looked nothing like the old man with the yarrow stalk, there was no doubt this was the same person. She could tell that his opponent, although he was younger and stronger, did not share his skill, and knew it.

The young duke fighting him was red in the face when he caught sight of La Môle and Françoise, and put up his sword, gesturing with his chin to show the fencing master they had a new audience.

Sainct Didier did not seem to recognize Françoise at all. He looked at them without emotion, without reaction.

La Môle said, "Forgive me for interrupting."

"Not at all," said Sainct Didier, still ignoring Françoise. "Monsieur, what can I help you with?"

"My own sword is out for sharpening, and I thought I might try something lighter. More flexible, perhaps. But I'll return when you and His Highness have finished."

"No, don't do that," said the young fencer laconically, sweeping his dull blade through the air. Then, without warning, he pointed the sword straight at the throat of La Môle. "You're in my service now, Huguenot, don't forget, and I don't want you caught without a weapon."

His face was pock-marked, his nose rather bulbous, and he looked very young, just barely old enough to shave. And yet he was a vampire; would he never look any older?

La Môle, unbothered, inclined his head. "Of course, Your Highness."

Françoise could not help staring at the duke—at the vampire. How ordinary he looked, with a bit of reddish beard, and colour in his cheeks like any man. Not very good looking, but confident, haughty, every inch the prince. He pulled his sword away from La Môle, and turned aside as if bored or disgusted.

Then the duke seemed to catch an expression on Sainct Didier's face as the swordmaster looked at La Môle. "Ah, swordmaster, you wonder at the fact that I have taken a Huguenot into my service, when the whole city is now baying for their blood. Well, as it happens, I am a freethinker, and contrary by nature, and when my mother, my brother the king, and their hangers-on all turn against whole families and even whole cities, I am inclined to look upon those people as my allies. Why not? We youngest sons of kings must find our friends where we can. Besides, my sister Marguerite asked me to do it, when she found this poor creature in pain after the massacre, and I refuse my sister nothing."

He finished with a chivalric flourish of his sword, and La Môle acknowledged the favour he'd done him with a nod of the head that was no more enthusiastic than it needed to be.

Then the duke, rather rudely, said, "And who are you, mademoiselle? Are you lost?"

"She was, but perhaps she is not any longer," said La Môle. "Have you got your bearings now, Mademoiselle d'Artagnan?"

Sainct Didier said quickly, "Monsieur, let's both see this lady to her destination, if you permit me, Your Highness."

The duke nodded lazily.

Sainct Didier strode to her, took her arm, and said over his shoulder, "Stay quiet."

The moment they were out of earshot, he said to La Môle, "I recognize you, sir. I know where you were wounded, having treated it myself. And the way you swing your arm, just so.

But how did you know me? You may speak. Mademoiselle d'Artganan is one of our kind."

Françoise was startled by this. "I thought we were not to speak of it," she whispered.

La Môle looked at her wonderingly, then back to the fencing master. "And I recognized you by your manner of fighting, sir."

Sainct Didier made a face. "By heaven, if you can recognize me that way, our enemies might, too. I'll have to remember to change my technique." He stopped walking, and explained to Françoise: "During the massacre, we few Benandanti who were in or near to Paris heard the drums, and we were called to protect the innocent."

Françoise thought back: she had arrived in Paris a few days after the massacre, and had heard no drums on her journey. Perhaps she had not been close enough to the city. She remembered the procession of the dead, and shivered, but did not want to speak of that vision in this sunny courtyard with men she barely knew.

"In Gascony, you said you were on your way to Paris," she recalled.

The swordmaster nodded and spoke very quietly. "Yes. I had received word from an old friend here that the Benandanti would be needed, that the queen had made herself a brood of hungry vampires, and they would have to be fed."

La Môle frowned. "I have been trying to determine the goal of all her schemes. Why would she turn so many into vampires, when she knows that vampires always turn against their own eventually?"

"It began in desperation, and desperation feeds itself," Sainct Didier responded. "She has been fighting for control of the throne of France for years, since the days when her two young sons were king in name only, and every faction tried to supplant her and control them. I do not know when it was that she herself stepped onto the path of the Malandanti, but she quickly began to use the powers of her kind to support her family. Vampires can influence the minds of others, but they exert a powerful control over the creatures they have newly turned. The more vampires she had under her thrall, the more she could use them like chess pieces, both inside the palace and further afield, in the city, in the estates, in the army.

"But as you say, sir, vampires become fractious over time. She found that her creations were liable to rebel against her, and to seek out the older Malandanti of Paris to ally with them against her. So she rooted out these older vampires, as she saw them as her rivals. The one you encountered, mademoiselle, the one called Madame Charbonneau—she is an enemy of the queen's who has somehow managed to evade her. She was not among the vampires who started the massacre, who took advantage of the mayhem to feed, camouflaged by the violence all around them. There were very few of us Benandanti in Paris and we were not able to prevent the massacre. But we did stop it, eventually."

"Then that is how you two met? In your spirit forms?" she asked.

Sainct Didier nodded. "I did my best to help this brave gentleman..."

He trailed off, and La Môle filled the silence, supplying first his long name and then the short version, as he had with Françoise.

Sainct Didier bowed in response. Then he said, "I am pleased to tell you that the vampires we encountered that night were all killed. But they were young and weak. The queen mother has turned so many. Too many. They are restless, undisciplined. I'm sure that she orchestrated the massacre as a sop to them, to satisfy their bloodlust and keep them in check."

Françoise took his arm and whispered, "You're in danger even now. I overheard Maître René speaking with the Duke of Anjou, who said his younger brother Alençon was a vampire, and that the king is, too. He wants to be made one himself."

The fencing master did not look behind him at his group of students. He did glance at La Môle, who was even more pale than before.

"You're sure it was him?" Sainct Didier hissed. "I thought she would stop short of destroying her own children. Every day I learn something that astonishes me. That was well done, Mademoiselle d'Artagnan, but all the more reason for us not to be seen together in the Louvre. I suggest you return to the Hôtel de Guise, and let me get back to my students."

"But surely you cannot put yourself in harm's way, now that you know. You were fencing with one of them!"

"Of course. We know they are among us. We know they could be anyone. They have long been afraid to expose their true natures to the population, lest the people rise up in horror and overthrow them. But Queen Catherine has been reckless, and created a reckless brood… We will soon know their names and their number, don't worry. Our safety is in keeping *them* from knowing who we are. In our waking forms, they have no idea we are Benandanti, unless we give them some reason to suspect. So let us not stay together now, and give rise to gossip."

"Gossip? Then do others know about the Benandanti?"

Sainct Didier shook his head. "Certainly not. Other than a few scholars and the old wise women who tell stories, no one knows our fraternity exists. The Malandanti know, though, because we give them reason to know. That is all I meant. Do not give them reason to wonder why we three, who had no connection until now, are suddenly talking together."

La Môle bowed to him. "I will be circumspect in all my dealings. But now that we know each other, can we not begin to fight back? We need not wait for the drums to call us. We can make plans and strike them where they are weak."

The fencing master nodded slowly, clasping the count by the arm. "I think the time has come. Where are you staying?"

"At La Belle Étoile, for now."

"Let me get some things in order and I will send word. It is very good to meet you, Monsieur le Compte."

Françoise fairly skipped as she left the Louvre and made her way back to report to the duchess. She had no orange blossom, but she had a great deal of valuable information, and she had hope for vengeance.

CHAPTER EIGHT

The Gibbet at Montfaucon

FRANÇOISE SPENT THE next few days at the Hôtel de Guise, helping the duchess with her toilette and wardrobe, and doing such an excellent job that no one found it surprising that she quickly became a favourite. Still, privacy was rare. Françoise slept with two other servants in the antechamber just outside the duchess's bedroom. She noticed that there was a small bed at the foot of the one where the duchess slept, yet it was never occupied.

One night, while she was brushing a perfumed powder into her mistress's long auburn hair, the duchess sighed and said, "The darkness is coming earlier. It will be September soon. I never used to be afraid of the dark, but I find it sends shivers down my spine now."

It was the opposite for Françoise. She used to be afraid of the dark, afraid that she would see ghosts in it. But now she had seen ghosts—for what else could that silent procession have been, on her way to Paris, but the ghosts of the slaughtered? And she found she no longer feared them. Terror had been replaced by something else: a fellow feeling that was more respectful than pity, more fierce than love. But as much as Françoise felt a new connection to the dead, she also felt for the first time that she had found her place among the living, here in the duchess's household.

Françoise looked at the little bed. "I would be happy to sleep here, if it would help keep the fear at bay."

The duchess laughed, stood up and took Françoise's chin in her hands. "You are delightful. There are reasons why a lady chooses to have privacy in her bedchamber, my dear. You need not worry yourself. I am never alone."

The gossip among the ladies was that Queen Marguerite, sister to the king, was the lover of the Duke of Guise, but the queen had not visited the Hôtel de Guise since the night of the massacre. As for the Duchess of Nevers, Françoise had no idea who her lover might be, and she saw no one visit. There was no way in or out of the duchess's bedchamber other than the room where Françoise slept on her pallet on the floor. It was a mystery.

Françoise thought long and hard about this, and other things. One possibility occurred to her: that she could have been sent here to spy on a vampire, and that the duchess did not occupy her bed at night. After all, what use was a door to someone who used the window? Sainct Didier had said the duchess was one of their kind, but perhaps one of their kind could be turned into a vampire, like anyone else.

The other possibility was, somehow, even more frightening. That the duchess, as a Benandante, regularly went walking in her spirit form at night, and did not want her sleeping body to be disturbed. Why this should frighten Françoise, she could not say. After all, she had done it herself, once, when the drums had called her. But to walk abroad at will—the possibilities it suggested, the doors it opened in Françoise's mind, were bigger and stranger than any she had considered in her young life.

She kept her ears pricked, and soon enough, she overheard some useful gossip among the ladies at the Hôtel de Guise.

Queen Marguerite had a new lover: a handsome young Huguenot called Count La Môle. He had contrived to take cover in her apartments after he was wounded during the massacre, and since then, a passion had arisen between them. Françoise had no doubt that this passion had been encouraged by the duchess, who spent so much time with Marguerite; it would give her a pretext to speak with La Môle, to make plans for the Benandanti. But what would those plans be, and when would they be revealed to Françoise?

She kept quiet and did her duties. A great deal of the latter consisted in preparing perfumed gloves and various oils and creams, powders and flasks; there were several small caskets on shelves in her dressing room where the duchess kept her cosmetics and salves. In the days after the massacre, she said, the latter had been depleted. Somehow it was difficult for Françoise to imagine the duchess out in the streets, healing the wounds of beleaguered Huguenots. The duchess tended to go where the power was, and the power in Paris now was not with the Huguenots. Whatever factions and counsellors had been in the ascendant when they expected the wedding of Marguerite and the Huguenot King of Navarre to bring about a new age of religious toleration, they were now in hiding, brought low, or dead.

In fact, she soon came to understand that the duchess's efforts had been on the Catholic side; the duchess was a firm believer in the old religion and had a horror of heresy. She did not support the massacre, not exactly, but she felt that the people of Paris had been manipulated into rising up to butcher their neighbours, and was forgiving of their crimes.

Many of these manipulated butchers had paid the price in their own blood, so the duchess was short on medicines. She visited the wounded daily and prayed for them at every Mass. It was difficult to say how much of the duchess's fanatical, nationalistic, political devotion to the Catholic cause was her own opinion, and how much was her gambling on which way the winds of power were shifting at court. After all, she moved in royal circles. In any case, she seemed quite eager to make her views known at every opportunity.

Therefore, it did not come as a surprise when the duchess announced she was going to ride out to the gibbet at Montfaucon to view the decaying corpse of the Huguenot admiral whose assassination, and the fear of reprisals following, had been the trigger for the massacre.

It did come as a surprise when she ordered Françoise to accompany her.

IT WAS THE first time Françoise had ridden Mistral since her journey to Paris. Although she had visited her mare in the stables, she felt awkward in her new clothing, riding behind the duchess on her magnificent white horse. They rode toward the Louvre, and as the palace came into view, Françoise gasped. A great crowd of people had gathered in the streets, most on horseback, and some on foot or with carts.

"Why are all these people here?" she asked the duchess.

"Queen Catherine has ordered that the entire court must ride out to view the corpse of the heretic. It is a show of loyalty to her and to the true religion."

Weeks ago, Queen Catherine was seen as a moderate, and now she was demanding shows of loyalty to the Catholic faith. No, Françoise thought. There was something deeper here. It was also a communal ritual in bloodlust. Tying everyone at court together in shameful mockery of the dead, so that none of them would feel clean, and all of them would feel guilty. So that they would justify whatever horrors the queen next deemed necessary to keep her brood fed and loyal.

With Françoise at her tail, the duchess rode straight for a beautiful woman on a pale horse, and they embraced. This must be Marguerite, daughter of Queen Catherine, sister to King Charles—and there was the king himself! He rode through the crowd, with a long cape the colour of blood, and a wide-brimmed hat that shaded him from the bright afternoon sun. He blew a horn as if this were a hunt. He was slim, and very ordinary looking, in an objective sense, but something about the way he sat on his horse and gazed out above the heads of the crowd made his position evident. Or perhaps it was the guards who rode behind him.

Despite the hat and its shadow, when the king's gaze fell on Françoise, she thought she could see two eyes glowing in the depths like those of an animal at night, and shivered. Any one of these fine people on their fine horses might have been among the vicious villains who came upon her in the form of bats in the southern mountains; or they might at least be of the same brood.

It was an hour's ride out to Montfaucon, as the vast company travelled slowly. The gibbet could be seen from a distance: On the top of a hill stood a square stone building with no roof, its walls riddled with openings where the dead dangled from crossbeams.

Crows rose into the air as the crowd approached. Françoise turned in the saddle and looked back. There must have been hundreds of people, all riding to demonstrate their eagerness to mock a Protestant corpse, just in case any of their neighbours were taking notes on who stayed home and who left the house. Surely most could not hope to curry favour with the king, who could hardly be expected to recognize anyone in this throng.

The duchess and Queen Marguerite were speaking to each other, the duchess leaning low in her sidesaddle, while Marguerite sat straight up. Marguerite looked nervous; she was biting her lip.

They were pointing at something—a group of riders coming quickly.

So quickly that one was going to run right into Françoise.

Clutching the reins, she looked to the right and left, but the throng was all around her. There was nowhere to go.

The rider bearing down on her was wearing a hat nearly

as broad as the king's, and as he got closer, she recognized the twisted smile of the Duke of Alençon. He smiled not out of any particular malice, or even any desire to hurt her. He smiled because he was a young man on a fast horse and he thought it was very funny to terrify everyone and force them to get out of his way. But there was nowhere for Françoise to go. She screamed at him to stop, and directed Mistral to step to the side, to the right, but there was no moving the crowd beside her.

With a thunder of hooves, a woman in black rode out from behind the king and took position next to Françoise, directly in front of the Duke of Alençon. She was draped in a long black veil, which fell from her small hat to her chest, in black lace that obscured her face even at this distance.

It was obvious, from the way she sat on her horse, that this was the queen mother. The head vampire: Catherine de' Medici.

She held out one hand and the duke grimaced, writhed as if in pain, and finally pulled the reins. The horse planted its feet, tossing its head and nearly tossing its rider.

One of the riders in Alençon's retinue crashed into someone, and there was pandemonium as the crowd tried to figure out what had happened.

Marguerite and the duchess moved out of the throng. Françoise, shaken, couldn't keep up; Mistral, was, understandably, nervous. She tried to ride toward the duchess, but she kept being moved farther and farther to the left, toward the front of the crowd, toward the gibbet.

Until she came a few feet away from the king.

This close, she could see his face under his hat. An ordinary enough face. He, like everyone else, was looking toward the place where the two riders had crashed. Both riders were still on their horses, holding up their arms to show they were all right. *Thank God*, Françoise thought, and she saw the relief on the faces of all the men and women around her.

But not on the king's. His expression did not change at all. He was gazing just as fixedly—not at the injured riders, but at Marguerite, his sister, who had ridden close to the riders and was gesturing with concern toward one of them.

Whether it was an injury she'd sustained in the crush of the crowd, or her nervous habit of biting her lip, Marguerite had a drop of red blood at the corner of her mouth.

The king, watching her, put his finger to his own mouth, as if mirroring it, then opened his lips and touched his finger to his own tongue.

There was something that horrified Françoise about all this, but she was about to be more horrified still.

Françoise knew little about the mother of the king, except that she was Italian by birth, and had been married young to King Henry II, who had died when Françoise was still a child. Her first memory of anything to do with the royal family was the celebration in the village to mark the coronation of Henry's oldest son; there had been games in the town square, and cake.

But after a couple of years on the throne, that new king had suddenly taken ill during a tennis match, and died, still in his teens. So his brother Charles became Charles IX, despite being only a child of ten, just a few years older than Françoise. Françoise barely remembered any other king but him, but for much of his reign, his mother had been regent.

This woman, veiled in black, the very mention of whose name struck fear into the eyes of the bravest man she'd yet met. Where was Sainct Didier, anyway? Surely he must be here; it seemed everyone in Paris was here. Perhaps he was in the midst of the throng somewhere.

"Let us give our greetings to the admiral," came the queen mother's voice, silken and soft, and yet seeming to carry over that whole fractious crowd.

As everyone moved toward the gibbet, Françoise lost her place at the front again. She didn't mind; she could already see quite enough of the shape of the man hanging by his legs in one of the openings, and the grotesque ball of straw someone had affixed where the head ought to be. She kept her eyes on the people around her and tried to find her way through them to the duchess.

When she found her, though, she found herself right behind the queen mother's horse.

Catherine de' Medici was facing the king, who was the nearest to the gibbet now. He was saying something—a poem or prayer perhaps—but the wind took his voice, and Françoise could not make it out.

Nearby, the Duke of Alençon had quieted his horse at last. She was close enough to see, under his hat, that pock-marked face, which she had first seen when he was fencing in the Louvre courtyard. He looked resentful, as if his mother had spoiled his fun. And perhaps she had. The way he had obeyed her silent command and stopped his horse had not looked voluntary. She had controlled him, by causing him pain.

Beside him, a much more handsome man she also recognized sat comfortably on a warhorse. This was the Duke of Anjou, whom she'd seen only for a moment on his way in to visit the perfumer, but there was no mistaking him. The small, triangular patch of beard on his chin made him look rather exotic, somehow, and it suited his face, accentuating the laughing quality of his mouth. Around the neatly trimmed beard, his face was shadowed by stubble, adorned by the glint of golden earrings. More than either of his brothers, he looked like a king.

The queen mother, like everyone else, couldn't take her eyes off him. She smiled in a way that made Françoise believe that this, her last remaining mortal son, must truly be her favourite. The one she didn't want to cause pain; the one, therefore, that she couldn't control.

Marguerite and the duchess were over to the right, their horses facing the gibbet. When she saw Françoise, the duchess gave a little nod, her expression saying nothing at all.

But it caught the queen mother's attention.

She wheeled her horse, and looked straight at Françoise. Behind that black veil, there were two eyes, and once again, as with King Charles, Françoise had the strange notion that they were glowing. She dropped her own gaze.

"Madame de Nevers, you have a new attendant," said the queen mother.

"Yes, Your Majesty. Her name is Françoise de Montesquiou d'Artagnan. She came to join the household of a family member here in Paris—you remember the Countess of Equitan. When she found that her protector had died, I took her into my house."

"Very generous of you, my dear."

The sky suddenly darkened, and the air cooled.

The queen mother flipped her veil up over her hat; it caught the wind, like the wing of a crow.

She brought her horse around and came very close to Françoise, near enough that she could put two gloved fingers under Françoise's chin. "Not bad at all. Very fresh. All that country air, I imagine. You know, my dear, about these women?" The queen stopped touching her face and gestured at the women on horseback in the crowd. "My flying squadron, people call them. My ladies and companions. Look, here is Charlotte de Sauve. And this little beauty is Guillemette of Ardouin. One has a king for a lover and the other a bishop. You could join their ranks, if you wished. The Duchess of Nevers used to be one of them. Chief among them, in fact."

Françoise did not know what to say. She tried to put everything Sainct Didier had told her out of her head, and respond like any country maiden who had just come to court for the first time.

"You do me great honour, madame," she said. Then, quickly, second-guessing herself: "Your Majesty."

The queen gave her a sour smile. "The sun has dipped below the horizon. It is time we were all going back to Paris, if we want to be back in the streets we know by nightfall."

THE KING AND his mother rode straight through the crowd so they could take up their positions in the front at the other end for the home journey. This required a number of attendants yelling "make way, make way!" and a willingness, on the part of the king, to ride as if having total faith that the people would hear and move in time. The Duke of Alençon rode in their wake, but Queen Marguerite was the hindmost member of the royal train and was soon quite surrounded. Marguerite had married the Huguenot King of Navarre, so the crowd did not part for her as willingly.

Françoise was starting to understand things.

As for Marguerite's husband, the King of Navarre himself, he must also be somewhere in the crowd, one of the many gentlemen with ostrich feathers in their caps and marvellous long cloaks, moving their horses through the crowd with some irritation. It would have been easier for the royal vanguard to just ride around the margins, but that would have sent the wrong message to the people. It was the people who must make way for the powerful, not the other way around.

A man on a tall horse pushed his way past Françoise, right up to Queen Marguerite as she passed. It was La Môle, but he made no acknowledgement of Françoise. He was, doubtless, heeding Sainct Didier's warning that the Benandanti should not be seen associating with each other too much. He said a few words to Marguerite, but she seemed to ignore him, staring straight ahead.

La Môle rode a little farther and set about clearing the way in front of Marguerite, to make her passage through the crowd easier. Because he was off to one side—and perhaps by design—this caused her horse to move to the side as well, into the less dense areas at the edges of the crowd.

The duchess followed Marguerite, and Françoise followed the duchess.

There among the deepening shadows, near a deserted and wooded area, La Môle and Marguerite drew close together and exchanged some words that Françoise could not hear. The man's face was so pale it almost glowed in the darkness, and he seemed very serious. Perhaps his wounds were giving him pain.

The duchess pulled her horse aside to wait for her friend and give her some privacy with La Môle—or perhaps, to keep some distance between him and the other two Benandanti in the crowd, namely Françoise and herself. She looked around absently. Then she pointed in the direction of the gibbet and asked, "Who is that man?"

Françoise followed her gaze, back the way they had come. In front of the gibbet there was a black shape, the cloak flying in the wind.

"I believe it's Coconnas," the duchess said softly.

Not softly enough to escape the notice of La Môle, who suddenly broke off his conversation with Marguerite, wheeled his horse and rode toward the duchess.

"By heaven, it is him," he said.

None of this meant anything to Françoise. Who was Coconnas?

The duchess stretched out one gloved hand in warning. "La Môle, keep the peace. He is merely gloating over the admiral's body."

"Peace? He does not have peace in mind. And he'll be gloating over another body soon, unless I gloat over his first."

"You don't know that he—"

"I know what I saw."

"You're mistaken. La Môle!"

But the young man was off, galloping toward the gibbet.

Françoise was slow to ride after the duchess; Mistral, who

had spent most of her life riding the sloping fields and country roads, was unused to crowds, unused to quick changes, and anxious at the rustling of branches in the shadows. Françoise felt the same, but what was to be done? The only safety was, surely, in keeping company with the duchess.

She rode up to the gibbet to see that the two men had drawn their weapons, the blades catching what little light remained in the day. The two women were calling out over the ring of the swords. Marguerite's face was stricken, but the duchess was comforting her, telling her that it was all in jest, that it would be all right.

Then came a thrust that hit La Môle's doublet, and the women cried out, and then, in a moment of sickening silence, La Môle answered it with a thrust of his own, which went right through the other man's body.

CHAPTER NINE

A Recipe for Theriac

IT WAS LUCKY that the headman of Paris was coming to the gibbet with a cart full of corpses, just at the moment when the two duellists were losing their senses, wrestling on the ground, their blood forming a growing shadow all around them.

At Marguerite's command, onto the tumbril went the two bloodied, pale men. "Get them to the Louvre, to the king's own doctor, and drive like the Devil is at your back," she told him. "It's Queen Marguerite of Navarre who commands you."

The duchess pulled Françoise aside to speak to her privately. "I will accompany Her Majesty to the Louvre and try to be of some comfort to her. You return to the Hôtel de Guise. Go into my dressing room, to the walnut cabinet against the wall, and press on the third and fifth drawers at once. This will open a compartment, where you will find a small jar labelled theriac. There is only a little—not enough. Using the ingredients you find in the rest of the cabinet, you will make more."

Françoise frowned. "Is there a recipe?"

The duchess's voice dropped low. "The time has come to let your talents guide you. Taste and smell will guide you. The lives of two young men hang in the balance, one of whom is a Benandante, and we can't afford to lose any more comrades."

THE SUN HAD set by the time Françoise returned to the neighbourhood of the Hôtel de Guise. The shadows deepened and pooled, until she was riding through dark, narrow streets lit only by lamps over doorways, and the occasional itinerant lamp-bearer, hired by someone with the money to pay for light.

She did not waste any thoughts on her own safety, partly because she was on an urgent errand, and partly because she was not an easy target, up on her horse and in her best clothing. Paris was full of easier targets: people whose deaths or injuries would attract no notice from anyone with the wherewithal to ask questions and seek revenge.

But she did not reckon on a quality common to newly made vampires: their arrogance, fed by the euphoria of their newfound condition, and a complete disregard for their own safety. Older vampires are more circumspect, more inclined to cling to their undead existence, more afraid of the whatever reckoning might follow it.

A caped shadow leapt down on her from above, and long claws raked her neck, while breath that stank of the tomb overwhelmed her. She wrestled with an attacker who was all claws and grey skin, and she felt the graze of a fang on her neck.

Mistral was having none of it.

She reared up, so that the vampire was thrown off.

Sainct Didier had warned her about the dangers of vampires learning she was one of the Benandanti, and at first she thought there must have been some breach in their secrecy, some conspiracy. But she watched the vampire lurch away, unbothered, looking for easier prey, and realized that the explanation was far more terrifying. The vampire infection had spread through Paris to such an extent that they were attacking passersby, boldly, unconcerned about facing the wrath and justice of the people. And perhaps they were right to be unconcerned. In a city led by vampires, why should vampires fear?

Françoise rode off, half out of her saddle, her hair coming undone and flying behind her. Mistral took her safely to the Hôtel de Guise, where the ostler asked no questions.

FRANÇOISE TRIED TO rearrange her yellow gown, her face and her breath. A quick pass of the hands over her neck and face reassured her that she had not been bitten. There was one scrape on her neck, but the ruff covered that nicely. All the same, she would never again forget the threat that lurked in a Paris street after dark.

It would have helped Françoise breathe more easily if she had shared the duchess's assessments of her talents. She knew a great deal about plants and herbs from her years in the garden back home, and she had learned even more in the few days spent with the duchess's salves and ointments. But to recreate a medicine? And one as complex as theriac? Her nurse had told her once that theriac could have dozens of ingredients, and needed years to age.

It was early evening and the other servants had not yet set out their pallets in the antechamber. She waited a few agonizing minutes for one of the maids to finish laying the fire in the duchess's bedroom, as Françoise pretended to check the rose-leaf sachets in the wardrobe. Then, when the maid had gone out, Françoise slipped through the little door beside the bed, and into the duchess's dressing room.

The walnut cabinet was behind an embroidered dressing screen, so at least she would be hidden from view if anyone chanced to come in. The last thing she needed was to be accused of stealing—or something worse. There was so much gossip about poisoning at court. The King of Navarre's own mother had been killed by scented gloves prepared by Maître René on behalf of the king's mother-in-law, Catherine de' Medici, or so people said. Everyone was fond of scented gloves in Paris; the floral and citrus smells covered up the smell of damp leather. But could such a thing truly kill?

Françoise had just tried to see Maître René herself; if she was caught tampering with the duchess's potions, people would gossip, and it would be difficult for the duchess to keep her on.

There was no point in these thoughts. The faster she worked, the less chance of discovery, and the greater chance that the two men lying senseless in the Louvre would recover. That was, if they had not expired already.

When she pressed the third and fifth drawer of the cabinet, from the top, a little door swung open on the side. There it was: a porcelain pot, bearing a simple painting of a stalk of yarrow.

She lifted the lid and sniffed. Thyme, cinnamon, cardamom, rose petals, and other things she could not identify at first. The compound was dark as pitch, and had a consistency like honey when she touched it with her fingertip. When she tasted it, a few more ingredients spoke to her. Saffron, valerian, and some sort of wood?

The knowledge of each ingredient started coming to her faster than she could put a name to it.

With a sudden burst of inspiration, she took down the mortar and pestle from its shelf and set to work. A little of this, a little of that, until the colour, smell and taste took shape. At one point she pulled a little tray of shards of something that looked like amber out of a drawer; the duchess had warned her away from that opium. She knocked a little off, ground it, and in it went.

For the wood, she shaved a little off the duchess's bedpost with her thumbnail, and it did the trick. Perhaps not the scented wood of distant lands that no doubt the recipe called for, but she did not have the recipe, did she?

Her feet and legs got sore, standing over the mixing table, tasting and smelling. After a time, her head started to swim, whether from lack of food or from tasting her own mixture so many times. She had a decent sized bowl of the stuff now, thanks to all the adding and mixing, but it wasn't quite right.

Françoise went to every drawer again. What could be missing? She felt she'd put nearly the whole contents of the duchess's stock into the bowl, and yet it was still not right. With her hands on the side of the table, leaning over it, she bit her lip in frustration. It hurt, which sharpened her thinking, and made her recall the way Marguerite had bitten her lip out riding today. The way the king, her brother, had stared at her as if entranced. No, not at her, perhaps, but at the drop of blood at the side of her mouth.

Blood. It was so clear to her now, it was almost as if she'd heard the word, resounding in the panelled room.

Françoise went out around the screen, to the more ordinary table with the mirror and comb, where the duchess applied her cosmetics. She picked up a pin from the dish and pricked her finger.

"Very good," said the duchess.

Françoise whirled around, holding her finger in her other hand, the precious drop welling.

"Go on then," the duchess said. "You must be close."

With a curt nod, Françoise dashed back behind the screen, added her blood to the mixture, and tasted.

It was perfect.

She allowed herself one breath of exhausted relief, and then picked up the bowl and went out behind the screen again.

"I imagine the recipe must be very secret, and that is why it isn't written down," she said. She didn't mean it to be chiding or complaining, but it sounded that way anyway.

The duchess gave her a sad smile. "The recipe isn't written

down because it changes with the mixer, with the need, with the seasons and the moon and the stars. If you had tried to simply replicate what I had done last time—or even if I had tried to do so now—it would have come out wrong. This is not what the quacks call by the name of theriac. This is the real thing, and you made it. Hmm, it looks a little thin, but that's all right, because I want to mix it in barley water for the men to drink."

This reminded Françoise of a question she'd been putting to the back of her mind. "You're going to give it to both men? You want to heal—what was his name?"

"Annibal de Coconnas. Yes, I want them both to live. La Môle is convinced that Coconnas is a vampire, because he saw the man with his teeth buried in another man's neck during the massacres. The simple fact is that Annibal de Coconnas is the sort of man who will use his teeth in a fight, when he's lost his sword and poniard and his arms are pinned by an enemy. Annibal de Coconnas is no vampire, and he lives in blissful ignorance of the existence of vampires at the French court, and while he may have killed many Huguenots a few nights ago, he only fought armed men."

Françoise felt light-headed; the repetition of the word vampire, here in this room, where the duchess dressed with her maids every day, felt like a wrong note in the symphony of the world.

"La Môle thought Coconnas was a vampire. And La Môle is one of our kind."

"Even we can be wrong, although of course that is not a condition I have experienced myself. But Coconnas is an ordinary man, who does not know the cause of La Môle's passion toward him, and he must not find out. Neither can Marguerite. The only hope of keeping the two of them with all their blood where it ought to be is to keep them ignorant of what is happening all around them. Keep all of this to yourself, and speak to no one but me, La Môle and Sainct Didier about any of it."

"I will not breathe a word," she said.

"Good. In any case, if they both survive, La Môle will soon finally have to admit that Coconnas is no vampire. One cannot bring a vampire so low with an ordinary sword wound through the lung."

It occurred to Françoise that it might be useful to know the ways in which one could kill a vampire. She would have to ask another day, though, because the duchess was putting a lid on the bowl of theriac, and preparing to go.

"It must be after midnight," Françoise said. "Is there no one else who can take this to the Louvre?"

She had not mentioned the vampire attack to the duchess, and she did not intend to. To admit how close she had come to danger might lead the Benandanti to keep Françoise out of things for her own protection, and that she would not countenance.

The duchess smiled at her. "I can protect myself on the streets of Paris, don't worry. Besides, it has to be me. The king's doctor is caring for them now, but I know a better doctor, a doctor who trusts me, who will see to it that these men drink some draughts prepared with this medicine. Don't be anxious. You've done well. If the men have any hope of survival, it will be thanks to you. The best things you can do now are to go to the kitchen and find yourself something to eat, and then go to sleep."

"I don't think I could eat or sleep," Françoise said, which was true, but not from worry. It was the heady thrill of mixing the medicine, just so, and perhaps the effects of smelling and tasting it so many times.

"Then pray," said the duchess, and she was gone.

Françoise did pray, kneeling down right there as if the cosmetics table were an altar. But sleep overtook her all the same. She woke some hours later, on the floor, from the deepest and sweetest sleep of her young life.

CHAPTER TEN

Intrigues and Infatuation

The next several days were [illegible] mistress spent most of her time [illegible] of her, but they [illegible] La Môle to die. There [illegible] a terrible blow. He had been [illegible] he had such a [illegible] not met, but the duchess [illegible] convinced he was as innocent [illegible] in this life could [illegible]

One day, a messenger came to the [illegible] of the duchess's husband [illegible] from one [illegible] Françoise declared that [illegible] news [illegible]

[illegible]

CHAPTER TEN

Intrigues and Invitations

THE NEXT SEVERAL days were easy for Françoise in body, as her mistress spent most of her time at the Louvre and had no need of her, but they were trying days in spirit. She did not want La Môle to die. There were so few Benandanti that it felt like a terrible blow. He had been charming and kind to her, and he had such a noble face. The other man, Coconnas, she had not met, but the duchess seemed worried about him, and was convinced he was an innocent—or as innocent as any sinner in this life could be.

One day, a messenger came to the Hôtel de Guise with news of the duchess's husband. He was still travelling, but moving from one city to another, changing his anticipated itinerary. Françoise declared that her grace the duchess must hear this news immediately. Although this was, in fact, not the sort of news that tended to interest the duchess at all, no one wanted to contradict her new favourite, who insisted on carrying the message to the Louvre herself.

It was still a thrill to know she could enter into that hidden hive of secrets and plans, where everyone seemed to know something, but nobody knew everything. It was a grey day, cool with a threat of rain. As Françoise passed the sentries and went through the postern, she came upon four men: Henri de Sainct Didier, the handsome Duke of Anjou, an equally handsome man she did not recognize, and Chicot. They were swinging tennis rackets and dressed in shirts and hose.

She curtseyed; it would be odd if she did not acknowledge them. Chicot gave her a wink.

Then Chicot said, "Monseigneur, may I present my friend, Françoise de Montesquiou d'Artagnan, who is a visitor here from the south, as I am."

How excellent of Chicot, she thought. Although he wouldn't know why it mattered, he'd saved Françoise and Sainct Didier from saying whether they knew each other.

But it transpired that he'd had his own reasons.

"I swear, Chicot, you know everyone and everything," said the duke, and there was a glint of satisfaction in Chicot's eye. He was trying to please the duke, for some reason. She felt oddly jealous, and then pushed that ridiculous feeling away.

"I hope the weather holds for your game, monsieurs," she said.

"Oh, no fear, mademoiselle," said Sainct Didier. "There are two lovely tennis courts, totally enclosed, just outside the palace."

At that moment, a gaggle of children came up with sticks in their hands, saying "Swordmaster, swordmaster!"

A smile twitched on Sainct Didier's mouth and he brandished his racket as if it were a sword, advancing on the group of children, boys and girls. Clearly they had come upon him before; it was quite charming to see.

As the children ran off, ushered away by one of the sentries, the duke's handsome companion laughed. "I see you brandish a tennis racket as well as you do your sword, Sainct Didier. Now I'm nervous about our game. And to think I was going to suggest a wager."

The fencing master lost his little smile as he went into instruction mode. “I play for the pleasure of it, my lord, and for the game’s benefits. Tennis is like swordplay in every way that matters. It gives students the mental acuity to face an opponent. Also, it strengthens the body. Strong arms and a fast eye.”

“Most importantly,” said the man she didn’t know, laconically, “it gives us a chance to show off our legs.”

He struck a pose, laughing.

The Duke of Anjou hit him on those shapely legs lightly with his racket, and then rolled his eyes as if sharing his exasperation with Françoise. “Everyone plays here, even my most unruly Mignons. I even know some ladies who like the game. Come and join us, mademoiselle, if you like, and we’ll rotate partners.”

She bowed her head. She had heard his voice before, and caught a glimpse of him, but to speak to him was a much more pleasant experience than her brief encounters with his brother Alençon. Never in her life had she thought that the heir to the throne of France would speak to her, and with such casual respect. “I would be honoured, even though I would be sure to slow everyone down. But I have a message for Madame de Nevers. Not an urgent one,” she said for Sainct Didier’s benefit, “but one I must deliver.”

“Then we take our leave,” said Chicot with a low bow that made her blush.

She hurried into the wing that held the apartments of the Queen of Navarre, but as it happened, she ran into the duchess coming the other way in the guardroom. The duchess looked exhausted, but she was smiling.

“Wonderful news,” she said, taking Françoise by both hands.

“Will they live, then? It’s been so long…”

The duchess nodded, and spoke softly; there were guards in bright livery lining the walls. "It was a near thing for a while, especially with Cocannas—his lung… The doctor administered a draught several times, and now he is confident he will live. They both will, thank God and all His saints. What's more, they've become fast friends. Now, tell me why you're here."

Françoise smiled mischievously. "We had a message that your husband will go to Lille sooner than expected."

"Ah." The duchess gave her a schoolmistress look. "Well, how good of you to come."

She took her arm, and they walked through the palace.

"May I ask you something?" Françoise ventured.

"Anything, my dear. Anything at all on this beautiful day."

"It's going to rain."

"Ask anyway."

"What's a Mignon? I mean, what does it mean here?"

At that, the duchess burst out laughing. "Where did you hear that?"

"I met the Duke of Anjou and he used the word—he spoke of one of his unruly Mignons, but he couldn't have meant a darling. It didn't quite fit."

"Did he use it of a young man? A beautiful one? He keeps a dozen or more of them, his favourites. All very good looking. I don't think he's actually sleeping with all of them, but he certainly doesn't mind keeping people guessing about which of them are actually his lovers and which are just his friends. If any heir to the throne can have true friends, that is. They drive his mother to distraction. She had one of them killed, not long ago, when the duke got too fond of him."

Françoise felt her smile freeze on her face. It was obvious that Chicot was trying to befriend the Duke of Anjou, and it seemed that kind of proximity could be dangerous. But what was not dangerous here, in a palace where the heir to the throne had two vampires for brothers?

As if the palace were listening to her thoughts, a tapestry twitched as they entered a small room just before the staircase. Both the duchess and Françoise froze. Behind them, the usher at the door noticed nothing, said nothing, kept his gaze steady. But the tapestry had twitched.

Then someone coughed.

A polite cough, a throat-clearing cough. A familiar cough.

The duchess made a face. Taking Françoise by the arm again, she walked casually toward the tapestry, and then behind it, where they found Henri de Sainct Didier with his finger to his lips.

He pressed a panel on the wall and it opened into a small chamber, with only a small, narrow window high up. When the door had closed again, he gave them a rueful smile.

"A secret room I didn't know about!" the duchess said, admiringly.

"You were playing tennis," said Françoise.

He grinned. "I hurt my ankle. So, what is the message? What is the news? You seem light-hearted—is everything well with our friend, then?"

Clearly, Françoise's attempt to convey that her message was not a serious one had not worked. But it didn't matter, because there really was news to pass on. The duchess shared it with the fencing master gladly.

"This is excellent," said Sainct Didier. "With five of us here, and known to each other, we can plan in advance. We can take the war to them, on our terms."

"Five?" the duchess asked with false lightness. "I count four, including La Môle. Unless you intend to persuade *her*."

"None of us can deny our nature forever, and we can't afford to squander any of our resources."

"Are either of you going to tell me who you're talking about?"

"An old friend," Sainct Didier muttered.

"And what sort of fight do you have in mind?" The duchess continued. "I have been here in Paris much longer than you, Sainct Didier, and I have cultivated my methods carefully."

"And I stand in awe of them. You are at the very heart of the court, and you know everything that happens there. But knowing is not enough. Being on guard is not enough. You must admit that something has changed in Paris. The sheer number of vampires the queen mother has created—this whole city will be a cemetery soon, one way or another. We must strike quickly."

"And you're happy to have another swordsman to strike with," the duchess said, with something between bitterness and empathy. "I understand the appeal. But do you understand the danger?"

The fencing master nodded. "Of course. We can strike low, to begin with. Weaken her in a way that will not draw her notice or her vengeance."

The duchess looked reluctant, but she said, "In a few days, the court travels to Chenonceau for a week."

"The whole court? Just for a week?" Françoise was amazed.

"They never stay in one place for long. If they do, the markets run out of food, and the parks run out of deer, so they go somewhere else for a time. New hunting grounds. Once that only referred to animals."

"But meanwhile, the lesser vampires will be in Paris," said Sainct Didier thoughtfully. "Madame de Nevers, can you contrive to stay in Paris when they go?"

She waved her hand. "The queen mother doesn't want the King of Navarre with them anyway, so he and Marguerite will stay here. Catherine will have left her men to keep an eye on her son-in-law, of course, but she won't have anyone watching me."

"Then we're agreed," Sainct Didier declared. "How will I let you know when everything is in position?"

"Tell La Môle," said the duchess. "Marguerite has a

weakness for him, which I'll encourage, so I'll have plenty of chances to see him."

Sainct Didier nodded, and then clapped a hand on each of their shoulders, in comradely fashion, and they said their farewells.

When they arrived back at the Hôtel de Guise, the duchess declared that she must not be disturbed, and she slept for a day and a half. She woke so refreshed that Françoise surmised that her spirit had slept as soundly as her body.

CHAPTER ELEVEN

Lovers

FRANÇOISE AND the duchess waited for word from Saint Didier, but they were not idle. There were potions to mix and ingredients to prepare. Most of the potions were salves and healing powders, or sachets to aid in sleep. The duchess warned her never to use too much of the thick, sticky chunks of what looked like amber: it was opium, and could be death in the wrong quantity.

One day, the duchess opened an oak chest in the shadowy back of the dressing room. A sulphurous stench immediately made Françoise cover her nose and mouth, and she tried to suppress a cough.

"We have a friend in the Church," the duchess said. "She has access to many old collections of books, and she found something for me a few years ago. A recipe for an ointment that claims to burn the skin of vampires. Not having much chance to try it on the skins of vampires, I thought little of it, until learning of Navarre's murder by poisoned gloves a few months ago gave me an idea."

She pulled out two pairs of white leather gloves, which looked ordinary but smelled like hellfire.

CHAPTER ELEVEN

Lovers

FRANÇOISE AND THE duchess waited for word from Sainct Didier, but they were not idle. There were potions to mix and ingredients to prepare. Most of the potions were salves and healing powders, or sachets to aid in sleep. The duchess warned her never to use too much of the thick, sticky chunks of what looked like amber; it was opium, and could be death in the wrong quantity.

One day, the duchess opened an oak chest in the shadowy back of the dressing room. A sulphurous stench immediately made Françoise cover her nose and mouth, and she tried to suppress a cough.

"We have a friend in the Church," the duchess said. "She has access to many old collections of books, and she found something for me a few years ago. A recipe for an ointment that claims to burn the skin of vampires. Not having much chance to rub the skins of vampires, I thought little of it, until Jeanne of Navarre's murder by poisoned gloves a few months ago gave me an idea."

She pulled out two pairs of white leather gloves, which looked ordinary but smelled like hellfire.

"I thought at least they would be protection against attack, if one were walking at night," the duchess said, "but I found I did not want to carry them around. Here, try these on."

The gloves were sticky inside and out once they were soaked, and the stench did not get any better. Still, the duchess seemed pleased with the fit. "Now we just need a chance to use them."

IT WAS NOT too long after that when the two convalescents came to the Hôtel de Guise, in the company of Queen Marguerite.

Françoise and a few of the duchess's other ladies prepared to file out of the room, but the duchess called her back.

Since La Môle and Coconnas were still in some pain, they all lay on beautiful velvet and brocade cushions on the floor, propped up on their elbows when they wanted to engage on a point, or lying back and staring at the gilt-patterned ceiling when they wanted to declaim. They all looked perfectly at ease with each other; it was clear that the two men had forgotten all their hatred of each other during their time at the gates of death.

"Françoise, you must be my representative for the south," the duchess said, smiling as if they all lived ordinary lives. "Monsieur de Coconnas has told me the most remarkable lies about Piedmont, and I want someone to tell me when I am being teased."

"Lies!" said Coconnas, smiling but a little red in the face, perhaps from the exertion of trying to get comfortable on the cushions with his wound still interfering with his breathing. In contrast to his pale-faced, dark-haired friend, he had ginger hair and the sort of complexion that always has blood in it. "Madame, I would never lie to you. I'll swear by any saint you care to name."

"Do you really expect me to believe that your homeland has an entire festival devoted to snails?"

"If you had tasted our snails, madame, you would understand.

We feed them on the most delicate and nourishing herbs."

"Tell us, Françoise, have you ever heard of this?"

Françoise settled herself on the floor, awkwardly placing the one remaining cushion under her elbow. It felt very decadent, and very vulnerable, to be lying on the floor with these gentlemen and ladies—with a queen, in fact! Marguerite was like the flower she was named after, pale and delicate, and she barely seemed to make a dent in the cushions. Françoise, by contrast, felt awkward, as if she had too many limbs.

"I am not from Piedmont, madame," she answered. "I could not say."

"But you're from the south. I thought you might have heard."

"She is from Gascony, is she not?" La Môle broke in, amused. "Nowhere near Piedmont, my dear duchess."

The queen laughed lightly. "You take her too seriously, both of you. Henriette knows perfectly well where Piedmont is, and Gascony, too. She probably owns land there. She is testing you, not the other way around. The fact is, you gentlemen are completely out of your depth when it comes to the ladies of Paris."

"That is true, Your Majesty," said Coconnas gravely. "When we arrived, before the misunderstandings that drove us apart, we were quite happy to have found each other. We arrived at La Belle Étoile and found the innkeeper most rude. He had only one room remaining."

"We were happy to share," La Môle said.

"Of course you were," the duchess said, poking Coconnas teasingly with her stockinged toe. "You two fell in love at first sight. I honestly believe La Môle is my greatest rival for your affections, Annibal."

Coconnas cocked his head. "I cannot deny it."

They went into peals of laughter, and Françoise wasn't sure whether they were laughing because it was true, or because they found it ridiculous. She was even more confused when La Môle put a tender hand on the muscled calf of Coconnas.

"I cannot be jealous," Marguerite said sweetly. "After all, I have a husband, albeit an understanding one."

"Mine is less understanding, but conveniently absent," said the duchess to Françoise, with a wink.

The queen went on, still addressing the gentlemen: "But you do have to admit, both of you, that Henriette and I have not tried to kill either of you, and you cannot say the same for each other. I thought you were both done for."

"As did I," said Coconnas. "It was very well done, La Môle. You fought better than any man in Paris."

"Any man save one," said La Môle, and inclined his head.

"Enough, enough!" protested the queen, still laughing. "Our darling Françoise will think us all ridiculous. We thank God that you are both restored to us. Life is short, and I will waste no more of it in pretending not to love whom I love."

This speech began in laughter but ended gravely. La Môle lifted his hand from Coconnas's leg and reached over for the queen's. "And all I had to do was nearly die."

Queen Marguerite hit him with a cushion, and then stood up, smiling, her hair dishevelled and her cheeks red. "We must get these two gentlemen back to the Louvre, or the doctor will be angry with us, Henriette. Besides, it will be dark soon."

The gentlemen rose, but La Môle stumbled, and was only prevented from falling by the queen catching his arm.

"Does the wound trouble you, my friend?" asked Coconnas.

La Môle nodded, his mouth tight, his face very pale.

"You must stay at the Hôtel de Guise tonight," said the queen, anxiously. "No, no, I won't hear of you going back to the Louvre tonight. You cannot ride in this condition, and not even in a litter would I have you travel. Henriette, you can find some room for him, can't you? There need be no impropriety, if—"

"Françoise will sleep with me tonight," the duchess assured her. "That will stop the servants from gossiping. Go, Marguerite, it will be all right."

In public, the duchess called the queen Your Majesty, but here among friends, it was Marguerite. Françoise took note of this, as she took note of everything. There was so much to learn about the ways of the court.

"I will accompany you, Your Majesty," said Coconnas, extending his arm. "La Môle, in the morning we'll send the doctor round. If you'll be all right without him tonight…?"

"I'm perfectly well, just a little tired," La Môle said, unconvincingly.

But when the queen and Coconnas had left, the gentleman made a miraculous recovery. He stood up straighter, and he grinned at the duchess.

"And so we are alone," he said.

The duchess nodded. "Noctu pro more," she responded.

Françoise started in recognition of the line she had heard spoken with Sainct Didier in the garden. La Môle looked as confused as she was.

The duchess laughed. "Sainct Didier and I have known each other for a long time. Last time he was in Paris, and a few times when he returned here after the massacre, we would arrange to meet at night, in our spirit forms. It is not easy to remember waking life, but we had a method for it. We would walk the streets and look for anyone who needed our help, anyone who had been attacked by a vampire. Once or twice, we even managed to fight one off."

"Sainct Didier asked if I am well enough to fight, and I am," declared La Môle. "I dare say my spirit form is stronger than this one, and this one is strong enough."

The duchess shrugged. "There are many connections between our day forms and our night ones, and those connections can be difficult to understand or predict. But we have need of you, La Môle, if you are ready."

"Show me the nearest bloodsucker, and I'll gladly skewer it. I am overjoyed to have company at last. It was only a few years ago that I heard the drums for the first time, at home in Provence. A few times I have seen others of our kind, in spirit form, but never knew who they were in waking life. And I never had a chance to fight—those times when I heard the drums, we simply roamed and gamboled, like animals. I remember… pure joy. But never have I walked in spirit form in the city."

"The joy is the same," said the duchess. "But here or in the country, our joy is a form of battle. You were on patrol when you gamboled, even if you did not happen to meet the enemy. Tonight, I guarantee that you will."

"Then lead on."

The duchess turned with a swish of her skirts, stepped over the pile of cushions and paused, holding out her hand.

La Môle hurried beside her, took her hand and they both walked toward the bedchamber. For a moment, Françoise remembered her nurse Sancia, who had been to Paris, as she was very fond of telling people. A cesspit of sin, she called it. What would she think if she could see this scene?

At the door to the bedchamber, the two paused, and the duchess looked back at Françoise, still holding the count's hand.

"Aren't you joining us?"

To Françoise's relief, La Môle took the trundle bed. The duchess patted the bed beside her, and lifted the sheets. They were fully dressed still, and Françoise had no desire to strip down to her chemise in front of the count—or even, for that matter, in front of the duchess. They intended to sleep, only to sleep… but that seemed, if anything, even more intimate than anything her nurse would have imagined.

"You've done it before, haven't you?" asked the duchess.

It was plain from her small smile that she was enjoying the double entendres.

Françoise mustered her courage, an action which manifested

as a small sniff, and then a nod. "But only once before." She paused, remembering that she was not to provide any more information than necessary, and considering what to say next. "I… will I take the same form, here in Paris? I'm afraid my form the last time was more suited to the country."

The duchess put her hand on Françoise's back, and pushed her gently up to sitting. She began to unloop her hair, so that her braids fell down her back. The count, sitting cross-legged on the trundle bed, watched them with a serious expression, as if this were a business meeting.

"You will take other forms," the duchess assured her. "Trust your soul to choose the most apt expression for the time and place. It feels like changing the expression on your face, like moving muscles, in a way. We tend to take human form here in Paris, but the only certainty is that the form you take will look nothing like your waking body. Your mind, too, will feel about your waking life as if it is a dream. That can make it difficult to remember plans, but all you need to remember is to stay close to me, and you'll be fine. And remember that your spirit body will be flesh and blood, while it lasts; you can be hurt and killed, in that form, as easily as in this one."

Françoise nodded. "But how will I know how to take spirit form at all? The last time, I heard drums. I don't even remember how it was that I came to be running in the hills."

"That's why we're here, together," said La Môle. "I am only a few years into this knowledge myself, and I still find it difficult to walk alone. It's easier when there are others."

"The drums you heard are in here," the duchess said. Taking her student's hand in her own, the duchess lay Françoise's palm over her own chest, just above the line of the bodice. She pressed it down, so that the flesh yielded. Françoise thought she could feel, very distantly, the heart beating within.

"The Malandanti take their strength from death," the duchess explained. "We take ours from life. From the heartbeat of the earth, of all living things. Eventually, you will draw that strength from your own heartbeat, when you need to. For now, feel this, and remember it."

She lifted her hand again and moved it up to her own neck, where the pulse was stronger.

They moved closer together, all three of them, with La Môle up on his knees as the trundle bed was lower. La Môle put his hand around the neck of Françoise, as the duchess put her hand around his. They felt the pulse running through them, an uneven harmony. The count's hand around her neck increased in pressure, just a little, his thumb finding her artery.

Françoise gasped.

The pressure ceased, the air cold in its absence, and she was alone again, with the thump still in her ears. La Môle's face was still as pale as it always was, but there were two small patches of red in his cheeks, and his eyes were bright. He toppled sideways onto his bed. The duchess touched her finger to Françoise's lips, and then fell back onto her pillow.

Françoise fell down beside her host, and stretched an arm up, feeling the drums course through her. Her fingers felt something under her cool pillow: the seams of a linen sachet, which explained the faint scent of lavender and lilac. She thought it would take her a long time to get to sleep. She thought that for less than one minute.

CHAPTER TWELVE

The Red Children

THREE CLOAKED FIGURES stood in the grand bedchamber and stared at each other.

Then they all looked at the bodies sleeping in the beds.

Françoise felt a distant affinity for the young woman with the braids lying over the coverlet, her face anxious even in sleep. Affinity was perhaps the wrong word; she remembered her as an aspect of herself, but at night, in sleep, Françoise was all aspects. She was everything she had tried to be until now, and everything she might be in the future. She felt protective of the sleeping woman, and protective of everyone in the city, and those feelings were only one face of her ferocity. As watchful as a hare, as honourable as a dog, as deadly as an owl.

She put her fingers to her face and felt a bulbous nose, cheekbones in the wrong places—the face of a stranger, and yet strangely familiar.

The spirit of the duchess stood in a long grey cloak, and on her face, she wore a leather mask, which covered everything except two large grey eyes. The mask smelled sweet, like the perfume they had made for the gloves. And indeed, the duchess was wearing her gloves, and handed Françoise a second pair.

La Môle wore a new face that had some undefinable beast-like quality to it, the jaw like a muzzle, and low bottom teeth that protruded.

They did not look exactly ordinary, but they looked like people, more or less. The one commonality between their three spirit forms, other than the cloaks, was their height: they were thin and very tall. Not giants, like the people Françoise had seen in the hills, but still, unusually stretched. The bedchamber looked uncannily different from this angle. She could see dust on the tops of the picture frames.

"You have made no choices so far," said the duchess. "You awoke in the form of a hare, when you were called to a meeting in the hills in the twilight. You awoke in this form to walk in the Paris streets at night, a human form, but tall as a shadow. Your form will be shaped by many things: your need, your companions, your environment. Some forms, you will never be able to take, because every form is an aspect of your spirit."

Françoise stretched her strange arms out in front of her. "How is this an aspect of my spirit?"

"That is for you to learn. That is the great education, and it ends only at our deaths, which I hope will be a long time from now."

"Try something else," La Môle urged her, watching Françoise as she quizzically inspected her own body. "Change your form. Draw on your needs, your desires, this room, this time, this moment. Draw upon us."

He put a hand onto her shoulder.

The heat and pressure of his touch made her shudder. She closed her eyes and asked herself what she would be in this moment. The shudder moved through her and she felt her fur ripple on her back, on her ribs. She stretched her long lithe body, her four paws on the ground, and nudged her nose onto La Môle's strong calf. She was small and safe, aware, vigilant, warm, full of fight and affection—everything catlike in her spirit found its expression.

"Good," said the duchess, cool and businesslike. "Now you must choose to fly, but to fly in this contained space, in these surroundings."

She had barely said the words when Françoise found herself shrinking further, further, until she was only the sound of her purring body, limbless, vibrating, in a world of monstrous size. She ran into a surface, and there were surfaces everywhere, pain everywhere, bright and dark and terrifying.

There was sound but she could not make it form words. She could not form words in her own mind. The world around her went pale and warm and she heard a whispering wind, felt it on her insect body, her fragile wings. The wind pushed her, forced her to grow, until she was a sparrow, panting, feathers ruffled on her small body.

There was softness all around her. Softness and comfort. Familiarity: the feeling of bedsheets. This was no place for a bird. She was herself, or something like herself. A woman, lying curled and exhausted.

That was my fault, the duchess said. It took a moment for Françoise to realize that the voice was in her mind, not in her ears, that the duchess had somehow spoken to her without making a sound.

That voice came into her mind again:

I did not prepare you, or tell you the limits. Very small forms, very large ones, very different ones, can be disorienting.

Françoise thought that was an understatement, but she was not sure how to say so, or what to say. She was not sure she could speak.

The duchess, standing beside the bed, put her hand on her arm, very softly. She spoke in the ordinary way again. "You are doing very well. I wish I could give you more time to learn, but we learn what we are by being what we are, and what we are is shaped by the Malandanti as much as anything. We are the weapons that can destroy them, if we choose."

Françoise drew herself up to sitting in the bed, and pulled the blanket over her knees. She was wearing a simple smock now, and she felt the chill as well as her modesty, even though this skin was not exactly her own. "How do I choose?" she said, her voice wavering. "How can I know what form will be dangerous to them and not to me?"

"You cannot," said La Môle, who was still standing near the fireplace, some distance from the bed. "You follow the needs of the moment and you hope. They have no hope; they walk the path of eternal death, and the only choices available to them are to survive at the cost of their own souls and the blood of other living beings, or to wither and crumble to dust. Remember that. You can choose, which already gives you power."

"And you have already chosen," the duchess added. She sounded triumphant and strong, and made Françoise want to feel the same. "You have chosen to hear the drums. Many who are born in the caul simply ignore it. They stay in their beds. Between the Malandanti hunting us whenever they learn our identities, and our fellow Benandanti refusing the call, we are very few these days."

"Then we should not linger," said Françoise. She felt the courage of her companions flow through her, and she feared that if she waited a moment longer, she would lose the will to join them. She threw the blanket off and rose out of the bed, rose into the tall, cloaked form that she had woken in.

La Môle clapped his hands together once, pleased.

"Then trust us, trust yourself, and follow me," the duchess said. She crossed to the window, opened it, and leaped out.

The bedchamber was on the top floor and yet, La Môle did not seem shocked.

Françoise moved without thought or intention, called by her companions. By the time Françoise was at the open window, the other two were floating down to the street, as if suspended by a kindly breeze. The same breeze cradled her. It was not exactly flying, but there was a lightness to her spirit body that she never experienced in the waking world.

At last her feet touched the cobbles, very lightly. They were in a narrow space between the Hôtel de Guise and an outbuilding, quite cut off from view. Françoise followed the other two through passageways and into narrow streets.

From time to time, someone passed them. Nobody remarked or crossed themselves, but nobody nodded or greeted them either. Françoise had the strong feeling that the people who passed were aware of them, but would rather not be. It made them uncomfortable to see spirits walking in whatever forms they chose, even if they did not name the phenomenon in their own minds.

There was a power in this. She liked it.

Before long, a vast darkness loomed ahead, cutting off the stars, in the shape of a tall castle with conical towers.

She heard the voice of the duchess in her mind:

This is the Temple. Built by the Knights Templar some centuries ago. For the longest time, it was the stronghold of one of their Order, a very old vampire, canny and strong. But we got him in the end. Forced him into sunlight, where he burned. The older they are, the stronger their powers of persuasion, attraction, control. Some of their other talents may grow in time as well. But they pay a price. As they age, they grow more vulnerable. Daylight becomes more than a nuisance; it becomes fatal. Garlic and moly and symbols of faith may do them great injury, instead of merely distracting and annoying them, as is the case for their younger creations. That is why Catherine de' Medici, who has only been a vampire for less than the span of a mortal life, has been able to take over Paris in a relatively short time. The older vampires can be killed quite easily by someone of strong will, and she always had that, even before she turned.

Françoise did not know how to speak with her mind, but she thought the words as hard as she could. *She killed them herself?*

Some of them, the duchess said. *Others, we eliminated. She still has enemies, but they have gone to ground, or left Paris. But because she is still young in darkness, her powers over the minds of other vampires are shaky and weak. That is why she has to placate them with gifts, including the massacre. The young vampires are restless; they do not see the need for secrecy, and some want to rule the rest of us openly, without resorting to disguises and tricks, without bothering with court etiquette or politics. She made too many of them, you see. She wanted to create an army for herself, just as she once made an army of seductresses out of her ladies in waiting. They all turn against each other, eventually.*

"The ladies in waiting?" joked La Môle, aloud.

The duchess laughed, and it was the same laugh, though the form was so different. It was startling to hear, but Françoise realized that they did not need to be silent; they only needed to make sure they were not overheard speaking of secret things.

The duchess carried on inside her mind: *Have I not turned against the queen myself? And I was a lady in waiting once, I remember it… She knows that she starts to lose them from the moment they turn; they are her creatures, and they find they must obey her, and thus they resent her. She will be the cause of her own downfall, that's certain. But in the meantime, she can do great harm to France, and its people, if we don't put an end to her and all her brood. Which is our business tonight.*

Françoise looked again at the forbidding castle and tried to swallow her fear.

Not there, said the duchess. *That wall, over to the right, leads to the orphanage. The Red Children, they call those foundlings. This is a feasting ground.*

But not tonight, growled La Môle.

He raised his hand high, looking down toward the end of the street. Two tall grey-clad figures were walking toward them. Françoise knew immediately they were Benandanti too.

She wanted to whoop in joy and greeting, like a werewolf—

she had never seen a werewolf, but she imagined them whooping.

As the two shadowy figures drew near, she smiled in deeper recognition, for the one on the left was Sainct Didier. The face was the same as he'd worn in the hills, but he was no giant here. The long, pointed beard trailed away into nothingness on the air.

The other person, she did not recognize. A pale, silver-haired woman with burning eyes. She realized with a start that it might well be someone she knew in another form in the daytime; the disguises of the Benandanti kept them strangers even to each other.

And yet, when it was someone she knew well, there was always something about the spirit body that was familiar. The way La Môle swung his arm when he walked. The laugh, in the case of the duchess. And for Sainct Didier, the voice. It had allowed her to recognize him in the garden, and tonight it brought her comfort and delight.

My friends, said Sainct Didier, in the silence of their minds. *I know you. I remember. We shall have good hunting.*

The duchess knew the silver-haired woman. She walked around her, sniffing like a cat.

The duchess said, *I never thought to see you in the world of night again.*

The silver-haired woman responded: *I could not ignore the drums.*

Leave if you wish to, the duchess snapped. *We want no unwilling participants.*

Then La Môle hissed, and pointed behind Sainct Didier and his companion. As if they were one body, the Benandanti moved into the deepest shadows, beneath the overhang of a house.

A waking woman was walking unsteadily along the street. She was thin, bent over the bundle in her arms, which could only be a baby. Françoise could not see her face, but her cloak was ragged.

She walked so softly on the cobbles. Her shoes barely made a sound. When she reached the wall of the orphanage, she gathered the baby in close to her, and a silent sob racked her body. How tightly she held the child, as if she could not bear to be parted from it.

And yet, she found the strength. Slowly, her arms uncurled, and she knelt, and lay the child down on the stones in a recess of the wall that looked as if it had been built for that purpose. There, the baby would be safe from the hooves of passing horses, sheltered from the rain and wind, for as long as it took the sisters of the Red Children to notice they had another charge.

The young mother walked back the way she had come, slowly, turning every so often, pausing, then leaving again. Françoise was glad she could not see her face.

The baby began to whimper, and then to wail.

Françoise darted forward, to cross the street and pick it up, comfort it.

But the duchess pulled her back, saying, *Wait*.

On the wall above the child crouched a shape. Not human, not animal, but watching. Barely detectable in the darkness. There could be no doubt that it meant to do harm, that this was a vampire preparing to take the child as if it were an offering. A child no one would miss; the mother would think it had disappeared into the safety and care of the Orphanage of the Red Children; the nuns would never know that the child had existed at all. A human life, a being with affections and fears, a small warm bundle of curiosities, about to be extinguished in service of indifferent gluttony.

It was intolerable.

And yet, the other Benandanti seemed all too willing to tolerate it.

She heard the duchess in her mind, answering her unspoken questions, saying, *Where there is one, there will be many. In their games and manipulations they are often solitary, but in the streets they are cowardly carrion creatures. They will steal each other's meat. They are drawn to the scent of blood and to the exultation of their own kind.*

The vampire alighted from the wall, as light as a dream, and swept up the child inside his cloak.

Suddenly, the child stopped crying, as silent and content now as if it were back in its mother's arms.

The vampire pushed back his hood. Françoise steeled herself to see a member of the royal family, but his face was that of a stranger to her. She remembered then that the royal family had left Paris for their celebrations at Chenonceau. This was one of the queen mother's lesser servants. Not rich or powerful in life, and abandoned to his own disgusting methods at night, and liable to punishment from his sire if he acted in any way that would draw attention, would endanger her control. Along with cruel hunger, resentment gleamed in his eyes.

Wait, cautioned the silver-haired woman who had walked here with Sainct Didier, whose name Françoise did not even know. How dare she command Françoise?

Still your mind, said the duchess. *Let your perception rise above the city. See everything. Do not move until the moment for movement comes.*

Françoise could not take her attention from the baby, not for a moment. They were treating this human child as bait.

Surely, though, they would stop the vampire before he actually harmed the child.

She believed this while the monster bent his head over the baby, while he used one long-taloned hand to pull the child's head back to expose its pudgy neck, while his fangs caught the moonlight.

Down went the monster's head, and the scent of blood filled Françoise's nostrils.

In her mind, she screamed, *You are all killers!*

She took a step into the street, not caring that her companions were urging her to stop, and she might have reached the vampire before he killed the child, might have reached him before he even noticed her, how deep was he in his pleasure.

But then a rush of wings came from above, and the vampire's head lifted up, away from the child of its own accord.

Sainct Didier pulled her back.

A great black bird flew at the vampire and pecked out its eyes.

The monster dropped the baby, and in that instant, the bird became a woman, and caught the child, seizing it as though it were a prize. A rivulet of blood ran from the child's body down to the street.

"How dare you?" the other vampire said, throwing back her hood.

It was Charlotte de Sauve, a lady-in-waiting, the leader of Catherine de' Medici's flying squadron. Françoise recognized her from the day they had all gone out to the gibbet to view the corpses.

The first vampire was pressing his claw-like hands to his injured face, and now he was covered in red blood.

Watch, said Sainct Didier. *A vampire does not bleed, except for after he has drunk. It is the blood of the child that leaves him now.*

This was the lesson, and this was her schoolroom. This dark, stinking street where monsters fed on the innocent.

Can we kill them now? Françoise asked, her hands fists. Her scream of horror a moment before seemed to have unlocked her ability to speak with her mind, and she intended to use it. She intended to use all her talents tonight, to take this evil out of the world.

More are coming, said the duchess. *Look. Rise and watch. That is why you are here!*

Tamping down her impatience, Françoise tried to do as instructed. She shut her eyes, and stilled her breath. She was aware of the city breathing around her. Aware of the smells rising from the alleys, from the windows. The smoke rising from chimneys. Aware of the stars in the heavens, and the coos of pigeons sleeping in the eaves, their heads under their wings. Aware of a murder of crows on the edge of a rooftop, two streets away.

Françoise shivered as she understood. A dozen of the queen's flying squadron. Every one of them a vampire.

She opened her own eyes just as the newly eyeless vampire complained aloud to his attacker. "I cannot be denied my prey."

"Can you not?" Madame de Sauve mocked. "You know the rules."

"This child will not be missed!"

"All the same. You should have had the self-control to take it to a private place, or waited for the nuns to do so for you. There is to be no killing in public view. Nothing that could alarm the good citizens of Paris."

"Nobody is watching," hissed the blinded vampire.

"Oh no?" Madame de Sauve countered. "What about them?"

She pointed straight at Françoise.

CHAPTER THIRTEEN

Fight and Flight

THE RUSH OF beaks and wings was like a sudden storm. Françoise put her arm over her face, as the crows flew at them.

Rise to meet them, the duchess said in her mind. *Do not be afraid.*

Something about her voice gave Françoise courage. She felt her arm becoming a wing, felt herself concentrate all her strength into wings, beak, claws. She was a flying weapon.

The three female Benandanti had become owls. Françoise did not know what to name their species, and she did not care, in her owl form. She was small, brown, large-eyed, nimble, while the silver-haired woman had become a great silvery creature with a cruel beak, and the duchess was a pale ghost with a wise expression.

Françoise soared over the street, and saw Sainct Didier below with a sword drawn. Before her eyes, a vine seemed to grow around its hilt and cover the crossbar with green. Its blade flashed and the point speared one of the birds, which instantly grew into the form of a woman, with the fencing master's blade through her heart. The weight of her pushed Sainct Didier down to the ground, flat on his back.

Another crow was wheeling to attack him. Françoise let gravity take her, dropped onto the sleek black body, let her claws find its flesh. The vampire wriggled in her grasp and its beak pecked her; blood and feathers rained in the street.

Below her, the men were still occupied with the dying vampire. La Môle pushed the impaled woman over to one side, allowing Sainct Didier to remove his blade, while La Môle's own sword slashed through the woman's neck. Her head rolled and La Môle breathed hard from the effort of the blow.

The damned crow was nearly free. Françoise only had one claw on it now, and it was pushing its own claws up into her breast. Again she spoke to gravity, and again it welcomed her. Down she dashed onto the cobbles, the crow bearing the brunt, its neck broken.

Françoise rose into the night to get a sense of the battleground. Two vampires lay destroyed, but the street was full of them, half in female form now, half still crows. Thirteen vampires to four Benananti—no, twelve, because the first vampire, the one that de Sauve had blinded, was running down the street, soundlessly, fleeing the battle.

And there on the ground, the bundle, the infant, left on the doorstep, inches away from La Môle as he wrestled with a vampire who seemed so strong he had no need of weapons.

Watch yourself, she heard the duchess scream in her mind, warning La Môle. *There's another one behind you.*

But La Môle had his hands full, so the duchess dropped in owl form, swooping over the vampire's head, distracting it, taunting it. When the vampire took crow form to chase her, the duchess dropped down into human form. She reached for the crow, and a foul-smelling smoke rose from where her gloves touched the feathers. She brought the bird to her face as if she would kiss it, and nuzzled it against her mask.

The bird smoked and hissed, making a horrible sound, and then a charred human corpse lay at the duchess's feet for a moment before she took flight again.

Another vampire down.

Françoise darted back and forth over the scene, trying to decide what to do. The baby was still lying on the stones across the street. Any moment now, it could be trampled, or picked up as a trophy by one of the monsters. Could she carry it away in owl form? She was such a small owl, and she did not trust her claws.

But if the duchess could change, so could she.

This third time she dropped to the ground, she was in human form by the time her feet touched the stones. Back in her green cloak, her gloves, her shoes, as if they had all been waiting for her. When she was an owl, she had no need of them; when she was in human form, she did.

In a moment, she had the child in her arms, but there was a vampire breathing over her shoulder, a hand reaching for her, and she leapt up, into the air, as high as she could in her light spirit body.

But she could not change form again, not with the baby clutched against her chest, her hand protecting his sweet downy head. She ran lightly along the top of the orphanage wall. Inside, she could see lighted windows; the nuns would surely take fright, if they heard the sounds of steel, the growls of the vampires.

She hesitated. Which way to go?

The baby mewled and wriggled, pushing his head back, unhappy in her arms. She did not have the gift of the vampire to calm it.

La Môle was near, fighting a vampire who had a sword of his own. La Môle's weapon had no vine on its hilt but a red stone that glowed like a sun the night before a storm.

He did not see when a vampire leaped up onto the wall to confront Françoise.

It was the other lady-in-waiting the queen had introduced her to that day at the gibbet. What was her name? Guillemette. Her face was just as lovely now, although the cheekbones stood out more, and the red mouth was curled back behind delicate white fangs. She smelled like roses, and for a moment, Françoise wondered what it would be like to stop caring, to toss this child onto the heap of forgotten lives, to live forever in her young and beautiful body, to be honoured and feared. To never be afraid again.

The vampire reached out her hands for the child.

Some instinct in Françoise saved her, and saved the baby, too. She raised her right hand, and the scented glove made contact with Guillemette's beautiful face.

It sizzled and burned, and the smell of roses darkened and withered into the smell of old leather. The vampire screeched and raked her nails across Françoise's face.

Françoise ran, directly into the vampire she'd just injured, knocking her off the wall. She kept running, hearing nothing but her heartbeat in her ears and the cry of the baby in her arms.

From the street, there came another human cry.

The mother of the child had, perhaps, had second thoughts, or heard the commotion, and returned for the child. She was staring fixedly at Françoise, and running down the street, tears streaming, her nut-coloured hair streaming behind her. She was young, younger even than Françoise. She paid no attention to the violence around her, only to Françoise, who was high enough to be beyond her reach.

Finally, she stopped, stooping to pry a cobble out of the street.

If Françoise leapt down into the orphanage yard, that would prevent her from being struck with a rock, but it would also abandon the mother to the vampires, and perhaps lead her to try something even more foolish. Besides, Françoise reasoned quickly, surely the mother would not actually throw the rock at her, for fear of hitting the child. It was a bluff.

And it didn't matter.

Just before the mother straightened back up, with the rock in her hand, a vampire appeared out of nowhere behind her.

His hood was down and his face was visible in the moonlight. It was a young face, fair and boyish, the face of François, Duke of Alençon, youngest son of the queen, and the most fractious. He had not gone to Chenonceau with the rest of the court.

The duke smiled with fangs.

The young mother was entirely unaware of him, but La Môle had spotted him. Thank God, Françoise thought. La Môle, with his blade now wet with blood duller and darker than the stone in his hilt, would run the duke through, surely. That was why they were here.

But he did not. La Môle simply stood in the street, staring at the duke, rooted to the spot. His eyes were glassy and he seemed almost asleep.

It was some sorcery, some power of the vampires, and meanwhile, the Duke of Alençon reached his arm around the neck of the mother and drew her into his body, hard and sharp.

At the same moment, Sainct Didier came running at them, his blade pointed straight at the woman and the vampire behind her. Françoise thought for a moment he was going to run them both through at once; it seemed the duke believed it too, for he let the woman go and leaped up, into the air, suddenly a swarm of bats like the ones who had been her first sight of vampires in the hills of Gascony.

And just like that night in the hills, she heard Sainct Didier's voice in her head, saying: *Run*.

Françoise stepped off the wall, floated down beside the frantic mother, whose chest was heaving as she tried to catch her breath and her bearings. With her right arm still holding the baby to her own chest, Françoise grabbed the mother's arm with her left, and pulled her away from the fighting, down the street the way she'd come.

After a few paces, she realized she didn't need to hold the mother's arm. She was running of her own accord.

"My baby," she panted. "Give me my baby. Please."

It did not occur to Françoise that her intentions might not be clear, even after she had pulled the woman away from the vampires. She handed over the bawling child and it gladdened her heart to see him calmer, though still breathing in great baby sobs, as his mother held him close.

The mother stopped in her tracks, then, hesitating.

"I am a friend," Françoise assured her. "You're safer with me than alone. Come on. I promise I won't hurt you or the child. I would give my life for you both."

The mother nodded uncertainly.

Which way to run? Not toward the quiet fields on the edge of the city, surely, but toward the more inhabited places, where even vampires might be circumspect. Back to the Hôtel de Guise? But that would give away Françoise as a member of that household, to the mother and to anyone who might see them.

She had no choice. They had to go somewhere.

"Come on," she said, and after a moment's pause, the young mother followed.

FRANÇOISE AWOKE IN the middle of the night, disoriented. She had been running. She remembered getting as far as the lane near the Hôtel de Guise, and then…

She sat upright. The mother and child. She'd abandoned them; it must have seemed as if she'd vanished. Curse her for waking up!

The duchess still slept beside her, and there was another dark shape on the trundle bed. La Môle. She considered waking them, but she was reluctant to interrupt them in their business with the vampires. It could be life and death for someone, to remove a fighter from the fight.

So she slipped out of the bed and padded through the antechamber in her bare feet, making her way through the rooms of the mansion in the direction of the servants' entrance. She had a dim memory of being close enough to see that lantern. She could only hope the mother was still outside near the door.

But when she reached the kitchen, she heard a baby crying.

To her astonishment, the mother was sitting at the kitchen table, bouncing her baby and wiping tears off her face, while the night cook said reassuring things and warmed some gruel on the stove.

Françoise wanted to go to her, but she realized in time that that would mean one person in Paris could associate her waking face with her night activities, which would put all her comrades at risk. She slipped away before the girl could see her.

CHAPTER FOURTEEN

The Queen's Sorcerer

It was not, it seemed, the first time the household staff at the Hôtel de Guise had been confronted with a wide-eyed young woman and an exhausted, fractious child. They found a room for them both in the servants' quarters, and the crying of the infant could not be heard in the apartments of the family and guests, and no more was said about it.

That was, until Henri de Sainct Didier came to call upon the duchess, who was still playing host to the ostensibly ailing La Môle. They formed their council of war in her antechamber, near the fire, as the day was chilly; the year was getting old.

"You did well, Mademoiselle d'Artagnan," said Sainct Didier.

Françoise bowed her head. How powerless she had felt when the vampire came for her and the child. In the end, the only thing she'd been able to do was run. "I did my best. I fear it was not good enough. I wish I could learn not to fear death."

The duchess smiled sadly. "That is not a thing one learns. If anything, it is the opposite. With each passing year, I regret more that I will have to leave this life. Do not mistake me, I wish to go to my Saviour, but… not yet."

"People say the young believe themselves invincible," Sainct Didier said, nodding. "But it isn't true. You, Françoise, who are not yet twenty. You know well enough that you *will* die one day, and you also know that you *could* die soon. A man or woman of advanced years, though, knows that they *will* die soon. That is the difference. The certainty of death never changes, but the nearness changes with every sunset. A swordsman, though, because of the frequency with which he faces death, now—now—now," he said, chopping the air with each repetition, "must adopt a perspective closer to that of an old man, even when young. It can be a lonely condition. That is why we seek each other out, why there is a brotherhood among us."

"Perhaps I could study to use a sword, as you and Monsieur La Môle do," she said.

Sainct Didier smiled. "Women fight in other ways. As you showed tonight. The three of you."

He said this last part with some significance that eluded Françoise.

"Who was the silver-haired woman?" she asked.

"An old friend," he responded. "That is all you need know. She has found safety in the daylit world with a new name, and she has no desire to join our council. But she will join us at night, when we call her."

"Or when she feels like it," grumbled the duchess.

"For now," said Sainct Didier, "we have more urgent matters to discuss. Such as what to do with the young mother you brought here last night, Mademoiselle d'Artagnan."

"The woman knows too much," said La Môle.

Unlike the response to her request to learn how to fight, Françoise had prepared for this line of argument. "None of us looked anything like we do in waking life. I told her only that the Hôtel de Guise was known for its charity."

"You once recognized me from my voice," countered Sainct Didier. "And now she has heard yours."

"Yes, but she does not have our talents. The night was wild, and noisy, and anyway, I will give her no opportunity to hear my voice again. She has not seen me here. The servants are the only people she sees."

"And perhaps she has already told them tales," said Sainct Didier.

"She does not seem like a gossip, my ladies say," the duchess argued mildly. "Her name, incidentally, is Marie."

La Môle waved this information away. "This is ridiculous. The girl must die."

Françoise could hardly believe her ears. "Die! I thought you would argue to send her away, to the country, but—you would murder an innocent?"

Sainct Didier turned his dark eyes on her for a long moment, an eloquent moment. It sent a chill through her, an understanding. The thought of killing an innocent did not horrify their companions, because they had done so before, or at least seen it done, or considered it. There was so much she did not know about this fraternity in which she found herself, purely by virtue of having been born in a caul. Would she choose these companions if fate had not chosen them for her?

La Môle said, in a gentler tone, "You have a kind heart, and that is to be commended. But we cannot rescue them all, Mademoiselle d'Artagnan. Both mother and child are already victims of the queen's brood. Our task is to make sure they can do no further harm. A little mercy now may result in many more mothers and children slaughtered."

He looked wan, haunted, despite his gentle smile. She remembered how the very sight of the Duke of Alençon had robbed him of action. She had heard of the power of vampires to control the mind and freeze the heart, but it had been terrible to see it before her eyes.

"You all think I am too soft," she said, trying and failing to keep her emotions in check. "But it is you who are soft, who would yield to your fears, who would protect yourselves at a cost to others. On my honour, I will not see that woman killed."

Sainct Didier looked at her with grudging respect. "I admit the principle. And I applaud your compassion. But we must be practical, or else we put others at risk. Including the very woman we would save. If we leave her alive, she could do great harm. There are already stories running wild in Paris about the vampires. She can connect those stories to us."

"She might forget," Françoise countered. "You told me yourself that the vampires benefit from the need people have to forget the hideous or unbelievable things they witness."

"She won't forget us," murmured the duchess. "Not without help."

At that, Françoise's ears perked up. "Help? Is there a way to *make* her forget?"

Sainct Didier frowned at the duchess. "Madame, tread lightly."

"Do not try to school me, monsieur," said the duchess, and drew herself up in a way that Françoise had never seen before. "I am two hundred years old, older even than you and a great deal older than Comte La Môle, and I have shed a great deal of blood, and if there is one thing I have learned in all that time, it is that we all become what we fight, eventually, if we do not listen to the young. Françoise is brave, and intelligent, and if she seems naive to you it is only because you have hardened your heart. Let her teach you again what it means to do God's work on this earth. Let her remind you of our purpose."

This astonishing speech robbed everyone in the room of the power of speech for a moment, but none more than Françoise. Two hundred years old! The duchess seemed to be still young, no more than thirty.

But Sainct Didier was unmoved. "Our purpose is, as it has always been, to kill Malandanti."

"But *why?*" The question burst out of Françoise. "Why is our purpose to kill Malandanti? Who decreed that it should be so?"

The duchess looked at the swordmaster. "You did not tell her the story, before sending her to me?"

"We have had little time for storytelling."

"It is our story that tells us what we are," La Môle argued. "No wonder the girl is confused. And you must be the one to tell it, Sainct Didier. It is a story of your country, after all."

They all stared at the swordmaster, like children pleading with a tired father to prolong bedtime. At last, Sainct Didier sighed and gave in.

"A very long time ago," he began, "somewhere north of Rome and south of the Alps, there lived a poor orphan girl, who grew into a beautiful and wise young woman, very gifted with herbs and medicines. According to the story, she was named Anthaia. Everyone in her village went to her when they had a broken leg or a fever. One summer, it all changed. Her neighbours stopped coming to her doorstep, and even began to shun her, turning away when they passed her on the road, or making warding signs. They began to call Anthaia a witch. They had sensed that there was a dark presence who walked beside her—or more accurately, behind her. They thought her powers had come at the expense of a bargain with a demon. But she had made no such bargain, and given no invitation. It was a vampire who dogged her steps, a vampire who lusted for Anthaia and wanted her for his own."

Françoise could tell that Sainct Didier had been told this story himself, perhaps more than once. It had the rhythms of a tale told many times.

"At first," the swordmaster continued, "the vampire hoped that Anthaia would give herself to him freely. When she refused him, he pursued her, and it took all her cunning to escape him. Since there was no one in her village who would help her or even open their doors to her, Anthaia fled into the hills, at the feet of the Alps. She ran as fast and as far as she could, but she could not outrun the vampire.

"She ran until her heart and her limbs were exhausted and she fell flat on her face in a field of corn. Panting for breath, she spoke a desperate prayer into the earth. She asked for help. And the roots of the corn heard her. The bones of the dead heard her. The insects clinging to the stalks heard her. The small animals in their burrows heard her. The larger animals listening for the movements of the small ones heard her too. Even the birds in the sky heard the whisper moving through the plants in the field, through the trees in the forest. Every living thing for a day's walk around Anthaia heard her prayer.

"They sent a small brown mouse to her ear and whisper their response. 'We will help you,' they said. 'We will destroy the thing that hunts you. But you must pledge some of your own kind to the fight. As long as evil walks our lands, we will mark some of your kind, who will join us in fighting them. As you have wakened the sleeping earth, we will waken your children. We will be their weapons and their allies, and they will be ours.'

"Anthaia agreed to this, and when the vampire came to that corn field, he was torn apart by wild things. But he was not the last of his kind. He had sired other vampires, and his tribe was known as the Malandanti, the Evil Walkers. We children born in the caul may be called by the drums of the earth to fight other evils, other vampire tribes, but the Malandanti are our most ancient enemies. They are the reason for the promise Anthaia made. They are the reason we have our gifts."

Françoise felt a kinship to this woman of some distant past. The story left her feeling sober and determined, but no less certain that the woman Marie should not pay with her life for knowing of the existence of the Benandanti.

She said, "We should use their gifts to fight every evil the

Malandanti bring to the world. The Malandanti attacked Marie and her child; we should not finish the job for them, simply to protect ourselves." She almost added that such a path was cowardly, but she stopped. She could see that the swordmaster was beginning to change his mind, and she did not want to overplay her point and cause him insult.

"But is there a way to remove her memory?" La Môle asked. "I have never heard of such a plant or elixir."

Sainct Didier was quiet.

The duchess said, "Many years ago, I encountered the aftereffects of such an elixir, and I tried to determine its ingredients, but it was beyond my skills. It is not something our kind can make. Our gift is for healing and growth; our weapons are lethal to the vampires because their nature opposes our own. We do not have the power to do harm to living mortals through our art, and destroying memory is harm, even if it is done for a greater purpose."

"Then who does have this power?" Françoise asked, eagerly, leaning forward.

"It is a sorcerer's art," the duchess replied. "And the only sorcerer in Paris who might have such skill is Cosimo Ruggieri, who came from Florence with Catherine de' Medici years ago."

"He is deep in the counsel of the queen," warned La Môle.

"And yet," said Sainct Didier thoughtfully, "that might be to our benefit. We need to know more about the queen's plans for her children, for Paris, for France. Access to Ruggieri might be useful. And a memory elixir is the sort of thing a woman might see a sorcerer about. An ordinary woman. This could serve more than one of our needs."

The duchess nodded. "It is a risk, but so is killing an innocent. Every body that washes up in the Seine has a story to tell, and the fewer stories we tell, the safer we will be. If Françoise obtains the elixir and we remove Marie's memories, will that satisfy you, La Môle?"

The count looked uncertain. "I will be satisfied. But mademoiselle, do not deceive yourself. An elixir from a sorcerer is a danger in its own right, and this may not be a kindness that we do."

COSIMO RUGGIERI HAD once been omnipresent at the Louvre, but in recent years, the queen had turned instead to Maître René the perfumer, who also dabbled in prophecies and horoscopes. So the ageing Ruggieri occupied a narrow house in a dark and quiet neighbourhood on the other side of the Seine.

A down-at-heel servant answered the door and admitted Françoise to a dim room that smelled strongly of the books that lined its walls, and the oils on the strange metal instruments that sat on any shelf space the books had ceded to them.

The magician was stout, red-faced, dishevelled, like a cross between an absent-minded friar and an overworked costermonger. He had a little bit of old sauce on the front of his robe, and a stray black thread in his reddish beard.

"What's your name, child?"

"Louise de Mirvaille, monsieur."

"You say you have a message from the Duke of Alençon?"

The magician looked at Françoise eagerly. She almost felt bad about deceiving him. The lie had been La Môle's idea; Ruggieri had been the duke's tutor, but the queen had dismissed him a year or two ago. The dismissal had probably coincided with the young duke's turning; perhaps Ruggieri was not to be trusted with such information.

Françoise let some of her uncertainty show. "I am afraid that message was a ruse, sir. I do not come with the duke's permission, but I do come on his behalf."

This was the delicate moment, the moment when he might throw her out, but he was curious. She saw it in his eyes.

"A riddle," he said patiently. "And what is the solution?"

She bowed her head demurely. "I am a... *friend* of the duke's. Recently, I was spotted leaving his apartments."

A pause. Then, "Young men do sometimes entertain young women. He is, what, seventeen now? And you are the same age."

A little older, Françoise thought, but did not say. She just nodded, letting the blood into her cheeks.

"The trouble is, sir, that I am married, and there will be a scandal. Oh, I don't fear for the duke. I know that he will prevail. I know he could slaughter my husband if he chose." She let a little light into her eyes at this, and smiled cruelly. "But that would bring disrepute, especially so soon after the bloodshed of Saint Bartholomew's Eve. My husband is a good Catholic, and as you may know, there are whisperings that the duke has Huguenot sympathies. And other whisperings besides..." She trailed off.

"Other whisperings?"

She shrugged. "Oh, people say he is cruel, evil, a monster, that he... I don't even know if I can repeat the things they say. They don't understand him. But if there were a scandal, and a duel, it would cause him to reveal too much about his nature, and not everyone loves that nature as I do. As you do, sir, being his tutor, and his friend."

The magician looked at her carefully. "You seem to know a lot about me."

"Because the duke speaks of you with such respect."

"He speaks of me? Really?"

"Frequently, sir. How else would I have known to come to you? He says you have a potion for everything. Potions for seeing the future, for falling in love... that one, we have no need of... and potions for getting rid of problems. He said you even have an elixir that will cause someone to forget an event."

He looked at her sharply. "And you want me to give you such a potion?"

"If I could get that servant to drink it, could I—do you think I could make the whole thing go away? I would be so grateful. And the duke would be grateful, too. Oh, I can't ask him about it now, because his pride wouldn't allow it—he would say he does not fear scandal. Truly, I don't think he fears anything! But he will be so pleased when I tell him that I tricked a servant into forgetting that she saw me. I won't tell him that I did it to save him exposure. I'll pretend it was for our amusement. He'll like that, won't he?"

"Yes, that is the sort of jest he enjoys. Tell me, what is the name of the servant you wish to ensorcell?"

Françoise had been prepared for this. She invented a name.

"It is not a name I know, but the palace does tend to go through servants quickly. So you intend to feed this person the elixir?"

"Yes. How the duke will laugh when I tell him what I did with your clever potion!"

The magician leaned back and rubbed his beard. "I see, I see. Yes, you were right to come to me. But I don't have such things lying around, you understand."

She let her honest anxiety show. "How long must I wait?"

He stood, and went to a table in the back, rummaged in some drawers.

"Not long. I will mix it up now. You may wait if you like. Are you hungry? Can I offer you some… well, I could have sworn there were biscuits."

"I don't need anything, monsieur."

"Well, at least have some brandy for your nerves." The rattle of a decanter. He placed a glass half full of dark amber beside her on the tray, and then returned to his worktable.

Could it be this easy? She was here, with Ruggieri, onetime magician to the queen herself, and he was doing as she wanted.

"The duke told me that you sometimes cast horoscopes," she said, casually. "That you have made them for all the queen's children."

"Indeed."

"But Maître René doesn't agree with your horoscopes about the royal family, I hear."

A pause. The magician paused, took a bottle off his shelf. "A horoscope is not a matter of agreeing or disagreeing. Any proper man of learning will tell his client honestly what the signs say. It brought me no comfort to tell Her Majesty that there were signs that pointed to the deaths of her sons."

"Ah, but there is death and then there is simply… no longer being *alive*," she said.

She'd overstepped. The magician put down the bottle with a thud. His eyes glinted in the dim room. "What else has the duke told you?"

Her only hope now was to seem as if she knew more than she should, but didn't have the wisdom to understand it. "Oh, you needn't worry, monsieur. The duke has been quite open with me. I know very well he is… unnatural. But I can't seem to resist him. I cannot help but love him, though he lives in darkness."

"He was such a sweet child," the magician said, sadly.

"But at least we can be sure that the prophecy has been fulfilled, and that his death has not taken him from us. That he will be with us for a very long time. He and his brothers."

The magician cocked his head. "Perhaps. Death may mean… transformation. As you suggest. But it may also mean utter destruction. And every creature that walks this earth may be destroyed."

Françoise shivered. The magician was telling her too much. Trusting her too much. That was a bad sign.

He walked around the desk and continued, "We have sacrificed black cockerels, searched the organs for more information. None of it is yet clear to me. But it will be. The queen has told me what I must do. I must make an examination of a human brain. There I will find the shapes that speak to me, the alphabet of the universe. Then I will know the fate of the Valois family. Then I will be given my due." He was very close to her now, and he was holding a knife in one hand. It gleamed, metallic, in the candlelight. "All I require for the prophecy is an innocent human brain."

She looked up at him, swallowed. He was so close to her now that she would not be able to get out of the chair and run, not without knocking him down first.

He flicked the knife out toward a withering chamomile plant beside her, and cut off one small leaf. He smiled.

"For the elixir."

Then he was walking back around his worktable, and Françoise breathed again, trying to stop her heartbeat from filling the room.

"It's a simple concoction, really," he said, tossing the leaf into the pestle. Then he shook something dark green out of a jar. Françoise sat up tall to try to see it. Her nose detected something unusual… chamomile, yes, but something else?

The magician glanced at her and noticed her posture. His eyes went hard, suspicious. "You're not drinking your brandy."

She smiled, sat back and put the glass to her mouth.

A sudden and certain knowledge struck her: brandy was not the only thing in this glass. Mixed in with the brandy was a tincture of something else. She sniffed surreptitiously. There was the chamomile, again. Fennel. Pine sap. It kept eluding her. If she could taste it, she might be able to catch everything—but then she would forget it. Because, she felt quite sure, this was the elixir of forgetting.

The magician had no intention of solving her problem by giving her the potion; he was solving the problem by *feeding* her the potion. He would go and take care of the servant himself with the one he was making—how fortunate that she'd given him an invented name.

But what choice did she have? He was watching her, and she had the glass to her lips. She could dissemble, pretend to shun alcohol, but it would raise his suspicions.

Françoise tipped the glass, let the liquid touch her tongue.

An ordinary person would have tasted brandy, and not very expensive brandy at that: cloying, harsh, thin.

Any Benandanti who tasted the brandy would have tasted the tincture, too.

Françoise tasted the brandy, tasted the tincture, and held it at bay. With every bit of determination and will she could muster, she walled off the effects from her mind, the effort of which immediately gave her a headache.

"When you give the elixir, you must find some excuse to say these words to the servant," the magician said, casually, mixing a spoonful of something that looked like honey in. "Say: you will forget this drink, you will forget speaking with me today, and you will forget that Louise de Mirvaille ever had any dealings with the Duke of Alençon."

She absorbed the words, knowing they would work their power on her as well. She would forget the conversation and the drink. But she fought it, hard. The effort was like a vice around her skull. She took another sip, and smiled, and watched the magician filtering some dark liquid through the paste he had made.

He held up a vial with the elixir in it. Françoise tasted the same elixir on her tongue, and she knew, at last, everything that went into it. She held onto the knowledge desperately, as it disintegrated and blurred.

"It's time you were going," said the magician.

She did not argue, and did not ask for the potion in his hand. He wanted her to forget; she wanted to get out, quickly. She needed paper and pen to write this down before it left her forever.

It was nearly night when she stumbled out into the street, repeating the ingredients of the potion in her mind, over and over. She should have just stolen the vial. She must learn how to be a thief. She must learn how to be a killer. So much to learn, so much to remember.

And it hurt so badly, hanging on to the information. She couldn't think and there was a haze before her eyes. The pain of it. She ran into someone, mumbled an apology, then looked up into a friendly, concerned face.

It took her a moment for the memory of his name to come into her beleaguered mind.

Chicot.

"What is it? Mademoiselle, are you ill?"

"Chamomile," she spat at him. "Fennel. Rosebud. Viper tooth. Copper. Limestone."

He grabbed her arms. "I'll fetch a physician."

It was too much. The effort of holding on to the memory was breaking her.

She repeated the ingredients to him, more forcefully, and then she fell to the ground, and knew no more.

CHAPTER FIFTEEN

A Game of Tennis

She awoke in the duchess's bed, with a cold cloth over her eyes. Sainct Didier was sitting nearby, reading a book with drawings in it. He looked calm, even content.

"Don't try to remember," he said.

Françoise frowned. What a thing to say! "Don't try to remember what?"

"Exactly. You went to see Cosimo Ruggieri, the queen's sorcerer, in hopes of obtaining an elixir that would remove certain memories from one who drank it. I don't know what happened there, but it seems he administered the elixir to you; perhaps you manipulated him into doing so, in hopes of discovering the ingredients."

She remembered the plan well enough, but the idea that she had been through an encounter with a magician and could now remember nothing of it was not a very nice one. The more she tried to remember, the more she felt as if some great hand were gripping her brain.

"I'm sorry," she said. "I hope I didn't tell him anything. I hope he didn't discover anything about us, from me."

He made a non-committal gesture. "I don't think he would have risked giving you the potion and sending you away if he had known you were a Benandante. He would have taken you to the queen mother as a prize, more likely. We cannot be certain, but I think it is likely he thought he was tricking an ordinary girl. But you are not ordinary. Not at all."

Of all the many things confusing Françoise at that moment, the pride in the face of Sainct Didier as he beamed at her was the most confusing of all.

"But I failed, monsieur."

"You did not fail. You managed to fight off a powerful magician's potion for long enough to remember its ingredients. Very few people could have done that, even among the Benandanti. The effort of it nearly broke your mind and stopped your heart. You managed to remember the ingredients long enough to say them to your friend Chicot in the street, and he carried you all the way here and told the duchess what you had said. She reproduced the elixir and has administered it to the girl, Marie, who is now living in a very comfortable home in the country and has no memory of any of us or of her time in this house."

She shook her head. "I do remember Chicot—I remember saying something to him. Something about vipers... But why Chicot, of all people?"

"Ah." Sainct Didier leaned back in his chair and looked troubled. "That is an excellent question, and one I had as well. At first, he tried to make me believe that he was following you because he was concerned that you were in an unsavoury neighbourhood, that he was being chivalrous, perhaps overprotective. Acting the lovelorn swain, perhaps."

"Lovelorn!" Françoise did not like the idea of any man following her.

"It would be a reasonable explanation, were it not for the fact that I had already noticed him following me, too. And the duchess. He has suspicions about us. I do not believe he is a vampire, but I wondered whether he might be trying to gather information on us to improve his standing at court. When he realized the game was up, he admitted to me that he suspected we were enemies of the vampires, and that he wanted to join our cause."

"But is he..."

"Born in the caul? No, he is an ordinary man. He knows far more than he should, but he might be a useful ally. But that can wait until you're feeling better."

Her head swam. "What can wait?"

"You can find out more about him than I can. He may have been following you out of the same curiosity that causes him to follow me, but there is no doubt he is also interested in you for other reasons."

She blushed. "If I can be of any use, I will."

"Good. The more you can speak with him, the better. But we must also learn what he says to others. The duchess says you have proven adept at hiding in the palace, overhearing conversations."

This sounded dishonourable, said out loud, but she could only nod.

"Then I suggest you find a quiet spot in one of the places he frequents, and see what you can hear."

Françoise knew the game of tennis as it was played in cloisters or in the market square, hitting balls off rooftops with beaten-up rackets, leather gloves or even bare hands.

But she had never seen a court as perfectly constructed as the one on the perimeter of the Louvre: a floor of gleaming flagstones, the walls smooth, painted all in grey. Along one side, there was a gallery for visitors, under the sloping roof where the players aimed many of their shots.

But there were no visitors in the gallery the day that Chicot had made a private reservation so he could play with the Duke of Anjou, because it was not open to the public. Françoise was the only one, sitting deep in the shadow of the roof, the rope netting hiding her from view. She got there early, so she would not be seen, and then she waited. It was a long time, and the bench was hard.

At last, the two men came in. Chicot, lanky and grinning. The Duke of Anjou, as handsome as ever, twirling a racket in his hand. As he inspected a basket full of white balls, he spoke as if he were carrying on a conversation that had begun before they came into the tennis court.

"Things seem to have calmed down in Paris, but elsewhere, Chicot, elsewhere, everything is going to get worse before it gets better. And will my brother the king have the strength of character to put it right? He is not himself. He has not been himself for some time."

"He was quite young when he was made king," said Chicot.

"That's not the transformation I mean."

"No," said Chicot evenly. "I hear the king has changed a great deal in the last two years. The old Huguenot admiral, Coligny, was gaining influence over him. And so your mother made sure that he would be guided by her. I've made a study of vampires. I know the signs."

There was a silence, as even Françoise held her breath.

Then the duke put a hand on Chicot's shoulder. "See, that's why I like you, Chicot. You tell me the truth. A rare quality."

"It gets me into trouble. But if it can be of any use to you, monseigneur, my honesty is at your service. And my curiosity."

"Your curiosity?"

"Yes. I might as well lay all my flaws at your grace's feet."

"And what are you curious about now?"

"You say His Majesty is changed, as no doubt he would be. You don't just mean his appetites, I take it?"

The duke grimaced, and reached a hand to his ear to fiddle nervously with his small pearl earring. "Charles takes these queer ideas into his head—he was never well, really, but he seems to have these fits now, when no one can reason with him."

"What happens when you give the strength of an immortal to a man who is fundamentally weak?" Chicot said.

"Exactly. Exactly, Chicot! You've hit it. And my mother knows just how to take advantage. But I never thought they were capable of such as a thing as this massacre, Chicot. As God is my witness, I did not."

The answer came in mild tones. "People say that you were one of the instigators, monseigneur."

Anjou poked a finger at Chicot's chest. "It isn't true. She doesn't control me, although sometimes, I admit, she is persuasive… I agreed that we had to knock old Coligny off the chessboard somehow, but I said nothing to anyone about any massacre. I will never forget my brother's voice, screaming, 'kill them all!'"

The duke had raised his tennis racket as he made his point, and it went flying, landing on the floor not far from Françoise's hiding spot in the gallery.

Chicot took three loping strides to retrieve it, but when he bent to pick it up, he contrived to toss it another few feet. Then he leaped upon it, shouting, "It's alive!"

This sent the duke into relieved laughter.

Chicot slowly stood up, dragging the racket as if it were an animal he'd hunted and killed.

As he rose, his gaze fell on Françoise.

Françoise froze. They stared at each other for a few heartbeats, saying nothing, neither of them moving.

"Come on, Chicot. Enough talk of my unnatural family and this godforsaken country they rule. You serve first."

Chicot made no signal to Françoise, just turned, walked back to the duke and said teasingly, "I will warn you that I'm incapable of letting anyone win, which I understand is de rigueur when playing a king's son."

The duke put a hand to his companion's cheek. "Darling Chicot, you had better steer clear of my mother."

"Why is that, monseigneur?"

"Because she always kills the men I like best. You came to me for protection and you may well find the opposite. Anyway, I don't plan to be beaten today, by you or anyone else. At least, not on the tennis court."

Once Françoise's heart had stopped pounding, she found herself enjoying the spectacle. The men were a sight to behold as they ran back and forth on their strong legs. No wonder Sainct Didier was always rhapsodizing about the virtues of the game.

The duke did win, although whether Chicot had let him or not, Françoise could not say.

They shook hands, and laughed a little, wiping their foreheads. Then the duke called for his servant and left.

But Chicot stayed, bouncing the ball idly. She opened the door of the little gallery and stepped out.

"You enjoyed the game?" he asked her mildly. "A dangerous one for spectators."

"So it would seem. And for the players, too. Tell me, did you let the duke win after all?"

"I hope it was not obvious."

"Not to me, at least."

He shrugged. "I'm trying to get into his good graces, you see."

"It would seem you already are. He confides in you—it could have cost me my freedom, if he'd known what I overheard. Thank you for not telling him I was here."

"I would like to claim I was being gallant, but I didn't want him to think..."

"What?"

"That I had brought a lady, to impress her." He hurried on. "A man may be in the good graces of a royal one day, and out of them the next. Paris is a dangerous place, and one needs the protection of strong friends."

"That is true, as I have reason to know. I admit that my new interest in tennis isn't everything that drew me here. I wanted to thank you for the service you did me the other day. When I was ill."

"It was my pleasure," he said, bowing, sweeping his tennis racket nearly to the floor as he did so. "And I was very worried. I kept pestering the servants at the Hôtel de Guise until they reassured me you were recovered and walking about."

"Very good luck you happened to be there," she said. "Sainct Didier says you've been following us. But what he can't work out is why."

"So he sent you to ferret it out."

She tried to look innocent. "He sent me to play tennis."

"Ha. In that case, let me teach you."

How eager men were to teach women things. "Now? But you must be tired."

"I've never felt more awake."

"Can I learn in a dress?"

"I don't know. Let's find out."

He walked over to a bin and pulled out a racket, then handed it to her.

"Sainct Didier says it is like fighting," she said, weighing the racket, sweeping it back and forth experimentally. "But I don't see how."

"I suppose it is like fighting, in a way. The court is like a body."

"A body?"

"Yes." He stepped back and seemed to survey hers. "When we fence, we think about where we wish our strike to land—the top right, for example." He pointed with his racket at her shoulder. "Or the top left." The other shoulder. "Or the lower quadrants." He pointed at each of her hips in turn. "So we carve up the court into targets as well. Go on, onto the other side, and I'll see if I can land a blow, oh, let's say under your… armpit."

He grinned.

She walked around the sagging net that divided the court in two, and stood waiting in a very good imitation of his own stance.

Chicot hit the ball onto the sloping roof, and it bounced to the floor. She whacked at it, but the racket seemed to absorb all the ball's energy, and the ball sank to the floor and rolled at her feet.

"That's to be expected," he said kindly. "It is harder than it looks, isn't it?"

"I didn't think it looked easy. May I try again?"

"Of course."

She had held back long enough. Biting her lip to hide her grin, she waited for his serve, then sent it back to him with a beautiful backhand, and it bounced twice on his side.

He dove at the ball, stopped it, and then stared at her. "Was that a lucky shot?"

"Not that lucky, or else it would have gone farther. I believe we now find ourselves in a chase position, Chicot."

"We do indeed," he said, rubbing his chin. "But who is chasing whom, I wonder?"

She laughed. "We may not have courts like this one in Artagnan, but I grew up playing with the boys in the local market. There was a perfectly sloping roof, although the woolmonger hated us. Women are allowed to do more things in the country than in the city, I am starting to think."

"You seem to have no trouble doing as you like here. All right then, shall we play to the point?"

They did, and Françoise won the game. By the end, Chicot was redder in the face than he'd been after playing the duke. But she charitably acknowledged that he had played two games straight, while she had played only one.

They sat down on the floor beside the gallery and Chicot shared a flask of water with her.

"I should have made a wager," she said.

"What would you have won?"

"The truth. The reason why you are so interested in my friends and in me. Why you seem to know so much about us."

He was quiet for a moment.

She practised patience, sitting still beside him, listening to the faint sounds of carts and horses on the drawbridge nearby, the occasional cheerful shout. People going about their business, while here in the heart of the city, she sat in this empty room with this man she hardly knew. She felt comfortable, at peace, safe. Perhaps it was an illusion, but perhaps an illusion was all she would ever have in this world.

Finally, he said, "I don't want to tell you anything that might put you in danger."

She snorted. "A bit late for that. Besides, don't you think there is enough secrecy and mistrust in this city as it is?"

"It isn't that I don't trust you."

"Good, because I trust *you*, Chicot. My friends may not yet trust you, but I do. You want to help us—that much is clear to me. If you truly want that, then let's be comrades, and face the enemy together."

"Always," he said, but then he gave her his hand to help her up. "We should leave. Someone else will be coming to play here soon, and I wouldn't want to tarnish your reputation. Although, if I were going to choose a place for a tryst, I would choose a more comfortable floor than a tennis court."

Her laughter rang off the walls.

CHAPTER SIXTEEN

The Vampire of Orléans

Françoise tried to run into Chicot for the next two days, but had no luck; he was always somewhere other than she expected him to be.

On the second night, as she lay on a pallet near the duchess's other ladies, she could not resist moving her fingertip to her throat, searching out the pulse there. It felt like a slight quiver under her fingertips, like a creature moving under her skin, a stranger. A force. At first it was as nothing, and then it was everything. It roared in her ears as she lost all sense of the world around her.

And then she was standing, cloaked and hooded, looking over her own body as if it were no different from those of the other women lying on their pallets, softly snoring, dreaming of ordinary impossibilities.

Françoise found it unsettling, being out in the streets of Paris after dark, even in her spirit body. Her spirit body did not breathe; did not have to. It did not hunger, did not thirst. It was only her mind, taking shape and wandering, but the shape of it was real and could be touched, just as her pulse could be felt. Like her pulse, her spirit form was not entirely her own, not entirely under her control. Once she found herself with her cloak wrapped around her and then she was a dove, wrapped in its wings. She had not intended that.

Walking in spirit form was a relief, in that she was no longer concerned in quite the same way about the cares of the waking world. Just as she had stared down at her own body, she felt curiously detached from the people she saw, and she did not think much about the duchess, about Chicot, about Sainct Didier, even about vampires. She watched the world and she did not put words to it.

She walked cloaked and watched everything and everyone. The prostitutes talking business with each other, the musicians stumbling home, the night-soil men on their rounds, the bands of young men shouting at each other and at the world. Paris at night was like the first verses of a round, each sound or smell or personality a melody, more obvious because more isolated. Later, when the dawn came, more strains joined in, until no one melody stood out from the rest.

She did not see any vampires, not even when she mustered her courage and walked past the Enfants-Rouges. Perhaps the vampires were avoiding it for the time being. What would she have done, if she'd seen one? She could not prevent them from doing their evil work, not on her own. All she'd be able to do was watch and witness. And yet, in this form, she had a need to witness, to let her eyes shine on all the evils of the world.

Once, when she turned a corner into an alley, she found it shrouded in strange mist, totally silent, without the little rustlings and bad smells of the real Paris. As if she had left the real world altogether, and entered a world of spirit indeed. After a few steps, the colour and life snapped back.

As morning came and her body started to waken, she could feel her spirit drawn back to it.

The next night, after she had walked for hours, she resisted the call of her waking body. She strode in the opposite direction. And yet, she returned, nonetheless. One moment she was on the bridge over the Seine, and the next she was waking on her pallet in the antechamber.

And the duchess was standing overhead.

"You were resisting," said the duchess.

Françoise sat up and rubbed her eyes. There was no one else in the room. Someone else had dressed the duchess, while she had overslept, oblivious.

She had worried the duchess would scold her if she learned that Françoise was walking in spirit form alone, but the duchess did not even seem surprised.

Françoise said, "Sainct Didier says it is possible to sleep for years, and our body stays alive, stays as it is, while our spirit wanders."

"So it is. I've done it myself."

"But I can't seem to prevent myself from waking before I'm ready."

"You'll learn, with practice. The trick is in nearly forgetting one's body, one's waking life. It can happen accidentally for some—for those who are desperate to forget—but for most of us, it takes some training. I find it unsettling. And I would not wish too hard to experience it. There is a cost."

"A sacrifice?"

"Say rather an effect. A consequence. The longer one remains apart from the world, the harder it becomes to remember that one wishes to rejoin it. It's not difficult in a pragmatic sense; one can return when one chooses, but the world is never the same as we left it. We find ourselves uninterested in our old friends, our old delights. It is a kind of grief, every time. As your nightly jaunts get longer, you will find they change your waking life more."

"You do not tell me to stop."

The duchess shrugged. "It is in our natures. We are solitary, and yet we are called to the world of spirit, the world of the collective. It is the paradox that makes us who we are. In spirit form, at least, we have more ability to fight and to hide than if we were simply women walking alone at night. But do be cautious. Remember that your spirit form does not have the same attachments to the world and to your waking life, and it may not make the same choices. And remember that injuries sustained to your spirit body will have their effects on your physical one, too. Not always the same effects. You know the way La Môle walks, with one arm always swinging?"

Françoise nodded.

"Well, I learned something about him. When he started to walk at night, when he first heard the drums, he ended up not with others of our kind but in the local cemetery, where he watched the ghost of a woman, sitting up in an oak tree, looking to the horizon. The dead will speak to us, sometimes, and even call us. But only seldom. They do not trust easily."

"I saw them," Françoise said, excited to have an explanation for an occurrence she had not connected to her nature as a Benandante. "I saw a procession of the dead, leaving Paris."

The duchess nodded. "I am not surprised. Murder and other abominations tend to make the dead restless, and we're more likely to see them after some great violence. The ghost La Môle watched had been murdered by her sweetheart, and everyone knew. It made La Môle angry. He's a man with a keen sense of justice. At night, he took a ghostly form himself, and haunted the village, walking up and down the main road ringing a bell, preventing everyone from sleeping. I don't know when he stopped doing that, but he kept that swing in his arm. He told me this in his cups the other night, with Marguerite and Coconnas."

Françoise tried not to look petulant about the fact that the four of them sometimes had evenings without her. Truth be told, she found their relationships rather dizzying.

"I will try not to adopt any odd habits when I go out tonight," she said dutifully. "And I am always careful."

"Tonight, you will not be alone. We hunt together, my

friend."

Françoise smiled, a little nervously. "At the Enfants-Rouges?"

"Not this time. Sainct Didier has been investigating tales of a vampire in Orléans."

Françoise started; she remembered Madame Charbonneau. That strange night at the inn, when the vampire had practically bewitched her, and then chosen to let her go. But she said nothing; either Sainct Didier had told the duchess about it already, or there was no reason to tell her.

"It's a long journey," said the duchess kindly, misinterpreting her reaction. "We will take animal form. Even so, we will be gone more than a night. So you'll have a chance to learn about spending more time asleep."

A DOZEN RATS left Paris by the Porte Saint-Jacques, and scurried through the fields and by-ways.

When they reached a shallow creek, rocks shining in the sunlight, they transformed into hounds, sleek and fast, as grey as shadows, making no sound but that of their breath.

And yet, as they ran, Françoise could hear the beat of a drum, coming from everywhere and nowhere. It called a few more to their number, coming one by one, joining without greeting, running straight for Orléans. A sense of urgency drove them as the sun rose. A sense that time was of the essence.

It was unsettling to be out in spirit form during the day. At night, people and animals seemed content not to look straight at the Benandanti, not to ask questions about the gliding way they walked, or their heavy silence.

It was perhaps because of that tendency toward silence and watchfulness that her comrades had chosen clerical disguise this day—a decision she'd followed, not needing to be told, as the thoughts of the others now seemed as natural as the beats of her own heart. She did not know which of them was the duchess, or Sainct Didier, or La Môle, as none of them had yet spoken to her, and the others, she assumed were strangers. Perhaps Sainct Didier's friend, the silver-haired lady, was among them, too.

By the time the evening was darkening into night, the company of Benandanti had reached the outskirts of Orléans, and they changed again into the shapes of monks and nuns, thin and cloaked.

How strange, to fight and die alongside comrades whose waking appearance and names one might not know, now or ever. But then again, there was a kind of freedom in it as well. Here, in her nun's habit and borrowed face, with her strong arms and set jaw, Françoise might be anyone. She might *become* anyone.

The company halted outside a slope-roofed shack, where a Benandanti woman stood outside the door, holding a broom. She was not holding it the way someone might who was about to sweep the threshold; she held it like a weapon. A Benandante in the guise of a friar approached and bowed his head. She regarded him for a moment, then handed him the broom.

Each in turn, they approached the woman, and found that she had a broom for each of them. Françoise took hers gratefully, not knowing why. The staff was crooked, rough in her palm, and the head was hardly more than a bundle of dried sorghum. Yet she felt even more powerful now.

She recognized the streets as the cloaked procession walked them, holding their brooms. People got out of the way. Some crossed themselves as if they were afraid; some crossed themselves as if they were grateful. No one spoke to the Benandanti.

For a moment, Françoise felt unsettlingly like one of the procession of ghosts that she had seen, the unspeaking, relentless walkers. Taking spirit form felt a little like dying to the world, but waking to something else. To the spirit of the night air, full of possibility.

She knew the smells of this place. She knew the inn when they approached it. The inn of Madame Charbonneau.

The friar who had taken the first broom turned and addressed the procession, speaking into their minds. Françoise was not surprised to hear him speak with Sainct Didier's voice.

We are about to meet a vampire who is very powerful. She has been here for centuries. Before the Malandanti came, she was here, a member of the vampire family whose very name has now been lost, except perhaps in her memory. We will contain her so that she cannot escape, so that her hunger and fear will make her unwise. Do not doubt that she can defeat any one of us. Our only hope is not to turn on each other, not to break. Our power is in unity.

At the word "unity", Françoise felt more power arise within her, a strength that came from the eagerness and anxiety of everyone around her, augmenting her own. Her limbs seemed to move of their own accord, and she found herself walking slowly to the right, taking her place in a circle of Benandanti.

Suddenly that power seemed about to overwhelm her, to take over her sense of self, her autonomy, the very freedom she had gloried in a moment ago. She felt as if she'd be absorbed by this company, so much larger than her usual companions—there must be more than twenty of them now, as so many had come from the countryside and within Orléans itself, drawn by the drums. Even the broommaker had taken her place in the circle.

Which of these nuns or monks was the duchess? They were all still cloaked, and none of them had any characteristics she recognized. She should have watched, while they were walking, for La Môle's arm swing.

The Benandanti stopped, having formed their circle around the inn. How was it possible the vampire within could be taken unawares?

She is distracted, came the duchess's voice in her mind, as if she'd read Françoise's thoughts. Perhaps she had.

Madame Charbonneau had spared Françoise, not long ago. But in the spirit world, she did not feel the memory so keenly. She could not quite feel the vampire's breath on her throat, or see her deep, dark eyes. She could not feel the warmth of her hand on her shoulder. That would make this easier.

As one, the Benandanti raised their brooms, holding them with two hands.

They laid them down on the ground, so that they formed a circle around the inn.

Something changed in the air. It was as if the brooms had created a wall, one that could not be seen or touched, but was there all the same. It stretched as far into the sky as it needed to. And Madame Charbonneau was within it.

Sainct Didier had said that her hunger would drive her to recklessness. Did the inn have guests within for her to feed on? Would the Benandanti have to stand here for days?

Within minutes—or at least it seemed that way; time was always a little strange in the spirit world—she had her answer. Dark smoke rose from the rooftop and resolved itself into a figure. A woman on the roof, in a dark dress, stooped as she surveyed the circle of her enemies, and plotted their defeat.

When Françoise recognized the woman's face, it sent terror through her, even in spirit form. For this was not Madame Charbonneau, but the queen mother of France, Catherine de' Medici. And she was not bothering to veil her power, not now. She stood on that roof not only as the mother of the king, the widow of another, but as the head of the Malandanti tribe, the most powerful vampire in France.

The mere sight of her sent a shock through the circle, but their resolve did not waver. They stared back.

A strange mist rose behind them. It crept with cold fingers around their legs, around their necks, dimming their view. It made Françoise cough.

Then a voice she did not recognize entered her mind, from one of the Benandanti who was a stranger to her. *With this mist, she hides herself from the people of Orléans. Even now she thinks she can hide her crimes and her true nature.*

The Benandanti laughed.

Then Françoise heard a voice she did recognize, that of the silver-haired lady.

She does not need the mist to cloud their eyes. They refuse to see what is right in front of them.

The voice came from the figure next to her, a very tall, slim figure in the habit of an abbess. These disguises were not only fitting for the Benandanti as they moved through the streets, Françoise realized; the crosses around their necks might also keep an old vampire at bay. An old vampire such as Madame Charbonneau. It would do little good against a newer vampire like the queen mother, even if the Benandanti's belief in the crucifix's power was strong enough.

Françoise tried to connect with the long string of days that had made up her waking life, tried to believe with all her might in the things she had been taught were true and good. Things she had been taught by her parents, who had rejected her. Her nurse, who abhorred her. By the priest who would have married her to a stranger. People who believed in those same ideas had slaughtered innocents throughout Paris, in the name of faith.

Her spirit form needed no words, no symbols. There was no need for faith because there were the drums. Her waking form might waver like a candle in a draft, but it was not her religion that had given her strength. Not the Catholic faith of her upbringing, not the Protestant faith of the rebels. She focused on the sound of the heartbeats, which never left her in this company.

Then came another familiar voice. La Môle spoke, addressing his words to the silver-haired lady. *We will protect them, whether the people of Orléans know what we have protected them from or not.*

Of course we will, said another voice, a man's, one that Françoise did not know. *You need not lecture us, whoever you are. We are here.*

What is she up to? Someone asked this in a voice that sounded timorous and young. This startled Françoise; could it be that she was not the newest of the Benandanti? Could this be the first time someone had heard the drums, as she had that night in the hills?

Could it end tonight the same way? With most of the company dead, their spirit forms leaving behind only scraps of blood, skin, fur, hair, while in some bed somewhere their waking forms never woke again?

The cold mist was strangling her, suffocating her. She couldn't see her colleagues or the broom. Even the inn was a dark shape looming; she could no longer see the queen.

Don't let them break you, warned the duchess, to everyone. To herself, probably, too.

What's that? said one of them, turning around.

What's that? cried another.

What's that?

What's that?

What's that?

Françoise felt the pull, the desperate need to know what it was that gripped her from behind. She knew that the hands on her shoulders were those of a hideous vampire, that his teeth would be buried in her neck. She felt his breath and it was not the sweet, warm caress that had escaped Madame Charbonneau's red lips, but the exhalation of a tomb.

But the danger came from ahead of her, not behind. She rooted herself to the spot.

On the far side of the circle, however, a Benandante in a monk's habit whirled to face the mist.

The circle was broken, there and in half a dozen other places.

Queen Catherine chose that spot as her opening.

Into the breach she came in the shape of an enormous black wolf, and she knocked the monk to the ground so hard his face was bloodied by the cobbles.

The silver-haired lady threw something at the wolf-queen—a powder of some kind, something in the Benandanti arsenal. It burned the wolf's fur and she twisted in mid-air, leaped onto the silver-haired lady and sank her great teeth into her throat.

The heartbeats were erratic now, weakening. Françoise lunged at the wolf with her broom, daring her to open her great jaws, to rear, to create some opening to use in her final moments, to inflict some damage. To break the body of this vampire queen, make her vulnerable, so that someone else could finish the job.

But between one moment and the next, the wolf was gone.

She had broken through the barrier, broken the circle of Benandanti, and their wall no longer prevented her from taking the form of a cloud of bats and vanishing in a sickly flutter into the eaves and chimneys of Orléans.

La Môle, in a monk's habit, screamed like a wild creature at the cloud of bats and brandished a sword, which seemed to be as much a part of him as his limbs; he always had it when he needed it. But he had come too late.

Sainct Didier ran to Françoise, his hand on her shoulder, while she tried to calm her heartbeat. How could her heart beat without breath?

They looked down at the shape of the silver-haired lady.

Sainct Didier bent and wrapped his hand around her throat, the same way La Môle had once felt for a pulse, on a silken bed in Paris. The fencing master bent to the silver-haired lady and said, "You will wake now, and Sister Marie will help you. You must wake. I am sending you home."

But the lady only looked at him sadly as red blood bubbled around his fingers. He tried to hold it in, rearranging his hands on her throat. Then she vanished, leaving only a patch of blood on the cobbles.

"Did she wake up?" she asked, hoarsely.

Sainct Didier straightened up. His hands were still cramped, hooked, and covered with blood. He grimaced.

She is gone.

Blood on the cobbles. Françoise remembered the fur she had left behind in the hills. These strange pieces of spirit-form that stayed behind, even after the spirit itself had re-entered the body, or paradise.

The mist that the vampire queen had called to protect her had all but vanished. There were only stray wisps, receding into the darkest recesses of the city.

Sainct Didier spoke aloud, gazing at the patch of dark blood, like shadows on the cobbles. "She was the only woman I have ever loved. And I killed her."

Françoise frowned, wanting to comfort him, not understanding. "It is not your fault. This is what we do." She switched to the voice of her mind, speaking only to him and not to any of the others. *We came for Madame Charbonneau. You could not have known the queen would be here. We were not prepared. Perhaps it was a trap.*

He put a hand to his temple. *We were not prepared. But I did know the queen would be here. It was indeed a trap. It was* my *trap, for the queen, with Charbonneau as bait.*

A terror she did not understand came over Françoise, suddenly. She ran into the inn, recklessly, not heeding the warnings of her broken and grieving comrades.

There was no one inside the dining room, except for Madame Charbonneau, who was pinned against the wall. Pinned by silver knives, with ebony handles. Pinned not by her clothing but by her own flesh, flayed and pulled back to reveal her viscera, her bones, even her unbeating heart.

She raised a bloody face to Françoise and began to laugh wetly.

Sainct Didier rushed at Françoise's side. He said, aloud, in a grim and exhausted voice: "I have my spies, just as the queen has hers. I made sure that the queen discovered the whereabouts of Madame Charbonneau at last, and I knew she would waste no time in coming here to deal with her old rival. The hideous sight you see there on the wall ruled the vampires of Paris for centuries under many names. And now I will put her out of her long misery."

Sainct Didier crossed the floor of the dining room. He said nothing to the ruins of Madame Charbonneau. From under his friar's cloak, he pulled his sword, which he drove into the vampire's heart, and deep into the wall behind it.

The sickly light went out of Madame Charbonneau's eyes.

Then Sainct Didier pulled out the sword and stepped back, a little to the side, as if he were demonstrating footwork for his students. The blade swung in the air, hit the wall again, and the vampire's head rolled at his feet.

Françoise looked away from the headless carcass on the wall. She felt as if she would be sick, and knew that she could not in this spirit form that did not eat or drink. The knowledge did not change a thing for the better.

Sainct Didier cleaned his sword and continued the lesson. "When Catherine de' Medici was turned, she found that obeying anyone was not to her taste. They are hierarchical creatures. They cannot work together."

"Neither can we, it seems," said Françoise, bitterly.

He shook a finger at her. "Never doubt that we can always do better than we have done before. If you have faith in nothing else, have faith in that."

"And yet you did not tell us who we truly faced tonight."

"Would it have helped?" Sainct Didier snapped. "Would you have been any braver than you were, had you known?"

Françoise had never felt so angry. She opened her mouth to say something, anything, that would show him just how angry she was, even though she could hardly put the reasons for her anger into words herself.

And she woke up in her body of the flesh, on the pallet in the Hôtel de Guise, with a raging headache and stinging eyes. She blinked a few times, turned to her side, and vomited.

CHAPTER SEVENTEEN

The Courtyard

THE FOLLOWING MORNING, the duchess called for white bread, water and wine, and sent everyone but Françoise out of her antechamber. They sat on either side of a small table, while the duchess presided over the wine and bread, putting some of each in front of Françoise, who felt a little as if she were expected to take communion. She was expected to swallow something, she felt sure, but what it was eluded her. The night before was already starting to feel like a bad dream, or like something that had happened to someone else.

And in the end, was it a tragedy? The queen mother had escaped, but that left them no worse off than before, except perhaps that now she might be more careful. Madame Charbonneau, who had been their stated target from the beginning, was destroyed. They had lost at least two Benandanti by the end, although neither of them were known to Françoise in her waking life, and it was to be expected that those who seek out vampires might not ever wake up again.

No, none of that was so terrible. And yet, Françoise felt out of sorts, out of body. She did not trust Sainct Didier. It came down to that. He had kept his own counsel, manipulating people and events in the way he saw fit, and people had died. And not trusting Sainct Didier, she did not know whom she *could* trust.

She had come to Paris to settle a matter of honour: her life debt to the swordmaster who saved her life. When would that debt be paid?

And, the more disquieting question: what would she do when it was?

Just as the duchess opened her mouth to speak, a servant came in with a message on a silver tray. The duchess dismissed the servant.

"She is dead," she announced.

"The silver-haired lady?"

The duchess nodded and said, "Sainct Didier blames himself. He will not recover easily from this. They were lovers once, you see. I knew them in happier days. Sister Anne. That was what she called herself in recent years. She became a nun, tried to repent, tried to leave us. She came to see our calling as sinful. Once, she told me that she saw it as little better than what the vampires do. She never was a person of strong constitution or firm resolve, but he loved her, and she did have her charms… Sainct Didier was devastated when she chose to leave behind this life."

"Can one?"

"Can one what?"

"Leave behind the life."

The duchess laughed bitterly. "I am telling you the story of a woman who tried, and last night you saw her nearly die. She turned away from us. Joined the nuns at the Abbey of Montmartre. And yet she returned, when she heard the sound of her old lover's heartbeat. What do you think?"

"But do we have no choice? Just because we were born in the caul?"

"Because God has made us this way. We are creatures of

blood and bone, of instinct and need. We may be solitary for a day, a week, a month, even years—God knows I've had my time in the wilderness—but when the monsters sniff at our door, we become hunted things again, every muscle frozen."

Françoise stared at her, remembering her first night as a hare, how it felt. She could see similar memories in the sapphire eyes of the duchess.

"Sainct Didier never lost his own resolve, then."

"Not in the same way. He went wandering, became a soldier. I did not think I'd ever see him in Paris or its environs again. But my warnings about the queen mother eventually drew him back. I knew that I would not be able to stem the tide here alone. The Benandanti are not city folk, for the most part. We tend to feel safest in the fields and forests. Even I feel that way, sometimes. Even I tire of the gossip and intrigue, and I used to look forward to the times when the court goes out to hunting lodges. Now I am just tired. Tired of all of it. City or country. I take little joy in the hunt, but I know that to not hunt is to risk..."

"What?" Françoise asked, boldly.

The duchess shook her head, made a vague gesture with her white hand. "To risk the total control of ordinary people by the monsters in their castles. Oh, I see in your face, you are young, you think, *the ordinary people are already controlled*. And so they are, but one thing that becomes clear when you live through enough history is that, generally speaking, the times can always get worse."

Françoise tore a piece of the soft, white bread, softer and whiter than anything she had eaten at home, except for on very special days. Feast days. Wedding days. Funerals. She had been given both a wedding and a funeral of her own, and yet somehow, she had never had any fine bread at them. And no cake, for that matter. But here she sat, eating fine bread given to her straight from the hand of the duchess, and it tasted like sand in her mouth.

"I thank you for your hospitality," she found herself saying. "But I need to be on my own for a time. To think about everything that has happened, and to think about what to do next."

The duchess showed no surprise. "Where will you go?"

"Ask for me at the sign of La Belle Étoile."

There was a long pause, in which the duchess tapped her wine glass with her fingernail, and seemed to consider saying many things before she settled on what she did say. "You may keep the dresses I gave you, and take the gloves and whatever plants you need to keep yourself safe. And do not hesitate to call on me if you need me."

But as Françoise was heading out the door with her small bundle, feeling like a servant who had been dismissed, the duchess walked over to her and took her arm.

"Françoise, another thing I have learned in all my years is that, just as the times can generally get worse, the times can generally get better, too."

"And do you believe that our times will?"

The duchess sometimes looked as old as her years, despite her perfect skin, with the hues and scent of lavender in her cheeks, and her brilliant, large blue eyes. What quality it was that betrayed her true age, Françoise could not have said. Something about the smile, perhaps; it had a great deal of pain in it.

The duchess said, "You have helped me to believe it possible, in this short time I have had you here with me. And for that I thank you, and I wish you well in your contemplation."

And with that, the duchess kissed her lightly on the cheek.

FRANÇOISE DID NOT see the duchess for months. Neither did she see Sainct Didier or La Môle. She avoided the Louvre and the Hôtel de Guise. She did not walk in spirit form and she did not hear the drums. At night, she had ordinary dreams in a narrow, scratchy bed.

The bed was in a servant's room at La Belle Étoile. Having spent the last of the money she'd taken from her parents' house, she offered her services to La Hurière, in exchange for board for herself and Mistral. The landlord had already hired a new cook, but he needed someone to clean the rooms.

Françoise had little experience with cleaning. She had taken care of Mistral's stall in the stables at home, but human mess was another thing altogether. She soon got a keen eye for signs of bedbugs, and she learned things about the night habits of the inn's clientele that would have shocked her a year before. She found incriminating letters; she found women's stockings left in men's rooms. She got to know the valets and maids who travelled with ladies and gentlemen, and found they usually had ghost stories to tell in the kitchen late at night.

Some of those stories featured vampires. She listened to them all. The story about the pale lady who was once pursued by two brothers, one a vampire, the other a doomed hero who gave his life to destroy him. The story about two children whose graves were opened by dogs, who were found to be as rosy and fresh as if they were sleeping. The story about the road through the woods where young women were warned not to go, for they would be taken as vampire brides. The story of a village left slaughtered, their inhabitants drained of blood, an act of hideous gluttony that must have been the work of a whole pack of creatures.

She kept them in her memory. So much sadness, so much death. It seemed to her a crime that no one was avenging the innocents, no one was stopping the vampires from swelling their ranks. And yet, she had lost her conviction that if someone should be stopping them, that someone could be her. At night, she dreamt of terrible bleak fungus growing out of graves, or of slavering dogs surrounding her bed. She felt a presence in the shadows.

One night just before Christmas, Françoise went to bed early, because she had finished her work and bed was the warmest place in her cold room. She was just drifting into sleep when all her limbs jerked and she lay staring at the ceiling, heart pounding. It was nothing but a sleep start; all the same, she felt suddenly claustrophobic, as if the blanket she'd been so grateful for a few minutes before was now a prison.

She went to her little window and looked out on the evening. The sun had gone to bed even earlier than she had, but there was a full moon, high in the sky. Françoise had always felt encouraged by any sight of the moon: a friend, a guide. Its pale light, broken by the buildings, illuminated patches of the dark courtyard below.

It took her a moment to understand what she was seeing in that courtyard, lying half in moonlight and half in darkness: a man lying right in the centre.

By the time she reached the courtyard in her nightdress and stocking feet, he was dead. She recognized him; he kept the stables. More a boy than a man. Charlot, everyone called him. He had been kind to Mistral.

And now Charlot was dead, with a pool of blood spreading from his bitten neck, melting the snow into red slush. La Hurière was short-staffed again.

The thrum of her anger, vibrating through her waking body, caused a storm in her ears and her sight went blurred, white and black mingling together, until blackness seemed to hem her in from all sides.

The pain in her neck came as a surprise. Sharp, excruciating, until the tides of blood surging through her body lulled her, until she was almost uncaring. Almost. A small stubborn part of her gave her the strength to shove her head back, straight into the skull of the vampire feeding on her.

That broke his jaw's grip on her neck, but it might not have been enough. As he snarled, she whirled. The motion of it was too much for her. Dizzy, weak, she pulled the phylactery on its leather cord from under her chemise. The wild moly and other ingredients did their work; he drew back. She got a look at his face, but it was not one she recognized, and then he was gone. Vanished into the shadows.

Her legs collapsed under her as the world went white.

She fell on the cold ground, insensible, the thrum of her blood in her ears.

The drum in her ears.

The vibration of anger returned, and lifted her off her feet. Her spirit woke, whole and ready, despite the injury to her body.

By now, there was no movement in the shadows. No matter. She did not need to give chase to find the vampires. She knew where the worst of them lived.

Françoise rose into the evening air in the form of a small wren and flew like a bullet to the Louvre.

It was not yet midnight; there was music and laughter coming from the courtyard. She settled on the top of one of the tall, thin, round stone chimneys and watched. An outdoor Christmas masque, with players in bizarre costumes: dragons and unicorns, wizards with enormous heads. Fires in braziers. Drums and tambourines.

There were real animals on chains, too: a monkey chattering on one top of a pillar, and a brown bear, chained to another.

In the audience was the figure of the queen mother, and beside him, the king her son. Neither of them had been the one to feed on poor Charlot; it had probably been one of their less favoured servants, out for a quick drink when the masters were busy. But what did it matter? The head of the snake was here.

And there was not much one small brown bird could do about it. She fluffed herself in the cold wind and dug her feet into the stone. She could find her way into the palace easily enough; a bird in the house was unlucky, her nurse always said. Perhaps Françoise could be unlucky for the vampires.

Poison would be satisfying, but what poison would kill a vampire? Could she take one unaware, stab or smother them in their sleep? She wasn't sure they did sleep.

Her frustration overcame her with an urge to move, and she darted through the air, swooped over the crowd and nestled into the hollow of a stone arch high on the central tower.

She looked down at the assembled revellers at a new angle and saw Chicot. He was standing with some other young men, holding a cup and laughing. Someone gave him a hoop, like something a child would play with after it came off a barrel. Chicot tossed it into the air a few times and then, without warning, tossed it over one of the old, bearded worthies standing near the king. The hoop fell cleanly around the man, sending the younger men into fits of laughter, while Chicot raised his glass to toast his own triumph.

In that moment, as she watched Chicot, several things became clear to her mind.

CHAPTER EIGHTEEN

Chicot's Tale

There was plenty of gossip in the inn about the Duke of Anjou, from the insinuation that the Mignons were all his lovers, to the insinuation that his sister was, too—that indeed, all three of the Valois brothers slept with Marguerite at their pleasure. This last rumour, Françoise was quite sure, was entirely invented, but the thread of real information that ran through all the rumours was that the Duke of Anjou's favourites slept near his bedroom at the Louvre. The most noble had their own apartments, and the others pallets in the antechamber.

It was a small matter for the little wren to return to La Belle Étoile, to carry in its beak a muslin bag with certain herbs in it on its return flight to the Louvre in the cover of darkness; to find an open window and slip between the bars; to flit from rafter to rafter until she found the duke's apartments.

It was a small matter to introduce certain herbs to the pallets after the servants had laid them out. When the attendants went to bed long after the masque was over, it was not only the wine they'd drunk that made them fall immediately to sleep.

All but one.

Chicot realized right away that something was afoot. He sat up and looked around in the dark room, in which the only light was moonlight through the windows. He listened to his friends snore. He looked carefully at the tapestries that hung on the walls. Then he turned his head a little, and saw Françoise standing in the shadows, against the far wall, watching him.

She was in her waking body again, in a dry chemise, a warm mahogany-coloured gown with a ruff that covered her bitten neck, and a black cloak. She was still a little weak and dizzy, but a glass of brandy and some beef broth from the kitchen had done wonders. Besides, the vampire had not managed to drink for long. All the same, it was not an experience she ever wanted to repeat. The thought of it made her more ill than the wound itself did.

Chicot was on his feet. They spoke to each other over the sleeping forms of other men.

"This is a surprise," he whispered.

"A bad one?"

"That remains to be seen. Are you here to murder me?"

"Why would I murder you?"

He stepped closer, over a sleeping companion, carefully stepping between the pallets. He had gone to bed in most of his clothing, perhaps too tired from drink and revelry to strip down to his chemise, or perhaps only cold. He was wearing a lovely blue doublet that had come partially unlaced.

"You have been avoiding me for weeks," he accused her.

"It is not you I have been avoiding."

Another step. "I'm glad to hear it. Shall we go somewhere where we're less likely to be overheard?"

"They won't wake up."

He shrugged. "All the same."

She thought for a moment, then turned and walked through the nearest door, into the outermost of the duke's antechambers. This room was dark, cold and empty, with no fireplace. There was a red patterned carpet on the floor, and moonlight breaking in interesting shapes through the leaded glass windows.

He followed her and took her arm. "Something is wrong. Is that why you've come?"

Suddenly she found herself unable to think of the right thing to say. "Many things are wrong. More things are wrong in this hideous city than are right. Everywhere I look, I see death, blood, torn flesh… but I would like to live, Chicot. I have decided I would like to live."

A smile broke on his face, but his eyes still looked concerned. "Then you and I are of the same mind."

"What do you mean?"

He let go of her arm, took a step away, with his back to her. "Oh, only that my desire to live is why I came to Paris in the first place."

"Tell me. Please."

She urged to him with her mind, as if he were a Benandante, as if she were in her spirit body, and able to speak without voice.

Whether by her mind or his own, he seemed persuaded. Chicot turned back to her, looking down at her face, and let out a deep breath before speaking. "In the spring, I was in the south. In Provence. Visiting a distant cousin at his chateau, trying to make something of myself, and getting into trouble. The usual. While I was there, the Duke of Mayenne came through with his army, on their way to join the fight against the Ottomans. A crusade, he called it. The pompous fool. Anyway, while he was there, he had the misfortune to become my rival for the affections of a certain woman."

"Ah," she said, and felt a chill. "And did he prevail?"

"No, I did."

"Ah," she said again.

He waved his hand like batting a fly. "It was a silly affair, the matter of three days, but I am nothing if not stubborn, and he is rich. He decided I had insulted his honour. I would gladly have fought a duel with him, but the coward never demanded it, and since he was the aggrieved party—or so he thought—I could not very well be the one to demand the duel. The duke and his men made life as difficult as possible for me, after that. I knew I would have a reprieve while they went to fight, but if Mayenne returned to France alive, he'd make my life miserable in a thousand small ways. He is a duke, and I am nobody."

"You are worth a hundred of him," she said staunchly.

He smiled. "And how would you know? Have you met the Duke of Mayenne?"

"I have not had that misfortune."

"Well, you're not wrong. But he's rich. I'm not. So I needed to find myself a wealthy protector, someone powerful enough to keep him at bay. Hence my project of finding myself a duke who would take me on as his attendant, and protect me as his friend."

"You seem to have succeeded," she said, gesturing at the room where he'd been about to sleep, in the duke's apartments.

He shrugged. "We'll see. He likes me, likes my advice, my honesty, my curiosity. But I know that honesty and curiosity can be double-edged swords."

"Aren't they all?"

He frowned. "Aren't all what?"

"Swords. Double-edged."

He laughed, then clapped his hand over his mouth; someone whom Françoise had not put to sleep might overhear them. "Most of them. Good point."

"That is what I lack," she said morosely. "A point, and an edge. I have no sword and I have no skill to use it. I have no way to fight the evil in this city."

"There are ways to fight other than with swords."

She nearly hissed at him. "So I am told. But why then must I cower in the shadows, a prey animal, hoping that a trick or a stroke of luck will save me?"

Chicot's face was unreadable. He cocked his face and stared at her, examining her, as if he was not satisfied with what he saw. "Why have you come here tonight, Françoise?"

"To find some way to fight. And you are the one man I could think of who might not laugh at me. The one man who might agree to teach me what you know."

He did not laugh. "When would you like to begin?"

"Really?"

"Really. But how do I know this isn't like tennis? How do I know you're not tricking me, that you're not an accomplished duellist already?"

She rubbed her temple, paced a bit. "I don't have a sword. Not even a wooden one, like a child."

"That's easily mended. But we don't need a sword to start the lessons."

She looked at him. "Do we not?"

He shook his head, and stepped toward her. With one hand on his hip, he held the other about a foot in front of his chest, palm to her, as if inviting her to some sort of dance.

"Do what I do," he said.

She copied him.

A moment later, the back of Chicot's hand was on hers.

He said, "You must learn to feel what your enemy is going to do, before he does it. Sense how much pressure he puts on the blade, and react to it. You always want to keep yourself in a good position, so you don't lose your balance, no matter how quickly he comes at you, or pulls away. This is something we can practice right now, if you like."

She nodded.

He pushed against her hand a little, and she stepped backward. A few more steps, then to the side, and then forward again. It was a dance after all. She kept her eyes unfocused, her gaze somewhere between their hands and his chest.

"Look at me," he said softly, pressing against her hand. "Look at my eyes."

She did, and was captivated, and immediately stumbled into him when he moved back.

He laughed and caught her. "You must always keep your eye on your opponent. Feel the blade, but watch the man. Are you all right?"

She nodded. "Should we try again?"

"I think one lesson is enough for tonight. I don't suppose you could use whatever sorcery you used to get in here one more time? I'm thirsty."

He said it lightly, but she could tell that he was digging, trying to understand her secrets.

She said only, "It isn't sorcery."

He said nothing for a long time, but eventually decided not to press. "Will you be here when I come back?"

She nodded.

He was gone for a few minutes, during which time she was able to think about the fact that they'd been gazing at each other, hand to hand, in this dark room. Her cheeks seemed to flush. She had been telling the truth; she did want to learn to fight. But she also wanted to be near him. She wanted to be with someone she could trust. In body and in spirit, she had found desire, a desire that could tether her to this broken world.

And yet, he kept secrets from her. He had followed her, and she still didn't know why. She had to be careful of her heart. She had to be careful in general.

When she felt him watching her, she turned to see him standing with a dark bottle of wine. He held it up in triumph. "Will you join me?"

THEY LAY ON the rich red carpet and drank the rich red wine, out of the bottle. They spoke about nothing for a little while. Françoise told him about her work at La Belle Étoile.

"You did not like the hospitality at the Hôtel de Guise?"

"I did not always get on with the company. Sainct Didier, the duchess, La Môle—they are good people, but I am not sure they see the world as I do. I don't know. I just needed to get away, to think a bit."

Chicot sat up. "La Môle?"

She nodded, feeling heavy from the wine. She had given away something; the cardinal sin. But what had she given away? There was nothing for it now but to speak lightly, innocently.

"Yes, he's a count from Provence. You know him, don't you? I'm sure I've seen him studying with Sainct Didier here. Haven't you heard the gossip about him and Queen Marguerite? And Queen Marguerite is often with the duchess, and the duchess is often with me."

He frowned, shook his head. "I know that Sainct Didier knew him, but everyone knows everyone. How odd."

"Why odd?"

"Let me think for a moment." Chicot traced the pattern in the carpet with his fingertip, while she took a nervous swig from the bottle. Then, without looking up, he said: "You asked me before why I was following you and your... comrades. Why I knew where to find Sainct Didier the day you came to Paris. Why I was there when you collapsed outside the wizard's house. I did not tell you because the true story, the full story, is one that could be very dangerous to me. And perhaps, dangerous to you. And I do not wish to be the cause of harm to you. But there is something I don't understand, and now I wonder whether silence is the greatest danger of all."

"I am heartily sick of silence," she said with vehemence. "I choke on it."

He swallowed. "I told you just now that I ran into some trouble at a chateau in Provence, that I found myself in need of a powerful protector. But I did not tell you that the Duke of Anjou was not my first choice."

The bite wound on her neck itched; the ruff was irritating it. She pulled the ruff away from it with one finger, annoyed. The room was very cold. "Go on, please."

"Well, I thought myself fortunate in that there were several important young men who had gathered at the chateau, to see the so-called crusaders off. Very exciting nonsense. One of the young men was the Duke of Alençon. Since he was very young, I thought he would be the perfect target—I would charm him, befriend him, and he would take me under his protection."

She was turned to stone. Chicot had sought the protection of a man she knew to be a vampire. Sainct Didier said he did not think Chicot had been turned, but how could he be sure? Vampires were magnetic, charming, and Chicot had certainly charmed her. She couldn't believe it, but she knew that she was not being objective.

Chicot, apparently not noticing the way all her muscles had tensed, carried on with his story. "I went to see the Duke of Alençon in his apartment. It was an old chateau, full of narrow corridors and shadows, and doors that didn't close properly. Perhaps that is why the door to his antechamber was slightly ajar as I approached from the empty guard room outside. I could hear his conversation with someone else. The duke was sitting with his back to me, and his companion was standing opposite him, so that he might have seen me. But he never did. The young man talking to the duke had an expression on his face I will never forget. He seemed to be in a kind of trance, as if he'd been drugged. The duke was laughing at him and the man seemed not to understand."

Françoise breathed out. Chicot had had a close call; he had seen the effect of a vampire working its spell, and he had escaped. That was the answer to the riddle.

"So you know that the Duke of Alençon is a vampire," she said.

The word seemed to echo in the cold, dark room. Now the wound in her neck throbbed.

He looked at her sadly. "I suspected, from that day. I went looking for information, trying to understand what I had seen. I read about old stories, about vampires and those who hunt them. I came across an old book about the Benandanti, the good walkers, who use witchcraft to defeat the vampires."

"It isn't witchcraft," Françoise said nervously.

"Whatever it is or is not, if it can stand against the weird power I witnessed that day, I am all for it. But that's not the end of my story, Françoise."

"Isn't it?"

"No." He pulled up his knees and picked at his fingernails for a moment. "I made my way to Paris, reasoning that if I could not gain the protection of the Duke of Alençon—or rather, if I did not *want* his protection—I must find someone else powerful to be on my side. And truth be told, I was curious about how the young duke could have such a terrible secret. Were there more of his kind? I took a room at Le Belle Étoile, walked as close to the Louvre as I could, and I began collecting information on everyone I met. I took note of who spoke with whom, and who went out late at night, even who avoided garlic at dinner. During the massacre, I watched your Sainct Didier arrive and meet with the Duchess of Nevers in the gardens of the Tuileries, and I noticed that they both carried sprays of wild garlic. Here were two people who seemed to know the secret, and they seemed to have secret business of their own."

"Is that why you sent me to the Tuileries that day? But how did you know Sainct Didier was the man I wanted to meet?"

He shrugged. "That was instinct. You had the same look in your eyes, something haunted and purposeful. I wanted to know whether you were one of the vampire-hunters too, and so I followed you as well, from that day on."

"You play a dangerous game, Chicot."

He put a hand on hers. "And one that you have been winning all along."

She shook her head. "Do not pretend to misunderstand me. Paris is not safe, especially not for someone who is determined to root out all its secrets."

"Oh, I know it's not safe. That's why I came, remember? Soon after I arrived, I arranged to meet and befriend the Duke of Anjou. I started in on my project of gaining a place in his retinue, and his protection against the Duke of Mayenne... or anyone else. I satisfied myself that he did not share his younger brother's curse."

"No, but the oldest brother does," Françoise said. "The king of France does."

Chicot nodded. "Yes, I have suspected as much. It is an evil time, Françoise. But at least, I told myself, there were the Benandanti! At least there was someone in this rotten world who was fighting back against evil. I was sure of it. You and your band."

She had lost all will to deny it. She said nothing.

After a while, he continued, not looking at her. "From what I read about the Benandanti, it seemed that one had to be born to it. Born in the caul, which I was not. It does not matter. I do not ask to be treated as one of you. But I will do everything I can to help. It was you, and your companions, who gave me hope. I thought that if I could join your cause somehow, support you in whatever way you needed, I would find some purpose for my life at last. So that is why I followed you—all of you. And, of course, at some point, Sainct Didier became aware of my movements. But there is one thing he does not know. The reason why I have kept this story to myself until now. I wanted to understand something, and I have not been able to do so."

"What? Perhaps I can help."

"That's what I fear," he said, and sighed. "Françoise, imagine my shock when I was walking outside La Belle Étoile one day and saw the very same gentleman who had been in that hideous conference with the Duke of Alençon, the gentleman in the trance. And imagine my surprise when you implied tonight that he was an associate of the Benandanti. Tell me. Tell me whether he is one of your kind."

She whispered in horror. "Do you mean—?"

He nodded. "The man who was so enthralled in the presence of the vampire duke was none other than Joseph Boniface de La Môle."

CHAPTER NINETEEN

The Honour of La Zinda

Saint-[illegible] [illegible] to the [illegible] [illegible] expression, his eyes [illegible]

They were sitting [illegible] where Françoise had met Saint [illegible] place for a private chat, [illegible] would feel [illegible] to talk about [illegible] she was [illegible] as if she were [illegible] again that girl who had [illegible] to listen to anyone [illegible] She [illegible] parts [illegible] and [illegible]

[illegible] at that [illegible] telephone [illegible] they [illegible]

But [illegible] probably [illegible] always [illegible]

CHAPTER NINETEEN

The Honour of La Môle

Sainct Didier listened to Chicot's story with a perfectly still expression, his eyes betraying nothing.

They were sitting on the bench in the Tuileries gardens where Françoise had met Sainct Didier. It had seemed the best place for a private chat, but not so private that either of them would feel the need to talk about the death of Sister Anne. But she was regretting choosing this place, now; it felt too much as if she were trying to go back to the beginning. She was once again that girl who had come to Paris knowing no one, eager to listen to anyone who would feed her a scrap of knowledge. She felt like the little brown bird who hopped on the garden path, looking so intelligent that Françoise wondered whether it could overhear.

It could be a Benandante; while they usually walked at night, all that was required was to be asleep. Some unknown person, napping, while they listened in on whatever conversations they liked. It could be.

But Sainct Didier was not bothered by the bird, so it was probably all right. He always seemed to know things without giving any indication how he knew them. And she must not let petty fears overtake her.

She sighed as she paced, which caused Chicot to break off his tale, while both men looked at her.

"You find this tedious, mademoiselle?" Sainct Didier asked. He had just started calling her Françoise, once in a while, before that night in Orléans. Now she was back to being mademoiselle. "You've heard Chicot's story before, I know."

"Not at all. I'm not bored. How could I be bored? I'm worried. And I'm sad. How could La Môle be one of them? Is it even possible?"

Sainct Didier thought for a moment. "It is certainly possible for a Benandanti to be turned, to walk the path of the Malandanti instead. I have heard of instances of it happening, and witnessed it once myself, long ago. But La Môle is no vampire; that I am sure of. He may, though, be under the influence. A slow turning, rather than an immediate one. They do like to play with their victims."

"I know," said Françoise pointedly, remembering the sight of Madame Charbonneau, flayed and pinned to the wall. There were some lessons she did not need to be taught.

They all paused for a moment, as two young women walked on a nearby path, holding silk parasols. Unusual items—Françoise had only seen them once or twice before. But these were fashionable young ladies; perhaps they wanted to look exotic.

Or perhaps they wanted to block the sun.

She was doubting everyone and everything today. And why not? There was reason to doubt.

Sainct Didier continued his lecture. "Sometimes the monsters take delight in forcing their victims to do evil while they are still—I will not say good, for which of us can say we are good? But while they are still mortal. Inevitably, though, the day will come when a mortal under the sway of a vampire will become fully vampire themselves, if their mind does not break first. If what Chicot says is true, then our friend is on a very dark path."

"You doubt my tale," said Chicot, not quite a question.

Sainct Didier cocked his head. "I doubt everything, until I am sure of it. Why did you not tell us everything you know sooner?"

"Out of self-preservation," Chicot said bluntly. "I did not wish to put myself at risk until I understood the lay of the land."

"Wise and prudent. But then, why have you decided to tell us now? What changed?"

Chicot blushed beautifully. "I find that I do not wish to put you at risk either."

"All of us, or one of us?" Sainct Didier asked, but then put up a hand to spare Chicot from answering. "It doesn't matter. All right, I will look into it. You must do nothing about this, and say nothing about this, monsieur. Do you understand? If you truly wish to protect her, and yourself, you must forget what you know. And if we determine there is some other explanation for what you saw in Provence, you must accept that verdict, or it will go badly for you."

Chicot bowed his head. "Believe me, I have no wish to expose myself any more than I already have. All I will say is this: If the day comes when one more sword could be of use to you, even a sword wielded by an ordinary man, then all you need do is say one word, and I'll be at your side."

Sainct Didier nodded. "Let us hope it will not come to that."

As December turned to January, Sainct Didier, the duchess and Françoise reached a kind of understanding, faced as they were with a new threat. Françoise remained at La Belle Étoile, but the other two kept her abreast of their plans, and included her when they could. She had the feeling they wanted to keep an eye on her, but whatever their motivations, she grudgingly liked the effect.

They each had their tasks. Sainct Didier would try to learn what he could from La Môle himself, bringing the conversation around to the duke, to his time in Provence, to the vampires themselves. He promised not to mention Chicot or give any indication that the scene at the chateau in Provence had been witnessed.

Françoise was to spend time with Chicot, a task she found welcome.

One day, he sent her a note to meet him in an abandoned quarry outside the city walls. When she arrived, she found him holding a long object wrapped in red cloth.

She unwrapped it and started to laugh: a wooden sword.

"It's too light to be much use in training," he explained, "but it is yours to keep, and perhaps it will make you smile, and light though it is, you can practice some of your skills with it."

"I have no skills to practice," she objected.

Then he stepped to one side and showed her two steel swords lying on the rocky ground behind him. They were blunt, for training, and very plain in design, but with these borrowed swords, she could learn to defend herself, if she wished.

She did wish.

They met on Wednesdays and Fridays in the abandoned quarry. She learned how to step, how to hold the sword, how to move from a guard into an attack or a counter. Unlike Sainct Didier with his precise methods, Chicot approached swordplay playfully. She liked learning from him and she especially like their private chats afterward, but the chats were of little use to the Benandanti. Chicot was more and more trusted by the Duke of Anjou, which meant he was less and less trusted by the duke's vampiric little brother. And as for the question of La Môle, Chicot had already told them all he knew.

The duchess had her own methods for learning secrets.

One day in February, Françoise had an invitation from the duchess to come to the Hôtel de Guise at her convenience, as the Duchess of Nevers would greatly enjoy her company.

She found the duchess sitting by a window, working on embroidery alone in the chill and even afternoon light.

"It's a ruff," said the duchess, holding up a pile of white linen. "I have an idea that it might be fortified against them—since it is worn around the neck—but the scent of garlic does not stay long, and neither does the perfume I use on my leather gloves. So I have tried my hand at spinning. Yarrow makes a poor thread for working, prone to breaking, but we shall see." She pricked her finger and popped it into her mouth. "Just my luck—I'll get blood on the ruff, and it will draw them rather than repel them."

The door opened, and a footman announced the arrival of the Queen of Navarre.

"Excellent," said the duchess, throwing her embroidery hoop down on the table. "Now we shall learn something, Françoise."

"Am I to come?"

"Of course. You are not a child, to be left out of things. You have made that quite clear, and rightly so. It has been so long since we worked as a group. I have come to understand that our habits of secrecy and silence have not served us well." She spoke to the servant: "Please seat Her Majesty in the green salon. We will be there presently."

Marguerite, the Queen of Navarre, was red with cold or perhaps excitement. She refused the offer of wine and the duchess sent the servants away. As for the presence of Françoise, it seemed to make no difference to the queen, who was no doubt accustomed to ladies in waiting, although she had brought none of her own today.

In their private conversations—and this one counted—the duchess called the young queen Marguerite, and they spoke to each other like sisters.

"My darling, do you want to know something astonishing?" said Marguerite in an awed tone. "I believe I am really in love with him!"

The duchess hesitated a moment, and did not look at Françoise. "With La Môle, you mean?"

"Yes, of course? Who else could I have meant?"

"Your husband, perhaps."

"Oh, no. That could never be. Henry of Navarre is a fine man, and we have become allies, even friends. But all of that would be ruined if we were to treat each other as husband and wife. Besides, he is head over heels for Madame de Sauve."

Françoise could not conceal a small wince at the mention of the vampire's name.

The queen caught it, and became briefly aware of her presence. "You do not like Madame de Sauve, Mademoiselle d'Artagnan? I admit I was jealous at first—even if one does not *love* one's own husband, one feels rather protective. But she is a sensible woman, I think. Perceptive."

"Perhaps too perceptive," said Françoise, trying to cover up her reaction with something mundane. "I was at the Louvre one day and a pin on my dress came loose, and her gaze went right to it as I passed her. So I remember my embarrassment every time her name is mentioned."

The queen laughed, brightly and briefly. "She does see many things. I think that is why my mother values her service so. My husband knows that Madame de Sauve does my mother's bidding, but he does not care. That is how love is. I understand now."

"What has Monsieur de La Môle done to make you feel this way?" the duchess asked.

"Oh, it's hard to say. He's so devoted, not only to me, but to Coconnas, to all his friends. He's so stiff with honour, which I wouldn't have thought would attract me to any man, and yet."

"And yet, stiffness can be an attractive quality," the duchess murmured with a twinkle.

The queen batted this away. "Hush, Henriette. All we've done is kiss so far. He's recovering from his wounds still, I suppose. He looks so pale even now. Anyway, I am here as you asked to tell you everything I know, because I know you hate to be left out of any palace intrigue."

"That is true."

"Would you believe, when I saw Coconnas last, he commented on how many plots seemed to be afoot in Paris, and then sighed, and said"—here the queen affected an imitation of Coconnas—"'At least Madame de Nevers is not mixed up in any of it.' Can you believe it? You have him fooled."

"I do like to stay at a distance from intrigue," said the duchess with a twinkle in her eye. "But tell me, what are all these plots?"

The queen counted on her fingers. "Well, first of all, my mother is trying to poison my husband."

"Naturally."

"She never does like any outsiders in the family. And yet, she's the one who made me marry him! But now, after the massacre, she fears anyone who might rally people against her, I suppose."

"Naturally. And is Madame de Sauve to be the assassin?"

"The instrument of assassination, anyway, but my husband will not be so easily done away with. Anyway, he has other things to worry about. My brother is also trying to assassinate him."

"I should think so. The king does everything your mother commands."

"Not the king. My other brother. François."

"The Duke of Alençon is trying to kill the King of Navarre? Why?"

"He says he wants to carve a—how did he put it?—carve a bloody kingdom out of France, and keep it for himself.

Something like that. He never used to hate his older brothers, but he resents them now. My darling little brother François. He used to always do what I asked him, but lately he is so changed."

So changed indeed. Marguerite, like the rest of the court, seemed incapable of seeing the truth about the vampires among them.

"Yes, I've noticed the changes in him," murmured the duchess. "So, since he cannot bring himself to murder his brother, the King of France, he'll murder his brother-in-law, the King of Navarre. But what is to be done about it?"

Queen Marguerite nodded vigorously. "Exactly my question! I spoke to La Môle about it. It is not in my interests for my brother to kill my husband, because my husband and I have decided we will be excellent sovereigns. We will go to Navarre and rule it, without interference from my family. And when we are there, I'll bring all my friends to join us. You, and La Môle, everyone. I told La Môle this, that he must not cooperate with my brother's plans to kill my husband. And La Môle said—'But can I, who belong to him, betray him?' It sent shivers up my spine."

"That is what he said? That he belongs to him?"

Marguerite shrugged. "As you know, I asked François to find a place in his household for La Môle. That is what he meant. As I said, he is very honourable."

CHAPTER TWENTY

There Is No Time to Waste

NOW THAT MURDER had receded to its usual levels, business at La Belle Étoile had picked up. That evening, the dining room was full of men, and a few women, eating the roast chicken for which the inn was famous.

It was not among the tasks assigned to Françoise to help in the kitchen, thank goodness, or in the dining room, which would have been even worse; she did not like the way some of the men looked at her. La Hurière himself served the tables, and Gregoire brought the plates up to any customers who chose to dine in their rooms. But a busy supper hour was hard work for her all the same. That was the time she cleaned the corridors and any rooms that were due to have their linens changed and boiled, and their floors swept and mopped, their tables scrubbed. It was hard work, but it took her mind off where she would be in a few hours.

The Benandanti of Paris would meet at the Holy Innocents Cemetery. Vampires often visited cemeteries; they found the very soil there restorative. Within the city, they could be found often at Holy Innocents but also at the Cemetery of the

Trinity, or the churchyard of Saint-Paul-des-Champs, or any of the other little patches of earth, marked and unmarked, throughout Paris. Sometimes they slept among the dead. The Benandanti did not dare to go to the larger cemeteries often, because they were places of power for their enemies.

But the duchess had declared that now that Sainct Didier's friend was recovered and the queen mother had taken no action against them, it was time for the Benandanti to recognize the sources of their own power, too. After all, did they not sometimes see ghosts? The Benandanti walked in the world of spirit, they rose from their sleep. The natural dead were their allies, just as the plants of the field were. It was time to stop being afraid.

But there was another reason. To the great relief of his conspiring comrades, La Môle had passed all the tests they'd put him to; if he was a vampire, he was very good at hiding it. When Sainct Didier asked him about the Duke of Alençon, he said he'd met him first in Paris. Sainct Didier said one possibility was that La Môle did not remember his encounters with the duke, and was unaware that his soul was in jeopardy.

And yet, they were all very aware of the fact that at every fight so far, something had always happened that prevented La Môle from harming the vampires. They noticed that he grew more pale by the day, despite the fact that the wounds inflicted by his friend Cocannas were slowly healing.

And as Sainct Didier also pointed out, there was still no answer to the question of how the vampires had found the meeting of Benandanti in the hills of Gascony. It was possible, although until now unthinkable, that someone among the Benandanti had heard the drums and alerted the vampires. La Môle had never mentioned being there himself, although he had been in that part of the country.

If the duke did have some sway over him, especially a sway he did not recognize himself, the longer La Môle stayed in that state, the more dangerous it was for the Benandanti. He knew everything.

Bringing him to the cemetery among vampires might force him to a crisis, force him to choose.

And if he chose the wrong side, all the Benandanti of Paris would be there to put him out of his misery and make sure he could do no more harm.

Françoise pulled the last sheet off a bed, punched it into a ball and stuffed it into the cart to go to the washhouse. From downstairs, she could hear laughter, a strain of drunken song. Once all the guests had eaten, the cook would leave a plate in her room with anything left over.

She would eat, and she would sleep.

It was not far from La Belle Étoile to the Holy Innocents Cemetery. The very walls always made her shudder when she walked past it—the place breathed death. A hawthorn tree inside the cemetery had bloomed out of season on the day after the massacre. People said it was a sign of God's approval. Remembering the grey faces of the dead she'd seen walking south of Paris, she could not believe that their murders had been acceptable to God. But then again, she was doing precisely what people accused the Huguenots of doing: she was plotting against the king. Against the king, and his mother, and his youngest brother, against all vampires.

There was a step on the guests' staircase; thank goodness she'd finished the rooms. Françoise got behind her cart and started pushing it with purpose, hoping to go right past whoever it was, in case it was one of the men who made her uncomfortable.

But she had hardly pushed it a few feet when the guest reached the top of the stairs and she stopped, staring at Chicot.

"What are you doing here?" she whispered.

He held up a key and grinned. "I've taken a room."

"Oh, no. Has the Duke of Anjou tired of you?"

"Far from it." He stepped closer, put a hand on her arm.

"Truth be told, I wanted to see you. Will they notice if you don't go back down right away? I have something to tell you."

She hesitated. He was smiling but his eyes were sad.

"Just let me get this cart down to the kitchen before the washerwoman comes for it."

"Oh, let me."

She shook her head. "There would be talk. Go on, I'll be there in a moment. I have a key." She grinned back at him, choosing to ignore for the moment her apprehension. Whatever he had to say, it was urgent, and so it could not be good.

CHICOT HAD BEEN assigned a gentleman's room with a single bed, neatly made by Françoise moments before. The valet, if he'd had one, would have slept in one of the servants' rooms. There was a chair and a table, which she had just wiped down.

Chicot was standing at the little casement window, looking out. When she let herself in, he turned to look at her.

"I'm sorry for bursting in on you like this. I did not want to leave without saying goodbye."

The hair stood up on her arms. "Leave? Leave Paris?"

He nodded. "For months, at least. I may not return at all."

She took a small step toward him. "What do you mean? What's happened?"

"You may know that the city of La Rochelle is under siege—that the Huguenots there refuse to accept the sovereignty of the king."

"I've heard some talk about it from travellers."

"It's not going well—for the king, that is. His negotiator has had no success. So he's sending both his brothers to break the siege. The Duke of Anjou is commanding. And I have to go, of course, as I'm Anjou's man now. At least, I hope I am, because the Duke of Mayenne is to be part of the force as well, and I'd rather not have to fight the Huguenots with a knife in my back."

She thought. "The Duke of Alençon is going, too? What about La Môle?"

Chicot shook his head. "La Môle's injuries won't heal; the doctor says it must be some infection. I fear it is something worse; I fear it is the vampire's influence. You must tell your companions about it, tell them that La Môle will stay in Paris. But perhaps that will put him out of the duke's influence, break whatever spell he may have on him."

Perhaps it would. Perhaps all would be well, except that Paris would no longer have Chicot in it.

"Can't you develop some injury, too?" she murmured.

He smiled. "If you fetch your wooden sword, you may try your best. I won't stop you." He put a hand on her shoulder. "But no, Françoise, if I'm to be Anjou's man, I must be at his side when he fights. He's eager to go to La Rochelle. Eager to make his own mark, and to get away from the Louvre, which seems to make him more and more restless each day."

"And you? Are you happy for a chance to get away from Paris?"

His voice roughened. "You know I am not."

Kissing him was as familiar as if she'd been doing it all her life, and yet entirely new, the taste of him, the smell of his skin, the feel of his hand behind her head, his shoulders beneath her palms. She pushed him toward his bed, and he pushed her back, lightly. "I did not tell you I'm leaving so that you would take me to bed," he said, into her ear. "We can stay like this all night, if you like."

She pulled back and looked at him sadly. "We cannot."

"No?"

"I have another appointment in a few hours. So there is no time to waste."

This time, when she moved him toward the bed, he did not resist. Only for a moment did she regret having made the bed so nicely, as they landed upon it and instantly dishevelled it.

"Your bed is more comfortable than mine," she said, pulling off his clothes.

"More comfortable than a tennis court would be, too. Although I'm still willing to try it."

SHE LAY IN his arms, their bodies still warm, closed her eyes, and thought that it would be pleasant to sleep there. No one would know; her plate would already have been delivered to her room, and no servant ever disturbed it. She would lie in his arms while her spirit walked the city, hunting vampires, conscious every now and then, perhaps, of a gentle kiss on her forehead. Did a sleeping Benandanti who was walking abroad look any different from ordinary sleepers? She would have to ask him, in the morning.

In the morning, when he would go away to war.

She might not find it so easy to sleep after all.

"You won't be missed at the Louvre tonight?" she murmured.

"No, my sweet. The Duke of Anjou keeps his own counsel tonight, and told his men they may drink and carouse as they wish. So here I am, carousing. I forgot about the drink, though. Should I ask Gregoire for a bottle?"

She hit his chest, marvelling at the permission she had to touch it, bare skin on skin, after so many times spent gazing at it, or trying not to gaze at it, when his shirt was on.

"The Duke of Alençon is the only one who isn't carousing tonight," he said, more seriously. "He's off to the Holy Innocents cemetery, to pray at the miraculous hawthorn. To commune with God, he says. More likely to commune with the Devil, and carouse in whatever way vampires do. Just think. If we're lucky, he might not come back from La Rochelle. Even a vampire may have difficulty reassembling what a cannonball puts asunder."

She sat straight up. "He's going to the Holy Innocents Cemetery? He said so?"

"Yes, what of it?"

She shivered. "La Môle told him. Just as he must have told him about the meeting in the hills. The duke will be there, tonight. Hunting us."

"That's where you're going?" He rubbed his face. "I would beg you not to, if I thought it would do any good."

"No more than I could beg you not to go to La Rochelle tomorrow. I must get there, as quickly as possible. Which means I must fall asleep. But how can I sleep? How can I sleep tonight?"

He lay back down, and pulled her down too, gathered her into his arms. "Shh. You will sleep, and I will hold you, and watch over you, and I will know that you are mightier in your dreams than any of the fighting men who are sleeping with their mistresses tonight, mightier than any vampire, mightier than the doubts or fears of any of your friends. And I will be here, with my arms still around you, when you wake."

She put her head against his chest. She did not say that if she did not wake, he would be holding a corpse. They both knew it. And after a time, his heartbeat in her ear began to sound like a distant drum.

CHAPTER TWENTY-ONE

The Holy Innocents Cemetery

THE BIRD THAT was Françoise was unique and nameless. A night bird, in variegated grey and black feathers, with large, swift wings, and a sharp, curved beak. Her claws were enormous.

Despite the moon's absence, her large eyes drank in the city in detail, a city of grey stone and black cobbles with a few scatterings of snow in corners.

In minutes, she was over the walls of the cemetery, and the charnel house just within, where skulls nearly spilled out of an opening in the rafters. The drums drew her forward. There were a few stone grave markers here and there within the cemetery, but most of it was open ground; the graves here were pits, for the most part, and unmarked. Here there was more snow than elsewhere in the city, as the ground was less disturbed: a thin white coverlet drawn over its crimes. For La Hurière had told her, with some gruesome pride, that more than a thousand bodies had been buried at Holy Innocents after Saint Bartholomew's day, and thousands more thrown into the Seine, into wells and quarries, into fields and farmland.

The whole city was poisoned with rotting flesh; God covered the city with snow like mercy.

She flew over the hawthorn that had bloomed miraculously during the massacre. Now it was withered and sleeping again.

On the far side of the cemetery, there was a great marble edifice where drinking water trickled out at street level, and two archways on the second floor contained a loggia. The drums drew her there, where a company of Benandanti stood and looked out over Saint-Denis. Sainct Didier had chosen the public fountain because vampires were known to shun running water. It was the safest part of an unsafe area. The Benandanti stood as pale and still as the statues carved in the monument.

In mid-air, Françoise transformed into a woman clothed in white, and floated in to take her place among them. Even though they were all in new forms, she recognized each of them now, by the way they stood, the expressions on their faces. Sainct Didier, La Môle, the Duchess of Nevers. Once they had been five; now they were four.

She spoke to their minds: *I have learned that the Duke of Alençon is coming here tonight.*

Sainct Didier looked at her sharply.

But La Môle said: *By dawn, he and the other vampires who dare to show their faces to us will be nothing but dust, here among the graves.*

His voice made her heart pound. Was his enthusiasm feigned? Did he still not know himself? If they could destroy Alençon here tonight, any hold he had on La Môle would be destroyed too, and the Benandanti would be united and strong.

In the form of rats, the four Benandanti slipped through the gates of the cemetery, and then took human-like form again, as pale as ghosts. La Môle swung his arm as he walked. He had the hood of his cloak down, and the form he'd taken was of a young man with long, straight black hair.

Sainct Didier was, as usual, in the form of a long-bearded old man; it matched his spirit.

They found their first vampire without even looking.

The interior wall of the charnel house was lined with an arched arcade, through which they could glimpse the faded and peeling mural that showed the skeletal Death dancing with various figures: an abbot, a knight, a farmer. Slouched on the floor against a column of the arcade, head lolling as if he were drunk, was a vampire, his fanged mouth slightly open, and blood trickling down his chin. Drunk on blood.

An easy mark.

It was La Môle who sprang at him, who ran his sword through the vampire's heart. He seemed to glory in it.

But as he was taking the creature's head off, the others attacked from above.

They came as black smoke, seeping through the skulls in the rafters of the charnel house, filling the sockets and gaps with such strange force that skulls began raining down on the Benandanti.

The duchess winked at Françoise before leaping into the form of a hawk.

But Françoise did not want to change. She had decided that her human-like form tonight would have a sword under its cloak, and so it did. She almost laughed, though, when she drew it and found it was a wooden sword. Her spirit form was limited only by her imagination, but this was now what she imagined.

She did not care. She also did not care that she was still a novice. She battered at the vampires who came at her, weaponless except for their hands and teeth.

It was not a conscious decision, when she grew to ten feet tall.

A vampire with a knife was coming at her. She recognized his face. Her heart pounded like a kettle drum, like a death knell, and her neck stung. This was the monster who had bitten her. He did not show the slightest recognition; to her, she was just meat. And he was a young vampire, not very powerful, and certainly not gifted with the charm that so many of his brothers and sisters had.

She raised herself up, higher, higher, higher, so that when she bashed his head with her wooden sword, it came with a giant's strength.

The sword cracked. Bloodied, the vampire staggered a few steps back, just long enough for the duchess to peck its eyes out, before Sainct Didier struck a beautiful blow that took the creature's head off.

Together, they had defeated it. It had not defeated her.

She stood tall, above everything, feeling strong, when something leaped on her from behind, hands on her shoulders, and dragged her down.

La Môle was coming toward her, his sword drawn. Without hesitating, he drove the point into her attacker's heart, and then offered her a hand to get up.

"Thank you," she said aloud, now standing three feet taller than him.

"My pleasure," said the pale man with the long black hair, and a small smile.

The smile faded, and Françoise turned to see why.

Two swordsmen stood atop a stone block in the middle of the cemetery, drawn and ready. One was the King of France. The other was his brother, Alençon.

The Benandanti rushed at them. Françoise brandished her wooden sword as if it were Joyeuse and screamed as she ran. But the swords of the two Valois brothers were already wet with blood, which dripped from their blades just as plants grew around the blades of the Benandanti. The vampire king and his brother drew strength from their cruelty, from their mother's power, from each other, from their own arrogance.

There were still several other vampires within the cemetery

who attacked the attackers, and it was a melee again. Blood spattered on the snow.

Françoise had a deep cut on one arm and her head had taken a knock, and she knew, with increasing panic, that even her size could not compensate for her novice skills as a swordswoman. Perhaps she should change into something like a bear or a wolf, but tonight her spirit body was not tractable. It took the forms that she could give it, and she could only give it what she felt in her heart.

She felt like a woman with seconds to live.

A voice rang through the cemetery.

It spoke Latin, and it seemed to freeze the vampires in place, as they all turned their faces toward the roof of the charnel house, where a man in silver robes stood, holding a great book before him, and reading what seemed like a sermon.

A whisper from Sainct Didier's mind: *It's Ruggieri!*

Françoise blinked and rose into the air, trying to get a better look. This was the wizard who had taken her memory. She did not recognize him, which was to be expected. His grey hair flowed behind him and he had his eyes closed, reading the words in a sonorous voice.

It would be a simple matter for Françoise or any of the Benandanti to kill him while he was in this trance, but he seemed to be on their side—or at least, not on the vampires' side.

And the Benandanti took advantage.

Françoise found that even a dull wooden sword could pierce a vampire heart, if driven from far enough above and with sufficient force.

Soon the cemetery was littered with the rapidly disintegrated corpses of the undead, their haggard faces turned to the night sky. But there was still a fight going on.

The king and Alençon remained rooted in place, gazing up at Ruggieri. They would not have been able to defend themselves.

But La Môle was defending them.

The same sword that had fought for the Benandanti now fought against them. Something had changed in him, in the moment that the magician turned his spell on the duke. Whatever the magician was doing, it was a real threat to the creature who had been slowly, viciously, turning La Môle into his pet for months.

La Môle, laughing, swung his weapon right into the neck of Sainct Didier and the swordmaster fell back, blood streaming.

Françoise felt her heart stop for a moment. It could not be. It could not be. For the second time, they had sprung a trap. For the second time, it had caught them more than they could handle.

They should have acted against him earlier. They should have believed Chicot's warning from the outset—and indeed she had believed him, but Sainct Didier had been cautious. And now Sainct Didier was bleeding to death.

La Môle changed from wolf to bear to bat to smoke, and every few seconds his sword reappeared to slice through Benandanti flesh. He was taller than Françoise now, taunting her. With her wooden sword, she was done for. It was only her to stand against him now. He had not been fully vampire when Ruggieri turned them to statues; now he was both vampire and Benandanti.

Then the duchess, in hawk form, flew from behind and pecked at Alençon's cheeks.

Her message was clear: don't fight La Môle; fight his sire.

La Môle whirled and swung his sword at the duchess, and bloody feathers flew.

Ruggieri's voice grew louder. La Môle seemed to fear that more than his fellow Benandanti. He glanced up at Ruggieri as if he was in pain, then pushed Alençon off the stone, and pulled at the king's arm, too.

At that moment, Ruggieri finished his incantation. A beam of unnatural light fell onto the stone, where the king still stood. Where Alençon had stood a moment before.

The king screamed, and fell to the ground, no longer frozen, but apparently senseless. He writhed as the beam of light faded.

Before anyone could make sense of what was happening, La Môle wrapped his cloak around Alençon and a cloud of bats rose into the air. Neither La Môle nor Alençon were seen again in Paris that night.

[illegible]

[illegible] Where [illegible] and [illegible]

Then [illegible]

[illegible]

[illegible]

[illegible]

[illegible] that night.

CHAPTER TWENTY-TWO

[illegible]

FRANÇOISE [illegible] woke up [illegible] wrapped in his sheets, drenched in sweat, [illegible] and blood in her eyes. [illegible] above her, she gripped his arm as he [illegible] with a damp cloth.

"You['re] [illegible]," he said, half [illegible] and half [illegible].

"You['re] here [illegible]

She blinked and [illegible]. [illegible]

her [illegible]

blanket on her lips.

"Blood appeared on your [illegible]

sleeping. [illegible]

you were [illegible]

afraid you would [illegible]

I tried to [illegible]

But you [illegible]

[illegible]

everything. [illegible]

tempers [illegible]

CHAPTER TWENTY-TWO

Reconnaissance

Françoise did not wake up in Chicot's arms. She woke up wrapped in his sheets, drenched in sweat, her body contorted and blood in her eyes. Chicot was there, a presence hovering above her; she grabbed his arm as he came at her with a damp cloth.

"You're here," he said, half wondering and half reassuring. "You're here with me. Can you breathe? Can you move?"

She blinked and sat up. The sweat was cooling. When he saw her shiver, he wrapped his cloak around her and settled the blanket on her legs.

"Blood appeared on your head and your arm, while you were sleeping. You were perfectly still, and yet blood appeared… you went pale and cold. I was wiping your wounds. I was so afraid you would die here, in your sleep, while I watched you. I tried to wake you up, and that's when you started thrashing. But you're awake, thank God."

"I'm awake. These are just scratches, I think… I can move everything. But my friends…" She remembered the bloody feathers, the sword blow to Sainct Didier's neck. She continued dully: "La Môle turned on us. He's a vampire. He made his choice."

Chicot winced. "And you fought him?"

"He fought us, yes. He was trying to protect Alençon. And he succeeded, I think. They got away. And the king—"

"The king!"

"He got away, too, I think... he had smoke rising from him, as if he'd been burned. He was hurt, I think. By Ruggieri. The queen's sorcerer. He seemed to be working some kind of spell against the vampires, and Alençon escaped it, but his brother did not."

Chicot rubbed his temple. "But you say the king is still alive? If Charles dies, then... Anjou would be king. Or perhaps Alençon, if he chose to contest it..." He stood up. "If you're really all right, Françoise, I should go to the Louvre, to see what I can find out. If the king and Alençon are still alive and not too badly injured, I imagine I'll be off to La Rochelle with Anjou at first light, which will not be too long now."

She nodded, and got out of bed, wincing only a little. They each got dressed in silence. When Chicot was ready, she buckled his sword on for him.

"I hope this keeps you safe."

He put his hand over hers, over the hilt. "You are the master of it and the master of me. Say the word and I'll stay, and take whatever consequence comes."

She was silent for a moment, and very aware of time passing, moment by moment. If only they could go into the spirit world together and never come back. "I do not think the Duke of Mayenne and the Duke of Anjou would be your only worries if you stayed. La Môle might not have told his sire everything when he was falling under his sway, but he certainly will now. The vampires will know our identities, those of us who are left."

He nodded, and put an arm around her, drew her close. "At least Alençon will be in La Rochelle. That's one at least you will not have to deal with. And the king may be injured, you say."

"But so is Sainct Didier, and the Duchess of Nevers, too, I think. Injured, perhaps dead. There was blood on all sides. We have been greatly weakened, and we will have to deal with La Môle, somehow." She pulled him close, then picked up his cloak from the bed and put it around his shoulders. "Go, and fight the Protestants, as you are commanded. But come home to me soon."

He looked very serious. "I know that I'm not a wealthy man. When we met, you asked me how I got the name Chicot. A boy started calling me that when I was young, because my family and all its estates had been destroyed, leaving only me, the stump. But I'm a stubborn stump. I kept the name, out of spite, and I intend to make sure you want for nothing."

She looked at him wide-eyed. Her first wedding had been a trap, one she had escaped. She had never considered that she might have a chance for another, a chance to marry a man purely because she loved him, and he loved her.

"What I mean to say," said Chicot nervously, "is that I intend to return, and when I do, I intend to ask you to marry me."

She found that she was too exhausted from grief and fear to say anything in response. So she simply laid her head against his chest and listened to his heart until he had to leave.

THE DUCHESS OF Nevers had a fever and a vermilion rash all down one side of her body. But she had left instructions to her servants that certain people, were they to come to the Hôtel de Guise, would be admitted immediately. Françoise was one of those people.

By the time she got there, the duchess already had a note in her hand. For a moment, Françoise remembered the day that Sainct Didier had sent the note to the duchess, confirming that Sister Anne had died.

But this time, the duchess passed the note to Françoise to read for herself.

It read:

> *My friend, I find I have a sore throat and cannot talk, so I regret I will not be able to meet for cards this evening. I expect to be well soon. Please write back and let me know whether any other members of our party are indisposed.*
>
> *Yours,*
>
> *Henri de Sainct Didier.*

Françoise read it and wiped a tear from her eye, which surprised her. She had no reason to feel such relief, but she did. "He's alive, and well enough to write."

"But not able to talk. Well, he's always complaining that he needs more time to write his fencing manual, so now he'll have time. If we're all spared."

"Do you know what happened to the king?"

"Ruggieri happened, although what he did and why, I could not say. He used to be the tutor for the Duke of Alençon. If I had to guess, he is dismayed at what happened to the boy—perhaps resentful—and decided to free him the only way a vampire can be freed. He must have his own spies at the Louvre, and knew where Alençon would be tonight, and thought it a good opportunity to find him out in the open. Perhaps he wanted to do it before Alençon left for La Rochelle." She sighed, and shifted a little in bed, uncomfortably. "As to whether Ruggieri's spell had any effect on the king, that you will have to find out. I can barely move, thanks to that pustulant traitor La Môle. Will you fetch some salve for me, Françoise?"

She did so, and applied it to the duchess's raw, red skin as gently as she could.

The duchess carried on: "Most vampires don't bother with revenge. They're simple beasts, really, only thinking about their next meal. Other people—whether vampires or mortals—do not enter into their minds as anything but meat. But the more powerful vampires are the ones who strategize, the ones for whom ambition is the greatest hunger. The queen mother is dangerous."

"And now that La Môle is a vampire, she may know all about us."

"Perhaps. Alençon resents his mother, and I think he will keep La Môle and his information to himself. La Môle himself, though, is unpredictable. He is both Malandanti and Benandanti, and he may come after us. And now we are too weak to stop him."

"Then I will have to find new sources of strength," said Françoise.

FRANÇOISE DID NOT want to see Queen Marguerite. The likelihood that La Môle would be in her rooms, behind a tapestry or a secret panel, was always high, and she very much did not want to see La Môle, not even in daylight and in the Louvre.

But she needed to know the status of the king, and for that, she needed to be in the Louvre, and there was really only one excuse she had for that: the duchess's friendship with Queen Marguerite.

Marguerite was distressed to hear that her friend was ill. Françoise deliberately made it sound as if she might not recover, in case La Môle was listening, or would find out from Marguerite later. Anything that might keep the duchess safe.

"I shall go and nurse her," said Marguerite loyally. "No, better still, she must come here with me!"

"If you think it is safe for her here. I heard the king may be ill. I am sure he will recover, but perhaps, if it is the plague…"

Marguerite waved her hand. "My poor brother has been prone to strange fits for most of his life. People are always saying he is ill, but the truth is, he is stronger than anyone gives him credit for. There is no reason for my dear Henriette to stay away. Please go and bring her to me as soon as possible."

FRANÇOISE WALKED THROUGH the long guard room to a wide stone staircase, where she immediately shrank back.

Catherine de' Medici was coming up the stairs.

Three of her ladies were behind her, and the queen mother was addressing a lecture to them, even though she was facing straight ahead. She took the stairs quickly, her black skirt in her hands.

"This is not what I intended!" the queen shrieked. "Something has gone awry! The king should not fall ill! It should not be possible! God does not allow it!"

Françoise felt her breath catch in her throat.

"The doctor says His Majesty will be well, that it is just a passing fit from exhaustion," ventured one of the ladies. "No different from anything he has had before."

Catherine stopped, her face a mask of anger. She turned and went back down two steps, facing the speaker, and forcing her down a step, too. The poor lady nearly stumbled down the stairs.

The queen said, "That is always what the doctors say. I watched my husband linger for six weeks with a piece of lance in his brain, festering and weeping, and the doctors said he would be well. I watched my first-born son stumble and faint after playing a tennis match, and they said he would be well, give him some water, and three weeks later he was dead. I sent my beautiful child Elizabeth to marry the Spanish king; the doctors had said her pregnancy was progressing well. They said my baby Louis was a strong child; and yet he died from a chill. They said that my darling Victoire would live even after her sister died in the womb—they said…" She stopped, and looked around.

Françoise took a silent step back into the room from which she'd come.

The queen continued, "My son, my Charles, is anointed by God to be king and remain king. It is impossible that he should be ill. And so something has happened, something I do not understand. But I *will* understand it. Come, is Maître René at the Louvre today? Find out. I will see him, as quickly as possible. I do not trust doctors."

At that, the fluttering procession came up the stairs and brushed right past Françoise.

As they walked, Catherine de' Medici turned her head to look straight at Françoise, a stare that seemed to penetrate her soul.

CHAPTER TWENTY-THREE

Ruggieri

IT WAS AN odd feeling, knowing that she had been to Ruggieri's house before, and having no memory of it. The servant did not want to let her in.

"Tell Maître Ruggieri that one has come who saw him last night," she said, and waited.

In a dimly lit room packed with books and strange objects, the magician stooped. His eyes were sunken, his face glistened with sweat, and his hair was wild; he wore no hat or cap. In the crook of one arm were two thick books; in the other hand he held a knife.

"You will have no need of that," Françoise said calmly.

He peered at her face, clearly recognizing her, although she did not recognize him.

"Yes, I am the woman you poisoned not long ago."

For a moment, his alarm betrayed him, before he drew back on his dignity. "I am no poisoner, mademoiselle."

"No? Then that potion that took my memory was a kind of medicine, was it? And that business in the cemetery last night—were you simply making a speech?"

It felt good to be frank. She was so tired of games and secrets. With Sainct Didier and the duchess both injured, she felt she had every reason to go about things her own way.

The magician took one step closer, the knife still gripped tightly, his face still in a grimace.

"You were in the cemetery last night?"

"I was, but you need not ready your spells and stakes. I am no vampire, I assure you."

"Then you are..."

"One of the Benandanti. You know the word, I think? You are a scholar of magic."

He walked around her, fascinated, as if examining some strange relic.

She took the time to take in her surroundings, too. Everything was in disarray. Several of the books had tumbled onto the floor, as if someone had pulled them down. Someone had, she realized: the magician himself was in the process of removing his belongings, or at least some of them.

"I will answer any questions you may have," she said, "if you will do me the same courtesy. I think you and I could be useful to each other."

He thought for a moment. He was a wreck, but he was still an intelligent one. With a nod of resignation, he put the knife back in his belt. "You are indeed a curiosity, but I have no time to waste here with you. I am leaving this city, and quickly."

"I will not let you go until I know what you did to the king. Will he survive?"

The wizard leaned against the bookshelf for a moment, and scratched his balding head. "You ask me to admit to treason."

"Is it treason to remove a vampire from the throne of France?"

"No," he said earnestly. "No, it is not. But be that as it may, the king was not my target."

"His brother, then? The Duke of Alençon?"

Ruggieri nodded slowly. "I had the raising of François.

He was a good boy, with a sharp mind. A very even-handed person, very fair, and skeptical. A contrarian by nature. He does not like to be told what to do. Natural, in a youngest son. I loved him as if he were my own. I still do."

"And yet, you tried to destroy him."

"He was destroyed already! And that was my fault."

"How?"

"Because I taught Queen Catherine to look for signs, not realizing the terrible actions she would take because of them." The magician pulled a large, circular brass instrument off the shelf, and looked at it lovingly, stroked its patina. Then he brandished it at her like a preacher making an argument. "Everything in the universe has a pattern; God is an artist, but most do not know how to read his signs. A drop of blood may tell part of the same story as a comet, for those who have understanding."

He put the instrument into the chest, and whirled around, looking for more objects to put in. There must have been hundreds of books in the room, and he seemed uncertain which ones to take. The most incriminating, or the least? Or was he packing the ones he thought would be most useful to him in future?

"You have been a magician for many years, and you have learned many things," she said. "That much is clear. And yet, you are outside of the bosom of the royal family."

He nodded sadly. "In the early years, the queen took great comfort and wisdom from my work, and I always made sure to encourage her to use my art only for the kinds of knowledge that could serve her. To choose auspicious days for travel, for example, or to plan for a negotiation. She did not ask me to tell her things a person should not know about God's plan."

"But something changed. When?"

In remembering, the magician seemed to have lost interest in packing his things, momentarily at least. "It would have been 1556, after her last accouchement, when she was delivered of a stillborn child, and another who lived only a few days. Something seemed to shift in her then. She had always been ambitious and clever, but now she became paranoid and manipulative. She was not the queen I had known."

"This was when she became a vampire."

He winced. "How it happened, I have never learned, although looking back, I have my suspicions. For many years I did not understand what change had come over her. I told myself it was only grief, when her husband died a few years later. But by then she was already obsessed with control, of both the present and the future. She invited a seer, Nostradamus, to prophesy about her children. He told her that her sons would be kings, but that they would all die young."

"I believe I have heard some reference to that," Françoise said, recalling the conversation with the Duke of Anjou she overheard when she first came to the Louvre. "At Maître René's."

"Oh, that charlatan, he only repeats the discoveries his betters made long before. He cuts open sheep and hens, points at the shapes of their livers, and tells the queen what she already knows, thanks to the talents of Nostradamus and myself. For the prophecy was true. There can be no denying that. I cast the horoscopes of all the children, and could see it plainly: they would rule, *and* they would die young."

"Both at least can already be said to be true of King Charles."

"Indeed. An outcome the queen herself brought about, in her fear and panic. The one way she could think of to give her boys eternal life—she did not care about Marguerite, she never has—was to turn them into creatures like herself. And yet, some mother's instinct must still live within that breast, because she has been reluctant to turn her middle child, Anjou. Her favourite. Perhaps it is because she knows that he would turn against her, as vampires always do… but he turns against her already, nonetheless."

"She turned Alençon, though."

"She did," the magician agreed sadly. "But only recently. She began with Charles. He was twenty-one when she turned him, the age of manhood. I don't know how she intends to explain his eternal youth to the people. Perhaps she thinks they won't notice. But now..."

"Now you have cursed him," she prodded.

He looked at her for a moment, biting his fingernail. Then he rushed to another bookshelf, across the room, and pulled one book out to reveal another behind it. It was large, with a faded blue leather cover. He took it in both hands, reverently.

"A Dutch vampire-hunter sent me this. He had it from one of his forebears. Many might read the book and never realize what it contained on one of its pages: a curse that may only be used once in a century."

"Why only once a century?"

He shrugged, looking annoyed at the question. "Perhaps the vampire-hunter who wrote it did not want competition while he lived, but he wanted to make sure he left some piece of his art behind, to be used in the direst need. Whatever the reason, I'm afraid the book is no good to anyone now. And neither is the king." Here a light of triumph crept over his face. "I do not know how long it will take, but the book says a blood-surfeit will come upon him, and he will slowly be destroyed by it."

"What is a blood-surfeit?"

Again, the wizard shrugged. For a scholar, he was remarkably incurious about some questions, it seemed. "We will find out. The king is still alive, today? You've come from the Louvre, yes?"

"I saw his mother there. She seemed upset... said that she had not intended this. I suppose she must have meant that she did not intend this when she turned him into a vampire."

"Perhaps," said the magician, stroking his beard. "Or perhaps she thinks it is a poison gone awry. She poisons so many people, sends her little gloves and pots of rouge out all over the palace, all created by that insidious perfumer... She should know that poison does not destroy a vampire, but she does not yet know about my curse. When she finds out, she will certainly kill me. If I am still in Paris to be found and killed."

At this, he began again to pile books and objects into the chest. Then he closed the lid, leaning on it to try to get it to catch. He was so desperate to finish his preparations and get out, as if he were the only one hunted in this city. It was not safe there for Françoise, either, but she had no intention of abandoning the fight. And she had no intention of going into the next battle unprepared. She needed all the information and allies she could muster.

"When did you turn against Queen Catherine?"

"I never did," he said, making a fist and banging the lid shut. "I swore my service to her when we came from Florence, when she was only a child. I swore that to the pope himself, her uncle. I swore to keep her and her children safe from the workings of the Devil and her father-in-law. And I discharge that oath faithfully still. I will save her one day, if I can. But I wanted to save him first."

"Alençon."

He nodded. "The poor boy—he's still only a child—he'll forever be seventeen. The queen would have waited until he was a man, like Charles, but there were signs that the smallpox he had as a boy had weakened his heart. She did not want Death to claim him when she was not in the room. So she panicked, and turned him, last year. He is no longer the boy I taught. No longer the boy I loved. But I wished to free his soul from its torment, and send it to heaven."

Françoise was taken aback. "To heaven?"

"If God wills it, yes. The boy's deeds committed after his own death do not damn him."

"If his mother performed the last rites before turning him, perhaps—"

Ruggieri shook his head. "I have left behind all that superstition."

"Then you are an adherent of the new religion."

Françoise was beginning to understand why Ruggieri had fallen from grace. The queen mother did not seem the type to toss aside a servant, even an irritating one, unless some perceived liability outweighed his usefulness to her.

He said, with patronizing patience, "If François was chosen by God to be among his elect, then his current state is delaying his true destiny. I wished to see him reunited with his God. But the curse I meant for him hit his brother instead."

She paced, thinking. "You have no other curses or spells that might work?"

He shook his head. "I have searched for years. The one I used was the only one I ever found. There are other vampire-hunters, wizards, alchemists, mages… I know them all, by reputation if not by letter. They all have their tricks, their herbs and plants, but in the end, it comes down to…" He mimed swinging a sword.

Time was even shorter for her than it was for him, although he did not know it, and it was long past time she found a safe place to sleep and go into the world of the spirit, where she could take any form she liked. The moment had come to press her point.

Françoise crossed the worn and faded carpet and put one hand on his shoulder. "But you did not know that you had allies, all this time. We are here. The Benandanti. You saw how we fought in the cemetery."

"You got in my way," he snarled. "It's because of you that the curse landed on the king and not on his brother."

"But now we are in communication, you and I, and we could work together. We can help you save Alençon. But first we must remove our greatest threat. La Môle has been turned. He knows all our secrets. At our full strength, we could not defeat him, and now we are weakened. We must find a way to eliminate him. That is why I came to you."

The wizard smiled sadly. "I have told you, I have no other curses."

"No, but I have learned that there are many ways to destroy a man in Paris. The queen will be out for vengeance as the king gets sicker. Even a vampire may fall to lies, gossip and the executioner's axe. You know the queen mother better than anyone. Tell me how we may accomplish this."

Ruggieri looked uncertain. He sat on the chest, which had finally closed. "If I stay, it will be me for the executioner's axe."

"We will do our best to protect you. Do you really think that running will save you? From vampires? No, your only hope now is to feed the queen's own curiosity, to use your wits and your knowledge to survive, as you have always done. And now you have us on your side."

CHAPTER TWENTY-FOUR

Two Books

In those days, the two main bridges over the Seine were still guarded by fortresses on either side, and the larger one, the Grand Châtelet, was the seat of the administration of Paris, as well as royal business.

On a summer day in 1573, the famous fencing master, Henri de Sainct Didier, was visiting the Châtelet to explain to an official why the Provost of Paris should purchase ten copies of the swordmaster's newly printed fencing manual on the single-sword.

Sainct Didier had been very particular about the room in which this conversation must take place: one room was dismissed as being too close to the stench of sewage from the river, the other too fouled by the smell of the slaughterhouses, both of which were likely to overcome his young female assistant, who carried the books and swords. One room was too small to allow for any demonstration of the art; another had poor light from the windows; another was obscured too much by smoke from some chimney nearby.

Eventually, Sainct Didier and Françoise convinced the official to hold a conversation in a room two storeys up from a cell known as the Gloriette, in which Cosimo Ruggieri was being held prisoner.

"Shall we begin?" the official asked, impatiently.

"A moment," said Sainct Didier, leaning against a chair and catching his breath.

His voice was still not quite the same, four months after the attack at the cemetery, but he'd had plenty of time to rest it. A ruff hid the scar. He and Françoise spent most of their time now in the world of spirit, walking the deserted, bleak outskirts of the city in disguises that changed hour by hour.

It was a necessary precaution, after La Môle had been seen prowling near the convent of Montmartre, where Sainct Didier was recuperating. And since the traitor knew the identity of Françoise, too, she had also gone into hiding.

She had given Mistral to La Hurière, in thanks for his decency, and because the mare needed someone to make sure she was well stabled, now that her mistress was spending most of her time sleeping in a hidden room at the Louvre, accessible only through a secret passage from the apartments of Queen Marguerite.

To get to the hidden room, one had to pass through the rooms belonging to the Duchess of Nevers, who had moved into the Louvre during her illness. She was totally recovered now, but Marguerite would not hear of her moving back out. They were inseparable, and so La Môle could do nothing about the duchess. Françoise thought it must have been terrifying for the duchess to sit there with La Môle staring at her, each of them knowing what the other was, but the duchess had a steel spine.

She had, at least, changed her sleeping habits, and now kept several ladies with her in the room at all times.

And at least the duchess was able to spend her days in her own body. Françoise, on the other hand, was revelling in the rare outing, even though the neighbourhood of the Châtelet did stink. She missed eating, drinking, walking the streets with legs that got tired. Her body was not as stiff and weak as she'd feared; the Benandanti gift allowed the body to sleep for as long as required without the need for sustenance or exercise. Even so, the stairs at the Châtelet had made her sweat—how glorious—and she was sure Sainct Didier was not entirely putting on his own need to catch his breath.

But the main reason for the delay was that their visit here needed to overlap with a visit Ruggieri was about to have in the cell far below.

Françoise positioned herself on top of a grill. From there, she could hear the conversation from below, when she tried. It was faint, but it was there, and she had always had excellent hearing. Like that of a hare.

At first, she heard only the groaning of prisoners in many cells, some of them little better than wet pits full of excrement and vermin. The groaning of the chains and pulleys that lowered them in or pulled them out, for the amusement of the guards.

Ruggieri would have a clean, dry cell, Sainct Didier had assured her, because he could pay. And in any case, the queen mother would not be taken to visit a prisoner in a cell filled with water and snakes.

The creak of a door, a bang, and then Françoise heard the voice of Catherine de' Medici, greeting her old friend.

Françoise gave Sainct Didier a tiny nod. It had begun.

"Very good," said Sainct Didier to the official, keeping him on the other side of the room, as far from Françoise as possible. All the same, their conversation intruded on her awareness. "Now, as you can see, my book is printed here in Paris and sold at the sign of the White Rose, on the Saint-Michel Bridge—why, we can probably see it from here. Come to the window, I'll show you. Not only would this manual improve the fighting skills of your men, but it is ensuring the prosperity of a hard-working Parisian family."

In the cell below, the queen said to Ruggieri: *You are lucky to be in prison and not dead. Did you think I would not hear about the book? About the cemetery?*

Ruggeri spoke softly, as if to himself, *You know that I come from the same Tuscany as you, Madame, where we both heard tales of the Malandanti from childhood, where we knew they were to be feared, not only because of what they could do but because of the dark bargain they made to do it... Never did I think the young girl I accompanied from Florence to France would be among their number.*

Françoise missed the next part, because Sainct Didier and the official moved away from the window and raised their voices.

Sainct Didier said, "You see, it is dedicated to His Majesty King Charles IX, and printed with the privilege of his king."

In the cell, the queen snapped: *The king is ill.*

Good. He should suffer, hissed Ruggieri. *You should all suffer my wrath for casting me aside, after my long years of loyal service. A mortal like me, an old man, weak and ill... perhaps I cannot destroy one of your kind but at least I can cause you pain, for a little while.*

The queen was silent, and Sainct Didier showed the official the illustrations in the fencing manual, took him back to the window, into the light.

The queen said, *Then the king will recover. Your curse will not kill him.*

It was Ruggieri's turn to be silent, calculatingly so. To make the queen think that he had not intended to reveal that. But of course, it was a lie. The king was dying. The trick was to make the queen think he was not—or not yet.

"Now let's you and I do what they do in this illustration, and you will see how easy it is to follow," said Sainct Didier. "I will be this figure, marked as the Lieutenant, and you can be the one labelled Provost. About time you had a promotion, eh?"

Below, the queen said: *But perhaps you are wrong, and the curse will kill my son, and you will be guilty of regicide as well as treason.*

Ruggieri barked a laugh. *Impossible. Believe me. The limitations of the curse are written in the book itself, in black and white.* A pause. *You can read it yourself. It's this one here, with the blue cover. The one that appears to be about falconry, to the uninitiated eye.*

—Hand it to me.

—I am too badly injured from this torture. Unable to move.

—Nonsense, they have not tortured you, but they will, if I command it. It will be the rack for you, Ruggieri. Now hand me that book.

A moment's pause.

Then, the queen: *Why do you hold it with your sleeves rather than your hands?*

Ruggieri sighed. *Because the very touch of the book on bare skin is death, to anyone, vampire or mortal. This is a book that kills. More surely than any poison that quack perfumer could mix for you.*

—And you would have watched me pick it up? Seeing that I had taken off my gloves in this heat… oh, you are wicked and deserve death.

—No, it is you who deserve death, whore of Babylon!

Ruggieri's scream was so loud that Françoise could hardly believe the others did not hear. Perhaps they did. But Sainct Didier calmly went about adjusting the official's foot position.

Ruggieri was playing his part well. Every note was believable. But there was one final point that had to be driven home. Françoise listened until she heard it.

The queen said: *I will take your book that kills, lest you try your trick on your guards. And I will be sure to wear gloves when I read it.*

You cannot take my revenge from me, shouted the wizard. *God will depose you. Your wretched line will wither and die before your very eyes and the King of Navarre will become King of France, no matter what you do. I have cast the horoscopes again and again. I have used every tool I know. The future is written and not even you can change that, whore of Babylon!*

Sainct Didier closed his fencing manual and said, “You will let me know of your decision. I believe we are done here, Françoise?”

She nodded. Everything had gone according to plan. They had been right to trust Ruggieri, even when he had not trusted himself.

FRANÇOISE AND SAINCT Didier walked briskly out of the Châtelet and into the late afternoon, and stood on a step, gazing out on a street full of hawkers and their customers, and people going up and down to the river.

Three guards were pulling a man in rags along the street. His wrists and legs were chained, and he bore a bright red gash down one side of his face. But they had not gagged him, and he was making use of that one freedom, screaming: “It was not me! I did not murder anyone! It was a vampire, a vampire in fine clothing, I saw it all! I tell you I am innocent!”

Drawing a sword, one of the guards smashed his pommel into the man’s head, and new blood trickled down past the old. The little drama passed by Sainct Didier and Françoise, forcing them to move aside. Then the man was swallowed behind the gates of the Châtelet, bound for the oubliettes from which few returned.

“One day we will have justice,” Sainct Didier grumbled. “Did Ruggieri say it all? Everything he needed to say?”

She nodded. “Perfectly. The plan is in motion. I almost feel badly for him. He is putting himself at great risk.”

“All the more reason for us to hurry, and make sure we don’t abandon him in this life. Come on.”

As much as Françoise understood the need for haste, she wished she could linger, to smell the oysters and eavesdrop on the gossip. Even in their spirit forms, even in the dead of night, she and Sainct Didier did not walk in the city often now. They preferred open spaces, where they could take the forms of giants, or spring into the air as owls, always on alert, always ready to fight.

Soon, she would be back in her secret bed, back in a spirit body. There was only an hour of sunlight left in the day. La Môle, being newly turned, did not hide from the sun, but he was unlikely to hunt in it—or at least, so they hoped. They kept to the crowds in the busy streets.

Someone grabbed her arm.

Françoise immediately wrenched her forearm out of the man's grasp, belatedly realizing it wasn't a grasp at all, at least not a malicious one.

She stared into the face of Chicot.

"I've been looking all over for you two," Chicot said, breathless.

"You're back," said Françoise, grabbing both his arms as if mirroring his movement of a moment before. "You're home."

"Not here," said Sainct Didier to Chicot. "At midnight, at… at the place where I took you to practice escape from an enemy. Come on, Françoise."

Sainct Didier took her other arm and she stared back at Chicot's face, ignoring the curses of the other pedestrians as she stumbled into them.

CHAPTER TWENTY-FIVE

Councils of Love and War

At midnight, three owls met on a weathered fence in a field in Montmartre, well outside the city walls. This was a place of strength for the Benandanti. The fields were crossed by many running streams, which vampires tended not to like. Yarrow grew wild by the walls and fences.

One of the owls fluttered down into the form of a man: it was Sainct Didier, looking much as he had the night Françoise had first encountered him in the hills of Gascony.

"I'll make a fire," he said. "For our friend Chicot to find us more easily. Besides, there is safety in it. I have never known a vampire who liked to be near fire."

His spirit body did not come with a tinder box, but he spoke to a bit of grass in his hand and before long, a small fire was crackling in a patch of dirt by a goat-cropped pasture.

Françoise took on the form of a woman, and so did the duchess. All three of them stood around the fire, gazing into it, as people will always gaze into a fire.

Then Françoise found the words to say something she had been meaning to say for many months. "I never gave you my condolences for the loss of Sister Anne. I know she was close to you."

The fencing master was silent for a while. He looked up at the dark mass of hillside behind them, past a lazily turning windmill, beyond which stood the Abbey of Montmartre. The woman who had taken the name of Sister Anne had chosen it as her refuge when she left the Benandanti, because of the streams and yarrow. None of it was proof against vampires, but they were reasons to hope that vampires would not simply happen along. But then, for reasons Françoise might never fully know, Sister Anne had rejoined the fight.

Françoise had never even seen her face, only her spirit form.

Sainct Didier took a long time clearing his throat before he said, "When a piece of wood is consumed, we replace it with another, but the fire does not go out. I know she is here with us."

"I very nearly thought you'd be flame without wood yourself, after that day in the cemetery," said the duchess drily. "And I'm still not sure you're well enough to go chatting at the Châtelet."

"It was necessary," said Sainct Didier. "We had to get Françoise in position to overhear Ruggieri, to make sure we were right to trust him. Everything is working as intended. The queen has the book, which she will use to try to kill the King of Navarre, because she refuses to accept the prophecy, and because she can't resist trying any new poison she learns about."

"She is always trying to poison the King of Navarre," said the duchess. "We did not need to give her a new kind of poison to know that."

"But this time we know *how* she'll do it," said Françoise. "And so we can arrange what will seem to be an unfortunate turn of events. We'll make it look as if the King of France found the book in his brother-in-law's rooms."

Sainct Didier nodded. "I have access to the rooms occupied

by the King of France, as I sometimes need to visit his armory. I'll take the book from the King of Navarre's room and move it to those of the King of France. He is already dying; when he reads the book, the queen will believe she killed her son herself."

Even in her spirit body, there was something endearingly familiar about the way the duchess waved her arm. "Well, I am glad to know you have your part in hand. My affair is going perfectly, of course. Thanks to her conversations with me, Marguerite is having doubts about La Môle's love for her. She says he is changed toward her, colder than he was, which of course is true, and I encourage her doubts. I have also told Coconnas about the love spells one can get from Maître René. It was clever of Ruggieri to suggest that; the queen trusts René and will use him in her schemes."

"But will this changed La Môle even care enough about Marguerite to try to win her back?" Françoise wondered.

Sainct Didier whistled. "Oh, a vampire hates to lose. Even if his heart has no real love in it for her, he will do whatever he must to make sure she belongs to him. Up to and including killing her, so I hope he goes for the love spell instead."

Françoise winced, looking at the fire again. "How we play with people's lives."

Then all three of them looked up, aware of something they could not have put into words; a shift in the wind, a feeling in the soles of their bare feet. In their spirit forms, they were always in silent communication with the earth and the sky, and they knew every insect and burrowing creature within a hundred paces. They could also tell when a human was approaching.

By the time Chicot reached the fire, they were waiting for him in forms that looked similar to their waking bodies, but not quite the same. There were small, uncanny differences in height, colouring, the wideness of the eyes. Still, Chicot knew them, and was unbothered by their changed appearance.

He strode to Françoise and embraced her, then embraced the other two in turn.

"Well met, my friend," said Sainct Didier. "We had not heard here in Paris that the siege had ended."

"It has not, but it will soon. Anjou is going to offer them a peace deal, which will allow the Huguenots to worship as they like in certain cities. It is very likely they will accept. A deal we could have made months ago, and saved many lives."

"Why make it now?" said Sainct Didier.

"Oh, then it seems the other news has not yet reached Paris, or at least not everyone in Paris." Chicot laughed bitterly. "The Commonwealth of Poland and Lithuania has been without a king for some time, apparently. Most of the candidates are unacceptable to the nobility for one reason or another. So they have been convinced to elect an outsider, someone who has no power base to abuse in Poland, and someone who brings alliances with them. I suppose any son of any king would do, as long as they don't already hate him. In short, the Duke of Anjou has been elected the new King of Poland and Grand Duke of Lithuania. He is to travel there in a few months, once he wraps up the siege at La Rochelle."

Sainct Didier whistled softly.

"I heard rumours that this was the queen mother's plan," said the duchess. "But I did not think it would come to pass."

Françoise was confused. "Why would she send her middle son away?"

Chicot said, "She tells him it is for his own protection, that her vampires are fractious, that it's best if he gets out of the way. To which he demands to know why she doesn't turn him, and she says it is because she loves him too much."

"I believe it," said the duchess. "Despite everything, I believe she does want to preserve him as he is, her one living son. Or at least, some part of her does. It may be that she wants to protect him from herself, from her desire to change him into a creature like all the others she has turned, and who turn away from her."

"Anjou believes she just wants him out of the way so he won't question her, so that she can use her other two sons as puppets, and I am not sure he's wrong," said Chicot.

"Perhaps all of it is true," said Sainct Didier. "And perhaps it is for the best. With Anjou safely in Poland, France will still have one Valois heir who is not a vampire, if we succeed in eliminating those who are. In the meantime, let the Poles have him."

"The end of the siege means young Alençon will be coming back to Paris, too," said Chicot. "And he's coming back angry. During the siege, Alençon chafed at taking orders from his brother, and more than once he sent vampires at night among the men to frighten them. If they hadn't already had their thirsts well satisfied on the battlefield, it might have gone worse. He'll lash out at someone now if he can't get at his brother, and the traitor La Môle will tell him about you, if he has not already. We'll have to find a way to neutralize them both, the Duke of Alençon and his man La Môle."

"We?" said Sainct Didier. "Leave that to us. You'll be in Poland, Chicot."

Françoise felt every part of her spirit body go on alert, as if some danger had approached; this possibility had not occurred to her. She shifted closer to Chicot, protectively.

Chicot shook his head in response to Sainct Didier's assumption. "I am released from Anjou's service. As a reward for, well, saving his life." He looked, charmingly, uncomfortable. "I still have his protection, but he's giving me an estate in Provence where I can make a life for myself." He glanced at Françoise, and she gave him a small smile.

"But you must go with him," said Sainct Didier. "You can watch over him in Poland, keep him safe. If Alençon resents Anjou, if he wants a throne for himself, he might well try to eliminate his older brother from the line of succession. Once King Charles is gone, Anjou will be the only one between Alençon and the throne."

Chicot looked somber. "I have heard rumours that the King is dying, but surely a vampire cannot die, or at least cannot die slowly."

"He's been cursed," Françoise explained. "And if he does go to his grave for good, that makes it all the more likely there will be violence between his younger brothers over the succession."

Chicot's eyes went wide, and she could see his thoughts churning.

"Our only hope of safety is to preserve the chance for a mortal king," said Sainct Didier, encouraging her line of thought. "One who can bear children, one who will do us the courtesy of dying eventually, and who will not bathe the country in blood out of caprice, as the queen mother and her puppet king have done. We cannot assume that anything is too horrible for Alençon to contemplate. He is a vampire now, after all, and without any scruple. He might send someone to harm Anjou, even in Poland… perhaps *especially* there, where Alençon can deny involvement when his mother asks. No, no. Anjou is France's only hope for a future free from servitude to monsters. You must go with him, Chicot. Keep him safe."

The duchess spoke more softly, but no less urgently. "You have already done us great service, Chicot. You warned us against the traitor in our ranks. You have shared information at great risk to yourself. Your name will be remembered by the Benandanti among our greatest allies, for as long as there are Benandanti to remember. In the fight against evil, anyone would say you have surely given enough for one lifetime. Nonetheless, nothing is enough when we who fight are so scattered, so few, so depleted. Nothing can be enough until the curse of the Malandanti is wiped from the earth. And so although it is not fair to ask you for more, I do ask it."

Chicot looked at Françoise. "I will go to Poland if Françoise agrees that I should. But I will not go against her will. I have made the duke no promise such as that I have made to her."

The fencing master and the duchess turned to Françoise, their faces a mixture of amusement and annoyance. The prospect of losing Chicot again made her feel dizzy.

And yet, was this not why she had left home in the first place? To fight the vampires, to act according to the dictates of honour, as her conscience led her? She mourned the loss of La Môle, the loss of Sister Anne, and she knew more losses would follow if the whims of the Valois family were allowed to run their full course. What alternative was there, except the one remaining mortal man whom the people would accept as their king? There was only one honourable course, and that was to fight to remove all vampires from power. Her own hopes and affections were a small sacrifice. Besides, when King Charles, Alençon and their mother were all destroyed, then life and hope would return, and on that day, she would do as her heart commanded.

She lifted her chin. "I would never command you, Chicot. You are a free man. Go where you will, but as a friend, I ask you to consider the needs of France, and the needs of the Benandanti. I ask you to go to Poland and help protect the Duke of Anjou from his evil family."

He bowed his head, so that she could barely see his tight mouth. At last he said, "But that leaves you the problem of Alençon, here in Paris."

"Alençon is a problem with his own solution," said the duchess. "If he does not succeed in getting his brothers out of the way quietly, he'll do so loudly. All the disaffected nobles, the Protestants and the moderate Catholics, already flock to him and hope he'll lead a rebellion against Charles. If we can encourage that, it ought to keep him busy—and perhaps he might even end up in prison, or beheaded alongside La Môle, if God smiles on our plans."

Françoise did not feel that God was smiling that night, and she did not bother trying to smile herself.

* * *

THE FIRE WENT out as if some unseen creature had stamped it. The duchess and the fencing master took flight, politely leaving Chicot and Françoise to make their own ways back to whatever bed they chose. Françoise went to him, tilted her face up to him, but he shrank back.

"What is it?"

He laughed nervously. "You're not yourself."

She let his hands drop, and looked herself over. "It's the closest I can get."

She realized that she wanted to kiss him to reassure him, to go through the motions, to communicate something to him. It was not quite the same as being in her waking body. The longer she spent in the world of night, the more that other life seemed like a remembered story.

"But your real body is sleeping somewhere. Somewhere safe, I hope. Let's go to it, and I will wake you up with a kiss."

She laughed, a little sadly. "Then you still don't believe this is truly me."

"It is you, but it is not your lips. I would feel as if I were being unfaithful. Oh, laugh at me if you will. I don't mind. I've missed you laughing at me."

She took his hand, and they walked toward the city walls. "The truth is, you are a soldier who has been away at war, and I am not your wife. Some might say you have no need to be faithful."

"Some would indeed say that. Many of my comrades did, in fact."

"You told them about me?"

"Certainly not, but I told them I had no interest in the women who did our laundry or provided other services. They all assumed I was saving myself for Anjou, but Anjou is not interested in me that way, although he flirts with everyone to keep them off balance. It isn't easy to get me off balance, and I think that's one reason he likes me. He will be happy to have me in his retinue for Poland."

"He seems like a sharp-witted man."

"He is indeed."

"And is he a good one?"

Chicot considered this, and for a while, the only sound was the crunch of dried grasses under their feet. "He loves life, and all the good things of the world. Art, music, fencing, friendship. I would not say he is kind, but he is never needlessly cruel. As far as scions of kings go, he's not bad."

"And he's not a vampire."

"Yes, he also has that to recommend him." He paused. "I *was* faithful, you know. At the siege."

"I did not doubt it. So was I. Although I wasn't tempted by lovely washerwomen, so I suppose it was easier for me."

"That's true. I've met the washerwoman La Hurière uses, and she's not very tempting at all," he agreed.

"I haven't been staying at the inn."

"Good. I'm glad you're keeping safe. Or as safe as anyone can, here in this bloody city. You know, Françoise, you could come with me. As my wife."

It came so casually, she almost had to ask him to repeat it.

"You're asking me to marry you?"

"Does it surprise you? You know I adore you. You are my beating heart. I seem to recognize your soul in every beautiful thing I see." He stopped, turned to her, and took her face in his hands.

"I will come to you in the body you know, just outside the city gate in an hour," she said. "You can't get in until morning anyway. Wait for me there."

In an instant, she was an owl again, silently moving against the scraps of clouds in the night. Too late, she realized that the transformation might have alarmed Chicot. But perhaps she should alarm him. He should know what he was getting for a wife.

* * *

Dawn came in creeping, grey and damp. They were filthy and entangled in each other. Françoise was restless, unused now to being in her waking body, this close to the city full of vampires. She frowned and looked out over the river while he arranged his clothing.

"What are you brooding about?" he asked.

"I have to stay here, Chicot," she said. "To see an end to this business with La Môle. I am the one Ruggieri trusts—we have so many pieces in play, and I can't risk it all falling apart."

He nodded, saying nothing for a moment. Then, lightly, he said, "Well, I'll be in Paris for a few months yet, because it will take time for Anjou to prepare everything for his entry into Poland, the coronation, all of it. So you and I can make the most of that time before we're parted. And then perhaps later..."

"Yes, later." She turned to him and took his hand. "Once King Charles dies, and Anjou takes the throne. But can Anjou rule Poland and France at the same time?"

"Also Lithuania, for good measure," said Chicot. "I don't know, Françoise. The way these families carve up the rule of the world is beyond me. I do not imagine he would sit quietly and watch Alençon take the throne of France, not after the way Alençon behaved in La Rochelle, the gruesome cruelty, the complete lack of interest in what outcome might be best for France and for its people. No, Anjou will not stay in Poland if Charles dies. I am certain of that. The only question is whether his mother will let him take the throne of France, or whether she'll put her other vampire puppet on it instead. Catherine does not like Alençon, but she can control him. This is the question Anjou will be asking himself."

"We will do what we can to help prepare the way for him. And for you. For a few months, then, we will be together."

She kissed him, because it was that or burst into tears.

* * *

Françoise was not able to come out of hiding while La Môle was still free. Most of the time, she slept, and wandered in her spirit body. She and Chicot met in different places in the wilds outside the city. Sometimes, she met him in her waking body. Once in a while, she even ventured into the city, always during the day.

At last, the day came when there were rumours La Môle would be arrested for plotting against the king. It was all going according to plan: the queen mother had left the book in the rooms of the King of Navarre; Sainct Didier had moved them to the rooms of the King of France; the King of France had taken a turn for the worse; the queen mother blamed herself, and was frantically looking for a scapegoat. And thanks to the duchess's sending of Coconnas and La Môle off in search of love spells to secure the loyalty of the beautiful Marguerite, La Môle was implicated in occult and unnatural business. The perfect scapegoat.

With La Môle on the run from his own problems, Chicot and Françoise felt safe enough spending the night before his departure in his former room at La Belle Étoile. She regretted that choice—not because La Môle or any other vampire found them there, but because she had truly grown to detest the greasy smell of roasted chicken.

"You will not see me in this body, but I'll watch the procession when you go," she said, looking not at his eyes but at their interlaced fingers. "And you must write, Chicot. And take care of yourself. Don't get into any duels with pompous dukes. Come home safely to me."

"Is that a command?"

"It is the only command I will ever give you. Take my heart with you to Poland, and bring it back safe."

CHAPTER TWENTY-SIX

It took four months for La Mole to be arrested and executed. [illegible] dove, watching the executioner's [illegible] destruction. Behind that window [illegible] in black, the Duchess of Nevers and Queen Marguerite [illegible] They looked out [illegible] called the Louvre. Today it was filled with [illegible]

Four months since [illegible] The king of France [illegible] running around the palace [illegible] the Duke of Alençon [illegible]

[illegible]

CHAPTER TWENTY-SIX

The Head of the Snake

It took four months for La Môle to be arrested, tried and executed. Françoise sat on a high windowsill in the form of a dove, watching the executioner's cart carry two men to their destruction. Behind that window stood two women in black: the Duchess of Nevers and Queen Marguerite of Navarre. They looked out over the patch of open land near the river called the Grève. Today, it was filled with spectators.

Four months since the Duke of Anjou had left for Poland. The King of France still languished in his sickbed, when he wasn't running around the palace screaming in agony. Emboldened, the Duke of Alençon had turned against his brother, just as Chicot said he would. Four months since Chicot had left. The noose the Benandanti was drawing around the royal family was tightening, albeit slowly.

La Môle looked about him with dazed arrogance, unbelieving that the queen mother would let this happen to him, would let a vampire be beheaded in front of all of Paris. And all of Paris had come out to see. People filled every inch of the streets the cart travelled. Some climbed monuments and walls. They didn't heap their insults on La Môle, though, but on his mortal companion, who was said to have confessed under torture. Torture, it was rumoured, had no effect on the brave La Môle.

His companion was his best friend, once his enemy: Annibal de Coconnas.

The duchess never said whether she had foreseen this possibility, when she suggested to Coconnas that La Môle could procure a love spell. Several people had seen the two men coming and going from the house of Maître René, and René himself (at his mistress's command) had given careful testimony about a wax figure he had prepared for La Môle, while not being aware of its true purpose.

And what was that purpose? the court asked.

To bring about the death of the king, through sorcery.

The king was not dead yet. It was, in fact, treason to suggest he would actually die. But it was not treason to charge a man with trying to kill him through sorcery. The king had clearly been under some influence: he was less and less rational with each day, and prone to fainting fits. He also had a tendency to bleed, spontaneously, from random parts of his body. Like some village saint, said Sainct Didier, at which the devout duchess looked disapproving.

Ruggieri told Françoise smugly, when she visited him in the Châtelet in bird form, that he believed the blood that abandoned the body of the king was all the blood of those he had murdered, returning to the world of the living. Ruggieri's curse had reversed the cause and consequence of one man's crimes, slowly and excruciatingly.

And La Môle would pay the price. The Benandanti would have their revenge on one of their own. One who was, they reminded themselves, already dead. Even when they couldn't quite convince themselves that the axe would be a mercy to La Môle himself, they took refuge in the certainty that it would prevent the deaths of innocents.

It was hard to remember any of that, watching the man go to his death. Vampires were charming, of course. It was one of their gifts. The whole crowd murmured that La Môle was so brave, so pale, so handsome, what a shame. And yet they were here to watch him die.

There could be no mercy for treason in France. Everyone knew that the country was on a knife edge. Alençon was now in prison for plotting open rebellion against his brother—just as the Benandanti had hoped he would—and the peace brokered at La Rochelle was fragile. No one argued against La Môle's death.

Yet they sighed.

Françoise, looking at the man in the cart, remembered the day he had been so polite to her, when she had just arrived in Paris. How he had looked at her as if she were a human being no less worthy of conversation and interest as anyone else. He didn't lecture her, or stare at her breasts, or belittle her, or ignore her. All of that put him head and shoulders above most men of her acquaintance, but it was more than that. He truly seemed not to care whether someone was a peasant or a queen, a scholar or a beggar, a Catholic or a Huguenot. Perhaps that was what had made Queen Marguerite fall in love with him.

That *she* was still in love with him, there could be no doubt. Her face was as white as a sheet and she clutched at the duchess's hand. The duchess, watching Coconnas go his death, revealed no emotion at all. It was as if her spirit were wearing her body, as if that were the borrowed form.

Coconnas and La Môle helped each other up the scaffold. They both looked to the window where the duchess and the queen stood, watching them.

Something that made Françoise nervous: a sense that La Môle should be fighting this, that it was not like a vampire to go meekly to destruction, even if his sire's sire, the queen mother, had orchestrated and organized it.

Somewhere down there in the crowd was Sainct Didier, although Françoise did not know what disguise he had chosen.

Françoise pivoted her dove's head to check on the duchess before going closer, to take advantage of her disguise and gain what information she could. She still felt unsettled in spirit form during the day, but she was getting very good at flying. A long, circular swoop brought her down to the flagstones near the scaffold, close enough to hear anything that La Môle might say. She had to work to shut out the hundreds of little comments from the crowd, to focus her attention on the man who was about to die for the second time.

La Môle said to the executioner: "You will not forget what I asked of you?"

The executioner reassured him he would not.

La Môle looked up at the window where Marguerite stood, and he smiled.

The axe took off his head with one blow.

The head rolled to the feet of the mortal, loyal, unsuspecting Coconnas, who was next to die through no fault of his own. There it came to a stop with the glittering black eyes staring at Françoise.

In the tower across the square, the Duchess of Nevers put her arm against the window glass and her head on her arm. As far as Marguerite was concerned, the duchess was perfectly silent, but Marguerite could not hear the conversation that took place between the duchess and a dove on the windowsill. In her spirit body, Françoise was able to speak with her mind, even though the listening duchess could not respond in kind.

Indeed, Marguerite could not hear much through her sobs.

The duchess had to repeat her question to Marguerite three times: "Was there any promise the headman made to La Môle?"

Marguerite dabbed her eyes. "A promise?"

"Anything that he might have asked the executioner to do on his behalf? We should make sure his wishes are carried out."

Marguerite frowned. "What good could an executioner do a man after death? Oh, but wait. There was a promise that La Môle once asked of me. I thought it a morbid fancy, but what could I do but agree?"

"What indeed?" murmured the duchess, walking to her friend and putting her arm around her. "Tell me what it is, darling, and I will help you keep your promise."

"His beautiful head," the queen managed, before the tears came again.

"What about his head? I don't want to rush you, poor thing. But time may be of the essence."

"He made me promise that I would have it embalmed, and keep it with me forever. So that we should never be parted. He might have made the arrangements with the executioner. What must we do?"

The duchess tapped her fingernail against her chin and paced for a moment. "I am sure he did make the arrangements. We will be sent for when they are complete, or perhaps someone will make a delivery. I'm glad we talked about this now, my dear, so you will not be too shocked when that delivery arrives. We should get back to the Louvre, where you can rest. There is nothing more to see here, and no more support we can give to those two brave men."

After one more tearful embrace, the queen obediently left the room for the spiral staircase, but the duchess went to the wall to retrieve the shawl she had left behind on a little bench before the window. Not being in her spirit body with its ability to speak with the mind, she whispered aloud to the waiting dove.

"I should have considered this. I once heard a story of a vampire who managed to get himself revered as a local saint, whose relics did untold damage… The head of a vampire could do much mischief to one who keeps it. We must get that head out of the Louvre, as soon as possible after it arrives, which I suspect will be later today. Meet me in Marguerite's rooms tonight—you can get there from mine—hide behind the screen in that closet, where she once showed us the ruby necklace. The king has ordered his sister to go to a ball tonight, so she'll have to leave the head behind. One cannot carry a head to a ball."

HAVING NO MORE specific instructions than "tonight", Françoise waited for some time behind the screen in the Queen of Navarre's closet. This was a small room where Marguerite kept some personal objects and a few devotional tapestries, including one that obscured a carved wooden screen behind which there was a prayer stool and a crucifix.

During the last year while they were trying to stay safe from La Môle, Françoise had not gone to Mass, although she and Sainct Didier had met a few times at the Abbey of Montmartre for confession and spiritual guidance.

Now Françoise found herself kneeling at a queen's prayer stool, and whispering the words that had always made her feel as if she were lying in a field, gazing up at a limitless sky. She doubted, though—not whether her catechism was true, but whether that feeling amounted to a faith strong enough to let her use a crucifix or holy water against a vampire. Sainct Didier always discouraged trying because, he said, no weapon was less reliable than faith. To him, a fight was won or lost on precision and predictability; if one did the proper things in the proper order, and did not falter, one would prevail. But that, too, took a kind of faith: faith in oneself, and in the point of one's sword. Faith in the moment, that it would not betray you and leave you lying on the ground, staring up but seeing nothing at all.

After a while, her knees got sore.

Now that La Môle was dead and she was hiding in a closet

anyway, she was in her mortal body, wide awake, and it did not suffer kneeling for too long. All the same, it was a relief to be out in the world in her own flesh again. During her months of hiding, she had been in the spirit world more than not, and it was starting to have a strange effect on her, as if everything were at a distance, as if she wasn't sure what was real and what was not. She reached out and touched the wood screen with her fingertips. Her own body felt odd, disjointed and aching, as if it were a stranger's. The constant sleep seemed to have suspended not only her hunger and thirst but even, conveniently, her monthly courses. As if her body were a vessel she had put aside.

But no longer. La Môle was dead.

Françoise was standing, staring at the back of the tapestry through the screen, going over fencing sequences Chicot had taught her in her mind, when at last she heard the voices of two women in the next room. The duchess said something reassuring about going to the ball. The king had ordered his sister to go, to demonstrate that she was not in mourning for La Môle. So the duchess said that she would place the head in the little adjoining room, that the room would become a shrine.

A few minutes passed in silence. Then the duchess opened the door and told Françoise she could come out.

To Françoise's surprise, the duchess was holding not one but two velvet bags, each sagging with a similar large, round burden.

"One of these belonged to Coconnas," said the duchess, lifting it. "Poor man. I was very fond of him, you know. Not that I wanted his head. What does the headman expect me to do, kiss it? It is ludicrous and, well, frankly, it's upsetting."

"Then why did you take it?"

"Because if I did not, the queen mother would have used his brain for her fortune-telling, which is even more upsetting. She's been eager to get her hands on the brains of the condemned ever since someone told her they were more accurate than hens' livers or sheep's stomachs. No matter what poor creature one dissects, one only sees one's own mortality, if you ask me. But perhaps a vampire thinks of it differently. Come, we have work to do, and it is not going to be pleasant."

She handed Françoise one of the bags, which was of red velvet, tied with gold silk ribbon, embroidered around the neck with little seed pearls. In her own hands, the duchess kept an identical bag, but in blue velvet instead.

Françoise sniffed; she recognized one of the duchess's preparations.

"Yes," said the duchess, "I perfumed the bags, as one would, to counter the odour of embalming, and to counter somewhat whatever power La Môle's head might have. I think our Marguerite would have very bad dreams if she were to keep this with her. She might find herself doing things she did not intend. So we must get it out, without alerting or upsetting the queen. She knows that La Môle's head is in this one." And here the duchess lifted the red bag. "So we must switch the heads, and put the head of Coconnas into the red bag, and take the blue one with La Môle's out of this place."

The lifting of the bag exposed the underside of the duchess's sleeve, streaked with blood. It must have been a gruesome scene at the headman's workshop.

A thought occurred to Françoise. "But what if Queen Marguerite takes the head out to look at it?"

The duchess made a face. "Believe me, she won't. It is not pleasant. I have no desire to make Coconnas into a relic, despite my fondness, and she will feel the same, if the head in the bag is not exerting any unnatural power over her. No, she'll let it be. Perhaps I'll buy her a little casket or reliquary to put it in, and seal it up. I think she wants to forget about him, if she can. To make a life for herself with her husband. But as long as she thinks the head is here in the bag, she'll feel she's kept her promise. All right, Françoise, this has to be done."

She reached into the red bag and pulled the head out by the hair. La Môle's eyes bored into Françoise. There was a cruel smile on the thin, purple lips. His livid skin did not look as if it had ever been human. And yet, she remembered the young man he had been, when the pull of the company of blood was still weak on him.

Coconnas, despite never having been a vampire, did not look much better. Françoise cringed as she grasped his ginger hair. They fumbled a bit as they tried to keep the neck of the red bag open, each with a head in one hand, not wanting to put their bloody, stinking burdens down on anything. But at last, the head of Coconnas was in the red bag, and the head of La Môle in the blue.

The duchess said, "I must be here when the queen returns from the ball; she might keep her appearance as brief as possible, just to satisfy her brother. So I'm afraid you must be the one to deal with La Môle, Françoise. Take the head out of the palace as quickly as you can, go out to the fields, and burn it in a fire as hot as you can manage." She put down the velvet bag on top of a chest, rummaged in a drawer and pulled out a leather satchel that Queen Marguerite used to carry books. "Here, put it in this. Less conspicuous."

With the head of La Môle inside the velvet bag and the velvet bag inside the leather one, Françoise went out of the queen's apartments, through the guard room, and into a narrow room that led to a little oratory. It would be quiet at this time of night with the ball on, and beyond the oratory was a small stair that would take her down to an exit.

She was so fixated on getting the head out as quickly as possible that she nearly ran straight into a lone figure in black, coming out of the oratory.

"Well," said Catherine de' Medici. "Françoise de Montesquiou d'Artagnan, it has been too long since I saw you at the Louvre."

CHAPTER TWENTY-SEVEN

A Conversation at the Louvre

FRANÇOISE CURTSIED AND waited for the queen mother to walk past. But as Queen Catherine stepped past her, she stopped and turned her gaze on Françoise again.

"What do you have there, Mademoiselle d'Artagnan?"

Françoise had just thought up an answer to this question. "Her Majesty the Queen of Navarre was kind enough to give me one of her old petticoats."

"Was she? How out of character. Let's have a look and I'll tell you whether it will suit you. I am an excellent judge."

Françoise bowed her head, thinking quickly. "I'm afraid it's soiled, Your Majesty."

"Soiled? My daughter gave you a soiled petticoat?"

Françoise said nothing; explanations would merely sound like lies, while silence might suggest an unwillingness to criticize.

"I think perhaps you should show me nonetheless," said the queen mother.

Françoise was halfway through opening the leather bag before she became aware of what she was doing, and was able to stop herself. She had not felt the vampire's power—she had simply acted as Queen Catherine wanted her to act. And even now, with her hand on the closure, she knew it was futile. Queen Catherine would see everything sooner or later; she probably already knew what was in the bag. It would be easiest to get it over with.

Footsteps from a nearby room made Queen Catherine look up, and listen. Then she grabbed Françoise by one arm and pulled her into the oratory. Inside, it was dark, the only light coming from one candle beneath a triptych painted with figures of the Holy Family. A heavily shadowed crucifix in pale wood loomed overhead. Objects of faith could hurt vampires, and yet here was a vampire who went willingly into their presence, who even—perhaps—prayed there. The look of reverence on the queen mother's face as she glanced up at the figure of Christ was undeniable.

It was difficult to believe Queen Catherine was a vampire, even though Françoise knew it to be true. She looked now like what she was: a small, stout widow with sharp eyes and a determined set to her jaw. She had been through war and plague and betrayal, and she was still here.

"You are carrying something dangerous, I think," said Queen Catherine gently, closing the door of the oratory. "Let's have a look."

The queen mother opened the clasp of the leather bag and reached her hand within.

Then she screamed.

The smell of burning was immediate, and horrible. Françoise recoiled as the queen drew her hand out and held it up, blistered and blackened.

She'd been burned by the velvet bag, the one that the duchess had infused with her perfume, the perfume that burned vampires.

Françoise stared at the burned hand.

A small smile appeared on the queen mother's face.

"I think now we understand each other," Queen Catherine said. "You are a Benandanti. And you know what I am."

Françoise shook her head, warily.

The queen waved her burned hand, impatiently. "Come, come, I am a busy woman, and if you waste my time, I will put you down on the floor and drink from you until I am satisfied. It has been too long for me; life gets busy, you see. Do not tempt me. I see what you know; there is no use in playing games neither of us can win, and neither of us can lose. If you do not tell me what I wish to know now, then I will simply turn you into my creature once I have tasted you, and then you will answer all of my questions like a good girl."

Françoise swallowed, uncomfortably aware as she did so of how it made her neck move, and how the queen watched the movement.

"I can tell you nothing," she said.

"Oh, I don't think that's true. Tell me what it is like to be one of your kind. The *Good* Walkers, you call yourselves, rather arrogantly, I have always thought. Why do you hunt us?"

"It is my nature."

"Then we are both killers by nature."

"I do not kill. One cannot kill that which is already dead."

Catherine smiled. "My heart might not beat, but my soul is neither in heaven nor in hell, and so I am not dead. My soul is here, with you, in this room."

Again, she looked up at the cross.

"You believe," said Françoise, wondering.

"Of course I believe," the queen mother snapped. "I believe in one holy Catholic and apostolic Church. I acknowledge one baptism for the forgiveness of sins. I expect the resurrection of the dead, and the life of the world to come. I am a true Catholic, ruler of a Catholic country."

"I believe your son rules, not you."

Queen Catherine laughed sadly. "For the time being. But I am the one who has kept this country together, against many threats and dangers. I have turned their enemies into allies, one way or another. I have done my best by my children, but I cannot save them from their own mistakes and from God's will."

Her face looked utterly serene as she said this. All had gone according to plan. King Charles had touched the poisoned book. La Môle had been blamed for it and executed. Yet the queen mother did not look racked with guilt or grief. Perhaps she had known all along that her son was already doomed, and merely wanted to be rid of La Môle for her own purposes. Or perhaps she was simply devoid of maternal love. Looking at her face, Françoise could believe her to be that intelligent, or that cruel, or both.

"You think I do not love my children," said the queen softly.

Françoise was startled. No one had mentioned mind-reading among the talents that vampires could possess. She stilled her heart and tried to compose her face. If the queen mother could truly read any thoughts she liked, the Benandanti would have been destroyed long before now. It was foolhardy to invent anxieties; all Françoise could do was stand her ground, one way or the other.

"Your Majesty's desire to protect your children is spoken of throughout France," Françoise said, honestly and demurely.

"Oh, I'm sure," said Queen Catherine. She cocked her head. "You Benandanti are born with your talents, is that right?"

Françoise was uncertain how to answer this. "Some say so."

"You have never had any choice in the matter, then."

Françoise did not reply.

The queen mother shrugged and looked away. "I also had no choice when I was made one of the Malandanti. I was chosen to walk the path of grief and darkness. A mother's path. Nine times I have given birth. I lost one, my darling baby Louis, when he was still learning his first words; he used to say 'thank you' so prettily, even when he could say little else… that was the first death. His other brother and his older sister are gone now, too. Each of these deaths has taken a piece of my heart with it."

"I am truly sorry for Your Majesty's losses."

"Oh, but there are more. It was my ninth confinement that killed me, as well as my two youngest children. Twin girls. Jeanne was dead in the womb, or so they told me later, but I think she was not dead until they killed her, trying to get her out. Victoire lived for a short time. I bled and bled—I remember being cold, so very cold, and my heart galloping, and then… one of the attending midwives was an Italian, a spy for my cousin Cosimo de' Medici, who had orders not to let me die, at any cost. I did not know she was a Malandanti. When I awoke from my long, cold dream of death and she told me what she had done to me, the first thing I did was stake her through the heart."

Françoise stepped back.

"Childbirth is difficult," said the queen, as if this explained everything. "You will find out."

"You are telling me these things because you're about to kill me."

"Do you really think I can afford to waste my time? No, my girl, I am telling you these things in return for what you are telling me."

"I have told you nothing."

The queen mother put a fingertip to her cheek. "Every flutter of those exquisite eyelashes is eloquent. That is why I am telling you. But you are right. I will kill you, at some point. I may make you my servant, if you are lucky. I have only restrained myself until now because of certain curiosities I have about your condition."

She smiled, and her moment of self-congratulation and inattention gave Françoise the fraction of a second she needed. She pulled the velvet bag holding La Môle's head out and threw it at Queen Catherine's face, and in the resulting burning, she lunged at the queen, trying to hold the horrible object to her face.

But the queen pushed her back with one hand, so hard that Françoise flew against the back wall of the oratory. All her breath was taken from her. The crucifix fell loudly, heavily, to the floor.

The queen mother put her hands to her face, and laughed. "This burn will take some time to repair. I see it will be veils for me for the next few days, unless I want to go about as dust or bats, or perhaps a wolf with a scarred face. It was bravely done, Mademoiselle d'Artagnan. But I know how I will be destroyed, and it is not by you. I tell you this one mother to another."

Françoise went cold. "I am not a mother."

"Aren't you? My mistake."

She glanced down at the floor, where La Môle's head lay grey and grinning, half out of its velvet bag.

"So there was more in your bag than tricks to use against my kind," said the queen. "I thought I sensed something, when I first passed you… The gall La Môle had, to try something like this!"

The queen bent down and peered at the grotesque severed head. She sniffed then, and then hissed and jumped back as if bitten.

"Take it away," she said, waving her burned hand. "You are doing my daughter a service, and I will do you the service of letting you live. Go on, now. I don't like looking at that smug upstart any more than I did when his head was attached."

Warily, Françoise pushed the head back in the velvet bag, and then enclosed it in the leather one again.

"Your Majesty, your daughter knows nothing of this."

"Oh, of course she doesn't. But you're doing her a service, nonetheless. I do not want—"

There were rapid footsteps outside, and shouting. The queen mother whirled and opened the door to the oratory. A servant in livery stood there, hunched, afraid.

"The king," he gasped.

And then King Charles himself came running down the corridor, clad only in a long shirt, which had been white and was now drenched with blood.

His face was so covered in blood that it looked as if someone had removed his skin. Blood streamed from the corners of his eyes, from his nostrils, from his ears, from under his fingernails. Blood seeped into his half-open mouth, and he desperately tried to swallow it in between his screams. He left bloody footprints on the fine old carpet and splattered the panelled walls red as he ran toward his mother, screeching with pain.

"Go," the queen mother growled to Françoise, and yanked her by the arm, marched her out of the oratory toward the approaching king, then pushed her to one side, out of the way. "Go now, and do away with it, and know that I may not hesitate to act upon *my* nature the next time we meet."

CHAPTER TWENTY-EIGHT

The King is Dead; Long Live the King

STILL STINKING OF fire and fear, Françoise met the Duchess of Nevers in the Tuilieries, at the same spot where she had overheard her talking to Sainct Didier nearly two years before.

"Is it done?" the duchess asked, wrinkling her nose.

"The traitor is nothing but charred bone now, and that is buried deep."

"Good. And did he give you any trouble?"

"Trouble of what sort?"

"I don't know, exactly. Black feelings, urges…"

"No, nothing more than the usual black feelings and urges one feels in a city ruled by vampires." Françoise hesitated. "I did run into the queen mother, though. She saw the head, and when the bag burned her, she knew me for a Benandante."

The duchess put her hands to both cheeks. "What? Are you serious? Then you're not safe, Françoise."

"It's not me I'm worried about."

"What, did she guess anyone else's names? What about the head—you didn't tell her it came from me?"

Françoise shook her head. "Of course not. But she knows me, and she will track my movements when she can. I am now a danger to the Benandanti of Paris. I should leave."

The duchess paced. "Perhaps. But then again, perhaps we can use this. Let me talk to Sainct Didier. In the meantime, it's best if you stay away from us, and away from court. Perhaps it's best if you go to sleep for a while, now that the queen knows who you are. Poor thing, I know you just got out of hiding because of La Môle, and now this."

Françoise nodded curtly, gazing at a patch of lily of the valley waving white in the May sunshine. Nearly four months since she'd last spent a night with Chicot. If only she had someone else to ask, but the duchess was the only woman and Benandante she knew, the only person who might know the answer to the questions she had.

"I've noticed that when I spend a long time asleep, as I have during these last months before La Môle was caught, my courses do not come when I expect them."

The duchess nodded. "Yes. That's an upside, I suppose. And thank heaven, because I've spent months, even years that way when I needed to, and can you imagine waking up to those sheets?"

Françoise swallowed. "But I feel now as I do when my courses are about to arrive. My breasts ache, and my back, and, well, I wonder how one would know if, well, what I wonder is what the signs are of something else. I don't know much about it. No sisters."

"Something else?" The duchess looked at her sharply, and stepped in close, her voice low. "Françoise, do you mean that you're with child?"

She bit her lip. "I don't know."

"How long has it been? Since you last bled?"

"Several months. I think perhaps five months."

The duchess looked away, no doubt calculating how long it had been since Anjou went to Poland, taking Chicot with him.

"And it's been four months since I was with Chicot," Françoise added, miserably, getting it over with.

The duchess looked her up and down, and Françoise was uncomfortably aware that she was a little thicker than she had been, a little rounder and softer.

"Why didn't you say something sooner? These things are best mended early, you know."

"I had no idea. I thought it was just that I'd been sleeping."

"Yes, well, perhaps. You haven't felt the child quicken, have you? Any movement?"

"I'm not sure I would know if I had."

"You'd know. All right, there's only one thing for it. Let's go out to the fields. We need to get some barley to soak in your urine. In a few days, we'll see whether it grows."

THE SECOND DEATH of King Charles IX was, like his first, a matter of exsanguination. It was the judgment of God for the massacre of Saint Bartholomew's Day, people whispered. The king, for his part, went to his destruction screaming that it was all his mother's fault.

From Marguerite, the duchess learned that there was one moment when the king seemed to be his old self again, human and repentant. He had asked, in that moment, for his family to take care of his baby son, an illegitimate child just born to his mistress. But then the moment passed again, and he became a wild creature, trying to gather as much of the blood that seeped from his pores as he could, so he could feed it back into his own mouth. It must have felt to him that he was dying of thirst, and drowning, all at once.

Many rumours swept through the Louvre in the king's final hours. It was said that Ambroise Paré, the barber-surgeon, upon rushing into the king's chamber as the queen was rushing out, smelled a terrible odour of garlic. It came from a book that had been placed on the fireplace and was already charred beyond all recognition. Why would a book smell of garlic? The matter was easily explained by every know-it-all in the palace who would hasten to educate their listeners on the strange fact that burning arsenic has a very similar smell to garlic. The book was clearly poisoned. Well, what wasn't soaked with poison at the Louvre in those days?

The rumours came to Françoise third hand and fourth hand, as she had moved back in to the Hôtel de Guise. The duchess would not hear of her taking up her old position at La Belle Étoile, even had it been available. Françoise found herself being served fresh milk infused with herbs; the duchess seemed to have made up her mind about Françoise's condition, even though they would have to wait another day or two for the barley to sprout, if it was going to.

Three days after the conversation with the duchess, Françoise received a message from Sainct Didier to meet at the old stone cross at the corner of Rue Saint-Honoré and Rue de l'Arbre Sec, in the same area as La Belle Étoile. It was a busy crossroads, where even a vampire would have trouble murdering someone without being noticed. There was a public fountain there with running water. And, taking no chances, Sainct Didier set the hour of meeting at noon.

He embraced her warmly when they met under the sun, near the fountain. Françoise almost wondered whether he knew about the suspected pregnancy, but surely the duchess would never break confidence on such a matter. Anyway, he said nothing about it.

Instead, he told her he was proud of her for coming through an encounter with the queen mother unscathed. "I have been trying to ascertain what I can about her mood and possible intentions, but everything is changing hour by hour, as the king is near true death now."

"Do you think I should leave Paris? If her spies see me with you…"

"I think the fact that she let you live is interesting. A

living Benandante may be more tempting to her than a dead one. Perhaps that was why Alençon turned La Môle. The satisfaction of gaining that kind of control over one of our kind... I imagine the mother would have the same instincts in that regard as the son."

"You think she will try to turn me?"

"Perhaps. I think you must be fascinating to her."

"Then I am even more dangerous to you than I thought, my friend."

He shook his head. "Mademoiselle d'Artagnan, you forget that are much stronger than La Môle ever was. I speak of character, not of your sword arm, although I suspect the latter is not far from the mark thanks to your lessons with Chicot—yes, I know about those. Still, best you take care not to find yourself alone with the queen mother again, until we can see which way the wind blows."

"Is the king that close to death?"

"He may be dead already. He has named the King of Navarre as his heir."

"The King of Navarre! Rather than either of his own brothers?"

"Anjou is in Poland and Alençon is a rebel. But the queen mother did manage to convince King Charles to let his youngest brother out of jail so that he could come to the deathbed. The old snake wants to be sure her vampiric son is ready to claim the throne, despite his brother's wishes. I think it's unlikely they'll even let the King of Navarre live, never mind take—"

There was a commotion down the street toward the east, and they craned to see what it was. Too late. A group of horsemen came galloping past the cross, stirring up storms of dust in their wake. All that Françoise could see of them were five black cloaks lifted horizontal in the wind. They screamed, "France! France!" as they rode.

As the last of them rode past, the dust cleared enough that

she could see his face as he turned and looked at her.

Chicot. Chicot on horseback, riding as if the hounds of hell were after him. His gaze locked on her eyes, but he did not smile, and then he was gone.

Coughing from the dust, Françoise did not realize at first that Sainct Didier had been knocked down. She helped him to his feet, while he insisted that he was not hurt, that he had only fallen when he stepped back to get out of the way.

The calls of "France, France!" had subsided, but now a new call came from the direction of the Louvre, on the lips of every person in a window or on the street, passing from one to the other like a plague.

"Long live Henri III!"

Sainct Didier put his hand to his temple. "Then the king is dead," he whispered. "But what are they saying? Henri III? Then has Henri of Navarre been named king after all?"

"Not Henri of Navarre," said Françoise, the grim face of Chicot still before her eyes. "It was the Duke of Anjou and his men who knocked you down. Henri of Anjou has come back from Poland to take the throne of France."

Wide-eyed, Sainct Didier turned to look down the street in the direction of the Louvre, as if he could get some knowledge from the sight of crowds spilling into the streets, proclaiming the new king. The handsome and beloved Henri of Anjou, the most tolerant and the wisest of the sons of Catherine de' Medici, had claimed France for himself.

And he had brought back his man Chicot with him.

In her belly, for the first time, the baby kicked. The duchess had been right. The feeling, though entirely new to Françoise, was unmistakable.

CHAPTER TWENTY-NINE

The Mignons

THE NEW KING required the members of the court to assemble, which included the Duchess of Nevers and her ladies. It might have been wise for Françoise to give her regrets and pretend to be ill; she should avoid the queen mother, after all. But she was desperate to know what was happening, and what might happen next. She wanted to see it with her own eyes. Anyway, she told herself, there was no real danger in a crowd.

So Françoise stood with everyone else in the ballroom at the Louvre, where the whispers bounced off the milky floor and walls. On one end, four tall marble women held up the musician's balcony, and it was on this balcony that Henri III appeared, surrounded by a half-dozen Mignons in velvet and silk.

They had returned to France even more lovely than they left. Curled lips and curled hair, the most beautiful men Françoise had ever seen. What had they seen in Poland to give their backbones confidence, their eyes such cynicism? They stared out upon the assembled crowd with the mistrust of bodyguards and the cool disinterest of courtesans.

To see Chicot among their number, vindicated, protected and protecting, might have given her a sense of pride or relief, if she had found a way past overwhelming wonder. Françoise had always found Chicot beautiful, but the arrangement of angles and shadows in his face now captivated her. She felt she could stare into his dark eyes forever. The deeper she fell into them, the further there would be yet to fall.

Chicot stared back. Over the heads of all the glittering ladies and gentlemen of the court, he stared fixedly at Françoise, with a curve to his lip that was not quite a smile, his brow lowered slightly, his gaze perfectly steady. They held whole conversations, whole trysts, just staring at each other. It was indecent. It was irresistible.

It stopped only when the queen mother swept past her, up the central corridor of the ballroom in her customary black, her veil pushed back off her face. No scars on that face, now. She must have had methods for healing them.

And she must not have shared those methods with her youngest son, or else he wanted to keep his scars. Alençon walked behind his mother insolently, his face now bearing not only the marks of childhood smallpox but also the pits made when the duchess had pecked at him in the Holy Innocents cemetery. He did not look at Françoise as they passed. Like his mother, he stared straight ahead, and up, toward the new king.

King Henri III laughed at the sight. "How do you like being let out of prison, brother?"

Alençon made a sweeping bow. "I am at your service, Your Majesty."

"No, you're not. You're at your own. You've been drawing all the malcontents in France to your side, hoping to push me off the throne and take it for yourself."

"Who has been saying such things?" Alençon objected.

"Don't take me for a fool," the king snapped. "In fact, even a fool can see what you are. Isn't that right, Chicot?"

"I see a man whose thirst for blood will be sated by his friends or his enemies, and he cares not which," said Chicot, laconically.

"There, you see?" The king said, gesturing toward Chicot. "My fool sees through your smiles, even if the fools who follow you do not. They are risking their necks, and for no reason. There is no cause for rebellion in my France. From this day forward, France will be a country where any man can worship as he likes."

"Toleration has always been our policy," said the queen mother.

The king raised one finger. "It was *your* policy, mother, once upon a time. Until you needed blood to placate your creations, and then you chose to sacrifice peace and tolerance along with thousands of your subjects. Or, forgive me, my brother's subjects. It is so easy to forget that you did not wear the crown when he did your bidding. But no longer. Your rule is over."

"Your Majesty will raise up men based on the measure of their... merit, and nothing else," murmured Chicot.

Nobody laughed, until the king did, and then everyone did. The queen mother was the exception. With a sour expression, she protested: "My son, I wish only—"

"Be quiet, serpent!" Henri interrupted. "I do not need anything from you now. Go and live in whichever one of your new houses suits you best. But Alençon, you must not leave Paris. And I will not hesitate to put you in irons again if I hear one word of sedition."

There was silence as the queen mother stared up at the son she had refused to turn, her best beloved son, the one she had not wanted to mar. Somehow, she had lost him anyway, and she knew it.

There was no reflection or sadness on Alençon's face, only the same resentment he had always worn for his older brothers. Now he twisted it into an evil smile and bowed his head, no doubt thinking he could do as much damage to his brother's position in Paris as outside it.

The king took one more moment to stare at his brother, then clapped his hands once. "Now, we will drink to the memory of King Charles IX."

IN AN INSTANT, everyone in the crowd seemed to acquire a destination—the goblets on the tables at one side of the room, or someone higher on the social ladder than themselves. Françoise had nowhere to go. She kept her dagger in her sleeve, and her eye on Queen Catherine, who was in close conversation with the Cardinal of Lorraine.

The new king himself was embracing his sister, Marguerite. And there was her husband beside her; the King of Navarre hadn't yet been killed after all, despite the rumours, and despite the long efforts of Queen Catherine. The man must have been charmed. Sainct Didier was talking with one of the Mignons, who was showing him the hilt of his sword, and the duchess was flirting with a duke, who was not her husband.

Everyone moved like the figures on a clock, in a pattern Françoise could only watch, and could not seem to join. She felt like the only fixed point in the universe, rooted like a tree, or like a frightened hare.

Then she felt someone looking at her.

Chicot's expression was the old familiar one again: amusement, curiosity, kindness… but with something new, some worldliness that she did not recognize. It frightened her and fascinated her. The idea that the man whose touch she had already known so many times might touch her again as if he were a stranger—that thought played in her head and drove everything else out. He strode toward her, his hand at his hilt, and put one arm around her waist.

It was not the sort of kiss one ought to have in public.

When Françoise pulled away, breathless, she said, "People will stare."

"Let them," he whispered in the hollow of her neck. "I have nothing to fear. The king has made me his jester."

"His jester! What, shall you perform antics like the queen's trained bears?"

He pulled away from her and grimaced. "He likes the fact that I tell the truth. I am always at his side."

She nodded. "I didn't mean anything by it. I was only surprised."

"Many things have changed since I last saw you."

She swallowed. "That they have. Might we find somewhere private to talk?"

He traced the side of her cheek with his fingertip. "I cannot leave the king's presence without permission. He needs me, Françoise. Things are not as they were. You and I cannot marry."

He said it so baldly, without any inflection at all, without any preparation. She was speechless for a moment.

Then she said, "Surely His Majesty would permit—"

There was a tumult at the entrance to the ballroom, and it drew every eye, including Chicot's. For a moment, he was like an animal himself, tense, on alert, sniffing the air. He drew his sword so swiftly and with such a flourish that a woman nearby almost did not jump back in time. Then Chicot walked down the length of the ballroom, his sword catching the pale light from the windows, and the crowd parted before him.

Someone yelled, "For God and Henry of Navarre!"

At the entrance, a man in a fine black doublet and a wide ruff aimed an arquebus, rather shakily, at the king.

Chicot's sword ran straight through the intruder's gut. Then Chicot raised up his skewered victim and kept walking, right out of the ballroom, as people scattered. Blood flew in a fine spray onto the marble floor.

Françoise ran after him, because where there was one man with an arquebus, there might be another, and Chicot's courage could get him into trouble.

In the empty anteroom, Chicot had put his victim back down and was pulling his sword out, with one foot against the man's chest.

Then the sword slashed against the traitor's neck. Another spurt of blood.

Chicot's sword clattered on the ground.

Chicot himself knelt by the dying man, put his mouth to his neck, and drank greedily.

It did not come as a surprise to Françoise, who stood like a block of ice and watched her lover drink the blood he needed. How he had been turned in Poland, she did not know, but some part of her had suspected since she watched him ride past her in the street. He, and the new king, and all the Mignons, had been changed, and not by Catherine de' Medici.

Everything that Françoise was as a Benandante—life, growth and nature—rebelled at the sight of Chicot on his knees, lapping at the man's blood. Chicot should never be on his knees to anyone, except possibly to her. He was greater than he had been, but he was also lesser. A slave to blood. And hers no longer.

She came close to vomiting on the marble floor. That would not have been any worse than what that floor had already seen since its construction, and what it would see as the night wore on. But she managed to keep her stomach from betraying her, as she walked toward Chicot and picked up the sword of which he had once called her master. Slowly, deliberately, she pointed it at his back, right where his heart would be.

Her hesitation was only a moment, but it was enough. Chicot was faster now. He was on his feet, one gloved hand over hers on the hilt, squeezing, the other around her neck, his eyes on fire and his mouth a snarl. The point of the blade was just to the side of his body. She no longer had control of it. The blood of a stranger dripped down his chin, over the little fashionable beard, so fashionable. She wanted to lick it off, even now.

She let go of the hilt, giving Chicot his sword back, tilting her face up to his, stretching her neck. Stepping in close to him, she let herself enjoy the feeling of his gloved hand pressing on her pulse. A gentle pressure now, a lover's pressure.

"You really would have destroyed me," he whispered. His voice held awe and sadness, but a look of triumph and possession was crossing his face.

"My love," she said as best she could despite his hand around her throat, "you have already been destroyed."

Her dagger entered just below his red leather jerkin, below the velvet doublet beneath, up into his guts as far as his lover could send it, but not yet as far as his heart. His grip loosened on her throat as his eyes went wide.

The duchess was pulling on her other hand, yanking her so hard she left the dagger in Chicot's belly.

Françoise briefly had an impression of a great dark shape behind in the air: her lover's sire, the king, protecting his own. But whether he was distracted by some other target, or too concerned about helping his injured minion, or whether he simply did not care enough, King Henri did not follow them for long.

CHAPTER THIRTY

By this time the duchess [illegible] Margarethe's apartment [illegible] servants [illegible] husband [illegible] safety [illegible]

The duchess [illegible] secret door [illegible] room where Saint [illegible] they were [illegible] and no windows [illegible] moment.

The duchess [illegible] each sat on the bed [illegible]

Saint [illegible] his [illegible] Catherine [illegible] another [illegible] rebellious [illegible] whom Catherine [illegible]

CHAPTER THIRTY

Blood in the Louvre

BY THE TIME the duchess and Françoise made it to Queen Marguerite's apartments, Sainct Didier had joined them. No servants were there to interfere; the Queen of Navarre and her husband had moved their household elsewhere for their own safety, even before the bloodshed began.

The duchess pressed the two carvings that opened the secret door, and then they were through, into the little room where Sainct Didier and Françoise had slept while they were in hiding. Two small beds, a chair and table, and no window. It was as safe a place as any, for the moment.

The duchess took the chair, while Sainct Didier and Françoise each sat on the bed they had occupied, as if by habit.

Sainct Didier pulled off his cap and ran his fingers through his thinning hair, looking exhausted. "It seems clear that Catherine did not turn this son herself. Could he have another sire from Catherine's brood? Perhaps if his sire was rebellious… or perhaps one of the older vampires of Paris whom Catherine has not yet exterminated."

Françoise shook her head. "I do not believe he was turned before he left. He was turned in Poland."

By "he", she meant Chicot, but also Henry. She had seen them both before they travelled east, and she would swear they had not been vampires then.

Sainct Didier looked pensive. "I know little about the vampiric tribes of Europe beyond the Malandanti. I have fought mainly in Piedmont, in Liguria, Provence, Tuscany, Rome. But Henriette, your lands lie on the roads to the east."

Françoise let her confusion show on her face; the duchy of Nevers lay south of Paris.

The duchess caught her expression, and said, as wearily as her comrade: "My friend, what he means is that I have been the Countess of Rethel in my own right, under one name or another, for more than three hundred years. A long way from Poland even so, but I do remember some travellers' tales. At one point long ago, when Hungary and Poland were ruled by a single king, a group of vampires called the Izcaci roamed from the Baltic all the way down to the Adriatic, and had some skirmishes with the Malandanti and the Strigoi. But then there was that revolt in Transylvania, and we heard nothing more of the Izcaci."

"It seems they still exist," said Sainct Didier. "Whoever sired Henri also turned his Mignons, or else Henri turned them himself. Françoise, what can you tell us about Chicot?"

What indeed? Where to begin? She felt too weary and heartsore to speak. Every choice they had made seemed to stretch out before her like a parade of ghosts, unchanging, relentless, set in their purpose. When she finally spoke, it sounded more petulant than she had intended. "I can tell you he was no vampire until we urged him to go to Poland, to stay close to Anjou. And now Anjou is King Henri and the father of my child is a vampire."

"The father of your child!" Sainct Didier sat up straight. He looked at Françoise and then at the duchess, who nodded.

Sainct Didier rubbed his temple. "But was he already... the children of vampires and mortals are said to have certain gifts..."

"I do not wish to disappoint you," said Françoise coldly, "but Chicot was a mortal himself when we last spent a night together."

"And what are your plans for the child, Françoise?" the duchess asked gently.

"To bring it into this world and keep it safe. And I swear that I will see that done."

When the screams had ceased, the three Benandanti walked out of the secret chamber and walked, room to room, back through the Louvre to survey the damage and the danger.

On a great marble staircase, several bodies sprawled. Blood was dripping down the steps. The attackers were nowhere to be seen, but their handiwork was clear. Red wounds on bruised necks, white ruffs torn aside, stained, ripped.

All of the dead were wearing velvet and brocade. These new vampires did not use the darkest streets of Paris as their hunting grounds; they used the Louvre itself. The Izcaci drank the blood of the rich and did not care who knew about it.

Françoise found it hard to move her heart to condemn it. She had seen the handiwork of the Malandanti all over Paris. The cowards who fed on orphan infants, who fed on and discarded men and women the way their families had always fed on the stags and boars of their fine estates. Perhaps it was time that blood was shed on marble and silk for a change.

But the Duchess of Nevers replaced the ripped fabric of a woman's torn bodice with reverence and affection. She had known this woman, whose blood still dripped warm out of her neck, whose eyes stared at the painted ceiling.

"This is civil war," she said. "France will be unstable with two tribes of vampires fighting at the top, and many will die because of it."

"Perhaps we should let them fight," Françoise said. She felt cold, distant, as if she were watching herself from a distance. Any one of these men and women might have been killed by Chicot. She could almost see the curiosity in his eyes as he sampled them.

"If we could let them fight without any harm to the innocent, and to us, that would be one thing," said Sainct Didier. "But two tribes of vampires, even if they hate each other, means twice as many killers loose, and they will recruit more and more to their ranks, until they turn this city into a walking mass grave. The way to exterminate vampires is not to simply bring in different vampires. Besides, Françoise, you know we cannot let Chicot roam free, for our own safety."

He said it so coldly, so plainly.

"Perhaps he will let us be," she objected, weakly. She remembered how he had pulled her to him, as if his will were all that mattered. "He doesn't know about the child."

The duchess shook her head. "You saw what happened with La Môle. Chicot knows too much about our plans, our safe places. He is already dead, Françoise, and the question is whether we honour the man he used to be, or whether we let sentimentality destroy us. And if we are destroyed, there will be no one to protect the people from the vampires."

The smell of blood threatened to overcome her, and she leaned against a tapestried wall, tried to stop the world from moving underneath her. The fact was that she was struggling to have faith that this world would ever be any less bloody. When was the last time she had felt hope? Perhaps in the Holy Innocents cemetery, watching Ruggieri's beam of light making a king writhe in pain. She did not know how to rid the world of evil. But she could at least stand in the way of some of those who made it multiply. And perhaps that would free her of the terrible pain in her heart.

Françoise put her hand on her belly to steady herself and soothe the rolling movements of her child. Then she nodded.

"When it comes to Chicot, I do not wish to be involved," she said, hearing her own voice as if from a great distance. "I will go somewhere safe to have my child, and I wish to know nothing."

"Good, then that is settled," said Sainct Didier. He stepped gingerly around one of the dying aristocrats. "But we cannot fight them all at once, the Izcaci and the Malandanti. We need to find a way to pull them in, one after the other. Like fish in a net. Izcaci or Malandanti, they're all linked to their sires."

"But to whom is Henri linked?" the duchess asked.

"He is linked to Queen Catherine," Françoise responded dully. "She may not be his sire, but she is his mother, and that has to count for something."

Few people could send a message to the queen mother summoning her to a meeting and expect her to comply, but Françoise d'Artagnan, it seemed, had become one of them.

They met in the Tuilieries gardens, designed by Catherine herself in more peaceful years, but abandoned, or put on hold, as she built herself darker places to hide in while she desperately orchestrated her purges and massacres. On open ground, they could speak privately, watched from afar; Sainct Didier and the duchess were watching, and Catherine doubtless had her own supporters somewhere near.

The real reason Catherine had abandoned the gardens, Françoise suddenly understood, was that they held no appeal or benefit to her now. What good was walking in the sun to a vampire? Fountains irritated them, as did many of the flowers. This, the queen mother's own garden, was not neutral ground; it was ground that favoured Françoise.

And yet, the queen mother came. She was veiled in black, as the sky was clear.

"You pique my curiosity," said Catherine. "I warned you that I might kill you, and then you sent me an invitation."

"I wish to open negotiations. We have a common enemy."

The queen was taken aback, then amused, then disdainful. "The Benandanti wish to make an alliance with the Malandanti? Oh, that would amuse me if the times were not so irritating. You presume too much. And you risk too much. It is enough to make me wonder whether your true purpose is something else." The queen stepped closer and put one fingertip to Françoise's collarbone, and traced it down, over her heart. It made Françoise's breath catch. "I think perhaps you take this risk because you are eager to become one of my kind. Perhaps you wish to meet your lover on his own terms. Will he not do you the honour of turning you himself? Not very gallant of him."

"I have not asked," said Françoise, keeping her tone and her thoughts even, letting the queen mother talk.

"Probably best to wait until you give birth. The child should have a chance to grow before it is turned. But do not wait too long. Learn from my mistake. And keep it close in the meantime. Never let it out of your control."

Françoise asked the question that had been weighing on her. "How did you know that I was with child?"

The queen mother laughed. "Oh, my dear, after you are turned, you will learn to see the world differently. Every heartbeat calls to you. I cannot explain how wonderful it is, when you learn that we are all one, when you hear the music of the blood that connects us. When you start to understand that there is no border between death and life. God made us to rot, just as he made us to rut. Creation requires destruction."

In her ears, Françoise heard a roar like that of the ocean or the mountain winds. She squeezed her eyelids shut and it faded. Nearby, she could smell spring roses. The world was being born again, as it was every year, and always would, whether it was populated by monsters or not.

But the queen mother kept speaking, in a low voice, a lover's voice. "Your eyes and ears will open. Every part of you will open. And you will look upon your old life as if you'd been a prisoner, shut away from the reality of the beautiful world."

Françoise opened her eyes. "If life is a prison to everyone who is not a monster, then you kept your son Anjou—Henri—a prisoner. But he found his own way out."

The queen spread her hands, like a benevolent madonna. "What choice did I have? All vampires are resentful and fractious; they cannot be loved, only controlled. And my son François, I can control. I am his sire. Henri has taken another path, and doomed himself. An Izcacus! I did not foresee such a thing. Nostradamus, Ruggieri—they did not show me this." Behind the black lace the queen mother's mouth was a taut line.

"No man can see the future clearly."

The queen mother made an expression that showed she was considering this. "Ruggieri could. In the old days. But I didn't want to listen. He could always see what I did not want to see. Perhaps I should let him out of his dungeon."

It was difficult to think clearly in Queen Catherine's presence. Françoise felt a thought trailing behind the conversation, tugging on her hem, and it seemed important. She bit her lip, let it catch up, and then she felt it grip her.

"Your Majesty," she began, a sudden attack of nerves pushing her back into forms and niceties. "You said you could tell that I was pregnant because of your gifts as a vampire. Then would every vampire—"

The queen waved her hand to interrupt. "Oh, my dear, we can all learn to see such things if we take the time, but most will not. Like all creatures, some of us are more observant than others. It takes practice for a vampire to understand what they're seeing, to sort all the beating hearts into their places. Some never learn that skill. Some are not interested in anything but their own next meal. So, if you are wondering whether all my kind would see the truth as plainly as I have, the answer is no. There are many reasons I am their queen, and they are my servants."

Françoise nodded. "You guessed correctly that the father is a vampire."

"Oh, there was no guessing about it. Everyone in the hall saw you and Chicot embracing. If he said nothing about the child, I think you can take it that he does not yet know. But my dear, everyone will see the truth soon enough, whether vampire or mortal."

"I will go away for my confinement. I have friends who are making arrangements."

"You are telling me a great deal about your plans."

"Yes. To show you that I am here in good faith. Do not dismiss the possibility of an arrangement with the Benandanti. We are ready to make a truce. If your kind leave our kind alone, we will do you a great favour."

"And what is that?"

"We will help you destroy King Henri," Françoise said, standing up straight. "He will be watching you, expecting the blow… and it may come from an entirely different direction. You do not need to be a king's sire to hold the power of life and death over him. You only need to be a queen, who makes allies, who makes plans, who will use any piece on the board when it becomes necessary."

The queen mother turned away from her, walking briskly, like any queen considering a question of state or family politics. At last, she turned back, sharply. "If your kind is attacking the Izcaci, they will attack your lover too."

"That is not your concern."

"Oh, but I like Chicot. I wasn't even planning on killing him, unless he got too close." She laughed sharply. "I did kill one of his toys once, you know. Henri gives his heart away too easily.

He could learn from *you*. Not everyone is able to harden their heart so quickly. That is something you and I share, it seems. But it took me a long time to learn to do it. A long time, and several civil wars, and betrayals, and so much grief. What was it for you?"

But Françoise had never hardened her heart. She had opened it to the world, that night when she left home, to settle a matter of honour. And in opening it, it was no longer entirely her own to do with as she chose.

"We have our arrangement," she said coldly. "You will leave my friends alone, and they will help you and Alençon defeat Henri."

CHAPTER THIRTY-ONE

Montmartre

FRANÇOISE WENT INTO hiding once more. This time, she did not wish to go into the spirit world. Knowing that her body was growing a child, it felt strange to leave it, even when she was asleep. Whenever she tried, she found herself anxious.

At the Benedictine abbey at Montmartre, she was met at the door by a middle-aged, black-habited nun who greeted Sainct Didier with a severe nod.

"When the time comes, Sister Marie will help you," said Sainct Didier. "She knew Sister Anne, and she can be trusted."

"I don't know how to thank you for this," Françoise said.

"Nonsense," said Sister Marie, taking her small bag with a strength that her small frame belied. "This is God's house. We are due no thanks."

The few months Françoise spent at the abbey would have been the most peaceful of her life, if it had not been for the ache in her back, the acid in her throat and the bruises on her hips from trying to find a comfortable position on her side in the narrow bed. Getting up from her knees became an awkward ordeal, and she was on her knees more than she had ever been.

The nuns were not cruel, but they did not admit the possibility of any life within their walls except a life of piety and simplicity.

They did not ask questions about the child. Françoise was told that she had to behave in a way that showed good moral character, or else she would be asked to leave. The evidence of her belly, apparently, did not stand against her in the eyes of the Benedictine sisters, who had no doubt met many young mothers before.

One day as they were carding wool, she said to Sister Marie, "I think I will call him Charles, if he's a boy. Charlotte, if she's a girl."

"After the late king?" the old nun asked.

"No. After a stable boy who was kind to me." She noticed the nun's expression, and laughed. "Not *that* kind to me. I barely knew him, in fact, but he deserves to be remembered. He deserved to live, and be happy, and have children of his own."

The summer was hot, or perhaps it just felt that way to her.

She was grateful for a breeze on an early September afternoon as she worked in the garden. With her belly, she could not help the hearty Sister Marie as she spread mulch around the roses. But Françoise used shears to harvest the first batch of rose hips for making jelly and medicines. Even the slight bending was enough to make her back twinge. It took her some time to notice that the cramps were coming and going, and getting worse.

Despite the fact that the experienced and competent Sister Marie had been planning to be at her side for months, she suddenly felt that she must get out of the abbey. She wanted to be out in the fields, like a wild creature, where she could take care of herself and her child without interference. She could not say why, but some instinct was driving her to leave the abbey.

She paused and put her hand to her back.

Sister Marie looked at her questioningly, raising one perfect nut-brown brow. She was the tenth child of a noble family; she had not seen many births until she came to the convent. Now she was an expert.

Françoise smiled. "Just stretching. But I could use a walk, and these roses could use some lime. I'll go down to the quarry and fetch some."

By then, her expertise with plants was well known, and Sister Marie did not question her judgment about the roses. But she looked concerned, her always-flushed cheeks even pinker than usual.

"On your own?"

"I still have a few weeks yet before this baby comes, and walking will do me good."

Sister Marie looked uncertain. "Just take care not to slip on those pathways."

"I'll be careful, and I'll return long before dark."

She did not return before dark.

HOW ALONE FRANÇOISE felt in that barley field, as the afternoon wore on. The baby was early, and coming fast. The pain tore her in two and she knelt in the field, grasping at stalks of barley, writhing and moaning. She drank from the flask she had taken, small sips. For a long time, she stifled her screams, as it might bring passers-by, who would alert the nuns, and she did not want to be touched or talked to by anyone. But a moment came, just at sunset, when she could do nothing but scream, and scream, and scream.

Someone took her hand.

She rubbed her eyes and looked into Chicot's face.

How strange it was to see a vampire look frightened. She would have thought it impossible. He was frightened, and he adored her, with an adoration that would be eternal and would brook no challenge.

"I am here now," he said. "Whatever you want you shall have."

She shook her head, tears running down her face. "Not whatever I want."

He was looking down at her belly, at the muddle tangle of her skirts. "You would have kept this child from me." Then back at her face, as he squeezed her hand. "And how can I blame you? But I swear to you, Françoise, I would not harm either one of you. I can be strong. I am stronger than you know."

She pulled him to her and kissed him hard, biting his lips so that she would not scream, and then pulling away in terror that her teeth might have cut him, that she might drink of him without meaning to, that she would turn—and would it be so bad, after all? To be with him forever, to let go of all the worry and self-doubt?

The pain racked her and she bore down, bringing their child into the filthy world, scrabbling at her lover for some kind of release and grounding.

"Come on, little one," Chicot said, putting his head on Françoise's shoulder, lending her all his strength.

She tried to remember the sight of him lapping at the blood of a woman on the marble stairs of the Louvre. But no image would present itself. There was nothing in the world except this field, and his cold hand in her hot one, and the child.

The child who was breaking her apart.

It was childbirth that had turned Queen Catherine into a vampire. All that blood; Françoise could feel it hot on her legs.

She leaned back on her elbows, and Chicot went down by her knees, guided his child into the world as she screamed and pushed. She could call it nothing but a miracle when the pain resolved itself into a stinging, a cramping, an exhaustion, and Chicot was holding their child, their wriggling crying child, who had come into the world veiled, wrapped, inside the caul.

Another Benandante.

Chicot regarded the little writhing mortal curiously. "He will have the powers of your kind."

Overhead, a hawk flew in a slow circle.

"Give him to me," she breathed, and took her child, unwrapped him, put him to her breast. She scrabbled in the nearby dirt for the garden shears she'd taken with her, and pushed Chicot away so she could cut the cord herself. She wanted him nowhere near her bloody body, or the child's.

But it was too late. Chicot's forearms were streaked with her blood. He held them up as if regarding a miracle, and sniffed one and then the other, rapt. He seemed to have forgotten Françoise herself, as he put the tip of his tongue to one streak of blood, and closed his eyes.

She closed her eyes too, giving herself a moment of grief for the man she had known, a moment to rest her aching, teary eyes as her child wept and she wept.

When she opened her eyes, Chicot was weeping too.

A vampire, weeping. It shocked all words, all thoughts, out of her for a moment. He was rubbing the blood off his forearms, using the ends of his shirt, and wetting it by wiping the tears off his own face. Water. They needed water, to clean her, and the child.

She looked at him rubbing the blood that he desired off his own flesh until it tore, this man who had fought to survive, this man with all his questions, this man who had held her baby in his hands and adored him.

Long ago in the faraway hills, Françoise had been saved by a giant with a long beard, wielding a stalk of yarrow.

Now, the same figure strode across the twilit barley field of Montmartre and swung a sword, festooned with yarrow, in a wide arc.

She looked up at the sky, and saw the hawk: the duchess, in her spirit form.

They were coming for Chicot.

Sister Marie had told them, and somehow, they had got word to Chicot. Someone he trusted must have told him that his beloved was giving birth to their child, in a field in Montmartre. Perhaps it was even Queen Catherine herself, keeping her bargain with the Benandanti. King Henri would not be their first target after all. They had not been honest with Françoise. They had tricked her, used her and her newborn baby as bait, because they had not known on which side her loyalties would lie.

And neither had she, until this moment.

"It is a trap," she whispered.

Chicot stopped rubbing the blood away, froze, and looked her square in the eye with an understanding that broke her heart.

By the time Sainct Didier's sword swung, Chicot had whirled to meet it with his own, and bits of yarrow went flying.

At her breast, the baby cried. She tried to soothe him—pulled down her bodice and offered him the nipple, but he searched for it like a blind mole. She was distraught, sore, barely able to see from exhaustion.

Overhead, the hawk dropped a stone from its feet, near Chicot. A warning? It was not like the duchess to miss. The hawk then returned to a field to get another, and dropped it. Again, it fell short of the mark. Was it caution? Where was the duchess who had pecked at Alençon's face? Or was she merely trying to distract Chicot?

Meanwhile, Chicot and Sainct Didier were fighting each other for control, their swords flowing from defence to attack to defence so quickly that Françoise could barely make sense of their positions and decisions. Sainct Didier took a step back and Chicot followed—and screamed.

The stones the duchess had dropped had formed some kind of barrier.

Upon hearing his father's cry, the baby cried louder.

Chicot, resentful, aimed his point at Sainct Didier's knee.

Once, in one of their lessons when they were falling in love, Chicot had showed her one of Sainct Didier's axioms. The swordmaster used to say that the best counter to a low strike was not to try to bat the sword away, but to simply move the leg out of danger while taking the opportunity to strike from above.

Chicot, it seemed, remembered this too.

When Sainct Didier went in for the strike to Chicot's body, Chicot's sword flicked upward and drove straight through Sainct Didier's abdomen.

All the sound of the world went silent for a moment and Françoise looked at Sainct Didier's astonished face, at Chicot's hideously triumphant one, and then at the face of Sister Marie approaching barefoot, in her human body, in her nun's habit, walking toward Chicot from behind.

She was holding a long ash stake, of the kind they used in the garden to tie up unruly branches. It was held with the point facing Chicot, as if Sister Marie were a jousting knight, and not a stout woman about to drive a piece of wood through the rotting corpse of the living dead. For that was what Chicot was; his heart no longer beat; how could it love? She tried to tell herself this, tried not to breathe in and steel herself, tried not to show her horror and grief.

She must have failed.

Chicot glanced at her, then, as if he saw what she saw, and whirled around, his sword swinging.

Sister Marie's head went flying off her body and came to rest in the field beside Françoise.

At that, Françoise screamed again, in a throat already hoarse, and Chicot looked at her with an expression of dull, cynical resignation that was even more painful than his look of triumph a moment before. Sainct Didier lay writhing on the ground, his breath coming ragged, blood seeping from his abdomen onto the dark ground. There was blood everywhere, but Chicot could not reach the bodies, imprisoned as he was in the circle of stones the duchess had dropped. What potion had she painted on them? Or perhaps it was magic from a sorcerer, Ruggieri or someone else. Another plan that no one had told Françoise about.

A vast shadow appeared in the sky and Françoise drew back, clutching her baby. Another vampire?

But as it flew closer, she saw that it was the duchess, still in the form of a hawk, and this time she was carrying not stones but a blood-red cloak.

She dropped it over Chicot.

He fell to the ground as if it were made of lead. Françoise could not see him, and he made no sound. Another of the duchess's tricks. She had been wrong to doubt her.

A whine on the air, out of nowhere, and a crossbow bolt went through the hawk's wing and she dropped to the ground.

For a moment, Françoise looked around at everyone she had once known and loved, battered and wounded.

She lay her baby down and scrabbled for the little pot of salve she kept in her apron pocket, the golden salve that she had brought with her from Gascony. Her nurse Sancia had believed it could cure anything.

On Sainct Didier's wound, the salve mingled with the blood as she layered it on, praying with every ounce of her strength that it would be enough. His betrayal would never heal, but she had no salve for that.

Sainct Didier took one long loud breath and then spoke bitterly, wetly. "You warned him," he said. "After everything, you warned him."

"And you lied to me. You put me in danger, and my baby, too."

He attempted a short laugh. "Danger? What do you think we are doing, Françoise? Oh, you are a pathetic creature. It would have been better for you and for us if you had just let him turn you immediately."

"I have not turned."

"There is more than one way for evil to take root in the heart."

He coughed at the end of this little speech. Françoise turned and looked for the duchess; the hawk had vanished, and now there was a woman, holding a wounded arm.

"Do not come near me," the duchess said to her. "I will kill you myself if you do. I would have already if it were not for the child."

The child, who was lying in the field, moving its arms and legs, as if it were any cot. She took him into her arms and rocked him for a moment, then stumbled to her feet. She had to get out. For the sake of her son, she had to find a way out of this field, before her friends decided to kill her after all, before the wielder of the crossbow found her.

It took a great effort to get to her feet, every muscle in her stomach screaming, while she clasped her baby close to her breast. But she had only taken three steps when Henri III, King of France, came out of nowhere. He stood over her and smiled.

Was it Chicot who had told him where he was going? Or perhaps Queen Catherine? If the queen mother, had she sent Henri here to ambush the Benandanti, or to be ambushed himself?

Somehow, she didn't care which. The whole world stank of betrayal and blood.

King Henri put a dagger to Françoise's neck, just above the sweet-smelling head of her child. His smile was still beautiful; he still wore golden earrings.

"Go and free your child's father, or I will skewer the baby."

She did not doubt his resolve. And she did not let go of her son. Slowly, she walked around the red huddled mass that was Chicot, and she took the stones away, tossed them into the field. They felt to her like ordinary stones. And the cloak, when she pulled it off him, felt like an ordinary piece of velvet.

Chicot rose to his knees, breathing hard.

"Now kill her, Chicot," said Henri. "And you can take the child."

Chicot looked at his sire, and nodded slowly, like a man in a dream. His sword lay on the ground beside him.

She could not outrun two vampires. But she would not let her child be taken. She would kick, bite, scream—she would offer herself to be turned.

There is more than one way for evil to take root in the human heart.

But Chicot stood, head bowed, still not killing her. He hesitated. There was love in him for her, even now, and it was fighting for control with the urge to obey his sire.

Françoise did not wait to see which way the decision would fall.

When Henri stepped closer to repeat his command to Chicot, Françoise was ready with Chicot's sword.

It might have ended in regicide, if Henri had still been alive, and if she'd been able to put a little more strength behind the strike. As it was, the blade hit the side of the king's head, took off a piece of his ear, and sent the vampire racing after her.

But Françoise had taken note of where she threw the stones, and she hoped they would work as well against one vampire as another. She stumbled backward behind the first one, then turned and ran as fast as she could, her left arm aching from the small but constant weight of her child. She ran into the night toward the nearest stream, and she was never seen in Paris again.

EPILOGUE

1825

EDMOND DANTÈS WAS concerned about his friend. He had only seen the abbé Faria look this dejected one other time. That was soon after they had first met, eight years before, when the abbé realized that the tunnel he had been digging did not lead out of the prison but into the cell occupied by Dantès.

They had both led each other out of despair, but Dantès thought he owed a great deal more to Faria than the reverse. Thanks to the secret passage that now connected their cells, the priest had taught Dantès several languages, and mathematics, and philosophy, and many other things besides. He had always seemed to Dantès to have a kind of supernatural curiosity and enthusiasm for life that matched his uncanny physical agility. Truly, a man of boundless resources. And it was thanks to those resources that the two of them had worked tirelessly toward their escape. The day would not be far off now. They would break free of the stone walls of the Chateau d'If and swim to freedom.

So why, then, did the priest look so sad? He had just been telling Dantès a story, a story that had taken place in France two and a half centuries before. A story of vampires, in the heart of the French court.

But at the very moment of crisis, when Chicot the jester had been parted from his beloved and his newborn son, Faria had trailed off, looking at the tiny window, high above. It was a cloudy day, the sort of day he liked, because there was no shaft of sunlight to bother his eyes, made sensitive from years of study and the dust created by tunnelling away with homemade tools at the stone walls.

"Did the vampires ever find Françoise and her child?" Dantès asked gently, hoping to bring Faria back to himself.

The priest turned his red-rimmed eyes to his companion. "What? Oh, no, they did not. The abbess of Montmartre hid her away in a vacant tomb, and Françoise and her child went into the spirit world, where they walked for many years."

Faria truly believed the story. This was why the guards called him mad: he believed all sorts of nonsense, they said. He knew the location of a secret treasure, which he had promised several times over to anyone who would free him, to no avail. But Dantès had come to believe that Faria was not mad at all. If he said there were vampires in the world, Dantès was inclined to believe him.

And yes, there were times when he had seen his mentor in the throes of something that looked like madness. Once, years ago, Dantès had gone into his cell and found Faria with a mouse hanging limp from his mouth, as if the man were a hunting cat. But what man had not found himself acting like an animal in this place, from time to time? It was the purpose of the labyrinth to turn them into beasts.

Long ago, Dantès had argued that their only hope of escape was to kill the guard. But Faria had argued that it was out of the question.

"Have you never thought about it?" Dantès had asked, frustrated.

"Incessantly," came the abbé's reply.

For even more years than Dantès, the abbé had struggled with his animal nature, and had learned how to prevail. That was not madness. But perhaps these stories of blood and loss were too taxing for a man who had spent so long on that battlefield.

How long, exactly? It was hard to say. Faria looked like a man in his sixties, but prison could age a man.

Dantès put his hand on his mentor's. "You're tired. And the guard will come with food soon. Best we both return to where we ought to be."

LATER THAT NIGHT, Dantès heard a sound, deep in the walls.

A wail, in a voice he seemed to recognize.

In a matter of minutes, he emerged from the tunnel in the abbé's cell, and saw his friend standing in a shaft of weak moonlight from his own cell's grated window. The abbé's face was white and contorted with something that looked, at first, like ecstasy.

The priest turned to Dantès, his eyes burning with pain.

"What is it?" asked Dantès.

"You know exactly what my trouble is, I think," said the priest hoarsely. "If two men in prison together cannot be honest with each other, what hope is there for this world?"

Dantès did not draw back into the tunnel, but it took all his fortitude to stay where he was. Here, in the darkness, his friend seemed less familiar, and his stories seemed less like stories. He had witnessed his friend overcome by fits of illness before. It was his heart, or so Dantès had assumed, by the distortion of the man's features and the attitude of his limbs while he was in the agony.

On those previous occasions, the abbé Faria had asked his friend to fetch the one remedy in all the world that would do him any good: a small phial, hidden in the hollowed-out post of his bed. Dantès fetched it now. There was still a little of the red liquid left. When the priest saw it, his eyes blazed and he snatched at the phial and drank the few drops down.

"That is life to me," he said. "For a little while yet."

He sank onto his small bed, looking shrunken.

"What more can I do for you?" Dantès asked. "You know that I owe you all the duty a son owes a father, for you have been like a father to me, these last eight years."

Faris stretched out his cold fingers and grasped his hand. "That is true. If there is a duty you owe me, well, there is a far greater duty I owe to you. But I will not say you are the son I never had, because I did have a son, long ago."

A creeping comprehension weakened all of Dantès' limbs. "But how is it possible that you were there, two and a half centuries ago?"

"You know the word. Say it."

"Vampire," Dantès breathed, like he was repeating a lesson. "You are Chicot."

"I am him, and he is me. The jester became a priest. I knew that the abbess had hidden her, but I could not make the woman tell me where. So I infiltrated the Church, and roamed as far as Italy, following clues. As a priest, I could search more easily."

Dantès thought about the possible meanings behind the phrase *I could not make the woman tell me where.* "But did you never find Françoise?"

"I searched for nearly thirty years, but could not find her. She stayed in that tomb, in that twilight existence, all that time, and her child remained an infant. They must have been like ghosts. But unlike any ghost whose story I have heard, François and her son returned to the world of the living. When it was safe; when the Benandanti who deemed them traitors were no more threat, and when I was in difficulties of my own. Then Françoise returned to raise her son. She found a dim but useful man—the son of a newly ennobled merchant—to marry her. When the boy reached adulthood, though, he heard of the deeds of a Malandante named Richelieu and went off to

Paris to fight, armed only with a sword, his mother's healing salve, and her advice never to betray his friends. He took her name: D'Artagnan. To my lasting regret, I never knew him."

"The musketeer! I have heard of him," said Dantès.

"Of course you have," said Faria/Chicot, with a father's pride.

Dantès knew that he should feel anxious for his own safety, but he could not. After all, Faria had been his companion for eight years. He had had plenty of chances to do violence upon him, and yet he had not.

"You are wondering why you are still alive," said Faria softly, as if he could read his friend's thoughts.

But Dantès was one thought ahead by then. He had started to put it all together. "You have sworn never to do violence. Not even to our guards and our persecutors. And every day, you taught me, spoke with me… the temptation must have been…"

"Very great," completed Faria, his dark eyes glittering. "The hunger is my constant companion. But it is not insurmountable. The tincture of blood in that phial, a kind of essence I learned to distil, has kept me alive for a long time, even here in captivity, but I do not have long now."

"We will escape together," Dantès said.

Faria looked at him gently. "I do not have the strength. The contents of that phial are not enough to give me my old powers. I would have turned to mist, or into a bat, or simply walked through these walls, if I had possessed the strength to do so."

Dantès was silent for a moment. When he spoke, his voice sounded strangled. "If you were to drink—not your small tincture but… enough, would that give you the strength to escape?"

"Yes." The syllable sounded to Dantès like doom.

There was no question in his mind or his heart. When he had met the abbé, Dantès had been on the point of suicide.

He owed the man eight years of his life. Dantès pulled up his sleeve and offered the pale inside of his thin wrist, where a blue vein seemed to writhe in response to the vampire's gaze.

Faria took the wrist in his long fingers, looked for a long moment at Dantès, who returned his gaze steadily. The vampire bent his face to the inside of Dantès's wrist, and his dry lips brushed the skin, a brief kiss.

Then he let the wrist drop, and shuddered.

He did not raise his head when he spoke. "If you think it is only the lack of consent that stopped me from drinking your blood, you are mistaken. I could have obtained it at any point. I could obtain that of the guard's, too. You would all go to your deaths willingly, if I willed it. I do not."

"But—"

"I do not!" Faria shouted with new vigour, and it rang off the walls. It did not matter; no one would come. The mad priest was known to shout, from time to time. No one had ever listened, except Dantès.

Dantès grieved the death he might have had, for a moment. Then he said, softly, "If you have nothing more to sustain you, then we must complete our escape soon."

The priest shook his head. "It is too late for me."

"Nonsense. You have been digging with me all this time. All you need to do is swim."

"I cannot! I have lost my strength, and the slightest patch of sunlight galls me now. I am old; I do not wish to return to the bright world. I know now that my efforts, these last years, have been not on my own behalf but on yours."

Dantès tried to keep the tears from coming to his eyes. "You must escape."

"I will not. But you will, my son. I will give you my strength. The strength you need, to escape from here, to find my treasure, to defeat all enemies." Faria lifted Dantès' chin, holding the lower jaw so that the younger man's mouth parted slightly. "All you need to do is ask for it. The choice is yours."

ACKNOWLEDGEMENTS AND AUTHOR'S NOTE

THIS NOVEL IS inspired by the novel *La Reine Margot* by Alexandre Dumas, usually titled in English as *Queen Margot* or *Marguerite of Valois*. It was also influenced by his other work, especially *The Count of Monte Cristo, The Three Musketeers*, and his vampire story *The Pale Lady*. So I owe the greatest thanks to him, and I hope this book leads readers to his work (or back to his work). I hope he would forgive me for the liberties I have taken in making the story my own (and adding the vampires). He was no stranger to taking liberties himself; wherever I faced a choice about whether to be true to the historical record or true to Dumas' timelines and characters, I went with Dumas.

My thanks as well to everyone at Solaris who has helped conceive of this wonderful series, gave me the chance to write in it, and helped bring the book into the world, especially my editor Amanda Raybould. Thanks are also due as always to my agent, Jennie Goloboy, and to my family and friends, whose support makes my writing possible.

About the Author

Kate [illegible]
novels, including [illegible]
[illegible]
bestseller [illegible]
[illegible]
[illegible]
the [illegible]
[illegible]
[illegible]
Book awards [illegible]
Canada [illegible]

ABOUT THE AUTHOR

KATE HEARTFIELD IS the author of several historical fantasy novels, including *Mercutio* (2026), in which Shakespeare's best character opens a rift to Faerie, and the *Sunday Times* bestseller *The Embroidered Book* (2022), about Marie Antoinette and her sister Maria Carolina. She has also written interactive fiction, and Assassin's Creed novels. She has won the Aurora Award for Best Novel three times, co-won the Nebula award for game writing, and been shortlisted for the World Fantasy, Crawford, Locus, Sunburst, Scribe and Ottawa Book awards. Kate is a former journalist who lives in Ottawa, Canada with a black cat named Minerva.

Charming
He'll pick your pocket while he's stealing your heart
Jade Linwood